Ghost of a Chance

Nikki Long

This is a work of fiction. Names, characters, places, and incidents either are the product of the author's imagination or are used fictitiously. Any resemblance to actual persons, living or dead, events or locals is entirely coincidental.

Copyright © 2021 by Nikki Long

All rights reserved. No part of this book may be reproduced or used in any manner without written permission of the copyright owner except for the use of quotations in a book review. For more information contact: emlong.lhp@gmail.com

First paperback edition September 2021

Book cover design by Karin Star

Author photo by Albert George

ISBN 978-1-7375566-0-2

Published by Long House Press LLC

Michigan City, IN

For Craig.

A man who doesn't believe in ghosts, but he believes in me.

Contents

Chapter 1

S leet bounced off the window, distracting Kate Murphy from the financial report flickering on the computer monitor. She rolled her shoulders to work the kinks out of her neck, then remembered reading an article in the *New York Times* about prolonged sitting in office situations. *Something to do with increased mortality and getting a big ass*, she thought. With visions not so much about her mortality but the possibility of a larger butt, she stood and walked to the window. The city below was silent, with only the ice pelting on the glass and the hum of the fluorescent lights overhead. From the twentieth floor the traffic looked like a mosaic made up of yellow taxis, long dirty-white buses, and washed-out flashes of red brake lights from the vehicles caught in the gridlock.

"Winter in New York. Fan-freakin-tastic," she muttered to the four off-white walls. She looked at her desk, the monitor beckoning her back into the abyss of numbers, and couldn't help thinking that her life was like the gridlock below—a lot of rushing to get nowhere.

Kate had been working at Sterling Bank for the last eighteen months, and it had all started with such promise. Fresh out of graduate school with her MBA and landing a plum job in the private banking sector, friends and family considered her to be on the fast-track to a long and profitable career. Everything was working to plan—she and her fiancé, Michael Francisco, would move to New York, get married, and kick ass in the world of finance. But those plans came crashing down when Michael took a job in Chicago. After a few months of trying the long-distance relationship route, it became clear their romance couldn't survive. All of Kate's planning for the future changed, and suddenly she was facing life without a road map.

Running her fingers down the glass, the chill brought Kate back to reality as her cellphone vibrated. *Eve Marsden*, the screen flashed as she settled back into her chair and connected the call. "Eve? How are you?" she asked, cheered to hear her best friend's voice on the line.

"I'm good. How's high finance treating you?"

"If I look at another spreadsheet, I'm going to lose my mind. I can't help thinking..." Kate trailed off, not quite ready to admit —even to her best friend—that maybe she'd made the biggest career mistake of her life.

"How's your social life? Last time we talked you were thinking about joining a dating service." Eve's voice softened. "You know, you can't spend every waking hour at the office, hon."

Kate knew Eve worried about her—had done so since the devastating breakup with Michael over a year ago. It didn't help that Eve was in Salem, Massachusetts—not far, but far enough that meeting up for their usual Friday night dinners was out of the question. Visions of grad school, laughing over pizza and beers until the wee hours of the morning surfaced in Kate's mind and made her ache for simpler, easier times. Now everything seemed unsettled, leaving Kate with a jumble of emotions she wasn't ready to deal with.

"Hey! Earth to Kate." Eve laughed. "You there?"

"Yeah, I'm here. As far as dating goes, I went to one of those speed dating events last month. Let's just say it was interesting and leave it at that." She shuddered at the memory.

"C'mon Kate, what happened? You can't leave me hanging!"

"I met seven guys. SEVEN! Each one crazier than the last. I think the worst of the lot was an accountant who kept saying how much he hated makeup on women. All while looking at me like I was a whore or something. God, what a lunatic! I kept looking at my watch, waiting for it to be over. When our time was up, he said he'd like to see me again, but only if I didn't wear makeup. Can you believe it?" Kate looked at the ceiling, shaking her head at the memory. "It was all I could do not to tell him to eff off right then and there."

Eve's laughter bubbled down the line. "I'm sorry, Katie. I shouldn't laugh."

A tear threatened to fall when Eve called her Katie. She cleared her throat to compose herself. "No, it's okay. Really, it *is* funny. Damn, I miss you. But enough about my epic dating failure. What's happening in Salem? How are things at the shop? Has *Potion* cornered the market on all things new age and occult?"

After graduation, Kate had gone off to hunt for a job, while Eve traveled through the United Kingdom, looking for inspiration. After visiting ancient sites and little occult shops throughout England, Eve decided to open a bookstore and occult gift shop in Salem, appropriately named *Potion*. It blended her love of everything mystical with her innate ability to sell. The whole occult thing did absolutely nothing for Kate, but she loved her friend and figured if anybody could make it work, it would be Eve.

Kate heard her friend sigh. "Okay. What's going on?"

"Oh Kate, I know I can make a go of this. I'm great at selling, but the actual running of the business—setting up plans for purchasing, marketing, financial management—that's just not in my wheelhouse."

It wasn't like Eve to sound so dejected. She had always been the unofficial cheerleader/supporter/counselor within their circle of friends. Whenever there was a problem, everyone counted on Eve's positive outlook to get them through. Kate knew it was her turn to step up and return the favor. "You need a business manager. Someone to run the back of the house while you do what you do best—charm your customers and sell them all manner of things that they really don't need but can't live without." There was silence on the other end of the phone, and Kate wondered if their connection had been lost. "Are you still there?"

"Uh huh.... Kate, I think I might have an idea. Don't say no until you hear me out." Eve started talking rapid fire, as if trying to explain her still-formulating plan before Kate could stop her. "Okay, look. You aren't happy in your job, right? Maybe you need a change. Get out of New York, find a place that has a slower pace where you can start over."

"Oh sure, Eve. Pull up stakes and just move? It's not that easy to do. And where would I go?"

Eve took a deep breath and dropped the big question. "Why not Salem?"

"Huh?"

"Why not? Look, you're the one who said I need a business manager. Why not you? Think about it, Katie. You could move to Salem, use your skills to get my shop running efficiently. We could get back to our Friday night dinner meetups!"

Kate's heart rate kicked up as she clicked the ballpoint pen on her desk in a frenetic, uneven rhythm. *Give up a high-paying job for an unknown business venture?* Click... click, click. *Shouldn't I stay at least five years at Sterling to see if this is going to be my career?* Click, click. But the thought of spending another year, let alone marking time for five, staring at monitors for hours and returning to a tiny New York City apartment night after night, made her want to weep. She threw down the pen as if it were on fire.

Eve continued her pitch since Kate hadn't said no to her offer —yet. "Look, I can't pay you the money Sterling is paying, but we can work out a salary, and you can have a share of the profits. What do you say, Katie? Give it a year and if you hate it, then you can walk away—no hard feelings."

The ballpoint pen Kate had thrown was teetering on the edge of the desk, ready to fall with the least little push. *There's some symbolism for you,* she thought. Kate realized she couldn't put up with another year in her current situation. But there was still the voice of that annoying adult in her head, telling her to be careful, and cautious, and... practical. So instead of diving head first into the unknown, Kate did what she always did—she compromised. "Here's an idea. I'll come for a visit and check out the shop. I have plenty of vacation time saved up. What do you think? A week in Salem and we'll see how it goes?"

"Perfect! How soon can you get here?"

She had to give Eve credit for her carpe diem attitude and hoped that maybe a little of it would rub off on her. "Let me check in with my boss and clear my schedule. I'll take the train and text you my itinerary as soon as I get everything settled." She could almost hear Eve vibrating with excitement on the other end of the phone. "Oh, and in the meantime, send me your most recent financials for the shop, okay?"

After ending the call and clearing her schedule, Kate sat in the relative quiet of her office and looked at her watch. "Two o'clock," she muttered. She weighed her options, then snatched the pen that was teetering on the edge of her desk, thinking maybe it was time to practice some of that carpe diem attitude. Without a moment's hesitation, she grabbed her coat and exited the office, feeling like a prisoner during a jailbreak. But looking around, everyone was either on the phone, in meetings, or they had already left to start their weekend—she would never be missed.

Outside, Kate couldn't help feeling a sense of excitement, and it took her by surprise since she hadn't felt it in so long. The cold January winds nipped at her cheeks as she pulled her knit hat down over auburn curls and turned up the collar of her coat. She took a deep breath and realized that if she moved, the last thing she would miss would be the smell of car exhaust and food vendor carts. There had been a time when Kate couldn't wait to get to New York—now she couldn't wait to see it in the rear-view mirror. With a sense of growing purpose, Kate walked down the street to the subway entrance, ready to put her future in motion. A future that seemed, with every step she took, to include Salem and a shop called *Potion*.

———◦———

The January wind was sharp, hitting Pete O'Brien like an icy hand as he exited Robinson Hall. The spring semester had begun, but the weather felt nothing like spring. He headed across Harvard Yard to the library after finishing his Irish history course, eager to get back to his research.

As Pete crossed the Yard, it was easy to confuse him with the students making their way to class. In his heavy wool peacoat with a Harvard scarf wrapped around his neck, he blended right in. Although with his handsome face, deep brown eyes, and dark brown hair, he gathered more than a few passing glances as he crossed campus. But Pete didn't acknowledge the interest because he was too deep in his research to notice or care.

"Hey Gina," he said, greeting the research librarian as he stepped off the elevator and entered the special collections area.

"Back at it again, huh, Pete?"

"Yeah. I can't stay away from the ambiance of this place," he laughed, pulling off his gloves and unbuttoning his coat. "I submitted a request to view some Celtic manuscripts. Are they ready?"

"Yes, they're here. Get comfortable and I'll have them brought out to you."

Pete headed back into the special collections room, smiling as he inhaled the scent of parchment. He loved libraries because they held knowledge and possibilities, and he found them comforting, especially after his mother's death. At the age of thirteen, libraries were a refuge from the world, and his deep loss. Through books, especially history books, he could set aside his own personal pain and immerse himself in other times and places. Pete settled in and looked around the room, quiet now with a few people scattered around. He took out his cell phone, checked the time, then sent a quick text to Rob. *Finally seeing the Dindshenchas manuscript copy. I'll report back if I find anything interesting.* He didn't expect a response, since the time difference in Ireland meant that Rob Mahoney was probably either having dinner or deep in his own research.

"Dr. O'Brien?" the library assistant asked, pushing a cart holding the manuscript, along with a selection of other texts.

It always surprised Pete when anyone referred to him as Dr. O'Brien. He put on a pair of white gloves from the basket on the table and helped the assistant unload the cart. Eager to review the manuscript in front of him, he settled in. "Dindshenchas—The Lore of Places," he translated to himself. The four-hundred-year-old text was a copy of a much older version in Ireland. The difference with this particular manuscript was it included a series of colored illustrations that interested Pete—illustrations that were not in the original. He and his friend and collaborator, Rob Mahoney, were looking for images to include in the manuscript they were writing on ancient Celtic deities. A manuscript that would hopefully seal their successful careers—Pete's at Harvard and Rob's at Trinity College in Dublin.

An assistant professor, he'd been teaching at Harvard for two years, knowing how lucky he was to have landed the coveted position. Of course, it helped that he'd graduated first in his class, finishing his PhD in history at the very institution where he now worked. Still, there were times when he couldn't help feeling a bit of impostor syndrome; that somehow, he had fallen into a job he wasn't qualified for, regardless of having the credentials to back it up. He had a fleeting thought about the cost of all that hard work, namely the complete and total destruction of his marriage that, in hindsight, never really stood a chance. Pete pushed the thought out of his head, focusing on the work in front of him.

He unpacked his bag and turned on his laptop. After adjusting the light on the table, he opened the manuscript, taking care of the fragile parchment. Anticipation flooded through him as he turned the pages. It was a feeling that always surprised him—as if he could feel the history through the parchment underneath his hands. Making his way through the first few pages, he carefully translated Irish into English, typing notes on his laptop. He was grateful his years of studying Celtic history gave him a serviceable knowledge of the language—along with hearing his father pepper Irish words into conversation since he was a small boy. Thankfully, he could run his translations by Rob for the more nuanced aspects of the language. It wasn't until he was several pages into the manuscript that he found the breathtaking illustrations. The colors were vivid, as if painted only days before. He turned page after page until he came across several illustrations of Celtic deities. As beautiful as the illustrations were, one stopped Pete in his tracks. It was a depiction of Áine—the goddess of love, fertility, abundance, and sovereignty. The drawing depicted a beautiful woman with bright green eyes and long curls of auburn hair, holding a sheaf of wheat in her arms. Her body was lush—draped in sheer ivory fabric, and she looked out from the page with a slight, knowing smile. He stared down at the image, unable to turn the page. *Damn, she's beautiful.* He shook his head to clear it. *Okay dude, seriously? Getting turned on by a drawing? How old are you?* he asked himself, feeling more than a little embarrassed—and weird. He stared down at the image for another moment, not yet ready to move on.

The phone vibrated on the table, startling him out of his goddess fantasy. It was a text from Rob, asking if he'd found anything interesting. Pete snapped a photo of the image of Áine and sent it back with a text. *I think we've found the cover of the manuscript. What do you think?*

Works for me, mate. But I think we'd better finish writing it first, Rob responded.

Pete laughed, texted back that he got the hint and continued his research, then with a reluctant sigh, closed the manuscript on the image of the goddess. For the next several hours, he continued to make notes on the various texts piled up around him on the table. It was around seven o'clock when his stomach rumbled with hunger. Pete returned the manuscripts to the cart, deciding to call it a night, as he grabbed his coat and headed for the exit, waving to Gina as he went.

Outside, the winds had subsided, but the temperature had dropped. Pete crossed the campus and headed to the train station to catch the *T* home to Salem. On his way, he couldn't erase the image of Áine from his mind or his visceral reaction to her. "Maybe it *is* time you started dating," he muttered to himself, pulling his coat collar around his neck as he picked up his pace toward home.

Chapter 2

K ate exited the train at the Salem stop and looked at the GPS on her phone. Once out of the station, rolling her wheeled luggage behind her, she walked in what she hoped was the general direction of *Potion*. She hadn't made it twenty yards when she heard her name being called. Across the street stood Eve, waving and grinning from ear to ear. As soon as the light changed, she raced across the street and grabbed Kate in a soul-enveloping hug.

"You're here," Eve exclaimed, pulling back to look at her friend. "This is so exciting. We're going to have so much fun!"

Kate laughed, taking in her friend's pale gray eyes, black pixie haircut, and petite frame. "Yes, I'm here! You look great, Eve. Obviously, Salem does wonders for you."

"I love it here. I think you will too. Come on. The shop's just a few blocks," Eve said, pointing in *Potion's* general direction.

The two women walked along, with Eve giving Kate a running narrative on the town, the people, and the history of the place. Kate noticed that along the main street there were a lot of storefront businesses—antique shops and trendy boutiques. But what really caught Kate's attention was the overabundance of witchcraft and occult shops, many of them out of business. The one thing those places had in common was an over-the-top, tacky feel—working hard to bring in the tourists intrigued by witches and the paranormal. Kate filed the worrying observation in her brain as they made their way to *Potion*.

"Is *Potion* open today?" Kate asked, as they turned right onto Essex Street.

"Yeah, I have a local woman who works a couple of days during the week. There isn't much to do this time of year, since the locals have little use for an occult book and gift shop. But I'm hoping that this summer I'll do well so I can more easily weather the off season. We usually ramp up in mid-May and things go gangbusters until the big blowout on Halloween. Well, here we are," Eve said, holding open the door to *Potion*.

Kate's first impressions? The large storefront was charming, with windows across the width of the shop looking out onto the quaint main street. While *Potion* specialized in magic supplies, books, and jewelry, what stood out to Kate was it didn't have that hokey, kitsch factor that most of the other places had. It was bright and colorful, with elements of the mysterious. Also, it didn't insult the Wiccan belief system, and it didn't cash in on the whole 'witches marched to the gallows,' story line that seemed to permeate a lot of the tourist trade in Salem.

There was something else about *Potion* Kate couldn't quite put her finger on—a sense someone was watching over the place. Shaking off the thought, she chalked it up to the metaphysical stuff surrounding her. One thing Kate knew, the quirky little shop charmed her. As she looked around, she resolved to do whatever she could to help her friend.

"Any takers today, Jenny?" Eve asked, before introducing her shop assistant to Kate.

"It's been pretty quiet, Eve."

"Well, it will be May before we know it. Did the UPS guy drop off the book shipment?" Eve walked toward the counter in the middle of the store, adjusting displays as she went.

"He did. They're in the hallway by the office. I'll lock up for the day, now that you're back. Okay?"

"Sure. Thanks for waiting." Eve said, checking the books before leading Kate to a small office at the back of the shop. "Well, what do you think of *Potion*?"

Kate looked at her friend's anxious expression and knew that everything hinged on her response. "It really is a beautiful shop. Your personality is all over this place. It's wonderful."

"See! You get me! I didn't want to open just another 'witchy' place," Eve said, using air quotes. "I'm glad that comes through. So, how do I get more business?"

"Slow down, girlfriend! I just got here. Give me time to get a feel of the place, then we can map out some ideas, okay?"

"Right! Sorry, I'm getting ahead of myself. I'm just so excited that you're here. Why don't we get you settled in, then we'll go out for dinner? How does pizza sound?"

"Perfect. Let's go." Kate grabbed her luggage and followed Eve up the back stairs to her apartment. As they reached the landing to the second floor, Kate felt a cool breeze scented with lavender brush across her face, raising the hairs on the back of her neck. She thought it was a bit odd, but didn't comment on it as Eve chattered away, unlocking the front door to her apartment.

"Come in and make yourself at home. The guest room is the first door on your right. Just drop your bag in there," she said, gesturing down the hall. "Do you want to unpack now or wait until after dinner?"

"Food first! I'm starving. I feel like I've been traveling for days."

After depositing her luggage in the guest room, they headed back out to the street, where light snow glowing in the light of the streetlamps greeted them. "We're going to *Sabatino's*. Best pizza in Salem," Eve said, locking the door behind her and pointing to her left. "Just a few doors down."

Sabatino's was everything Eve promised. The sounds of laughter and Frank Sinatra playing on the jukebox greeted them as they entered. There was a long mahogany bar on one side, and on the other were tables and booths, all draped in red and white checkered tablecloths with candles in wine bottles. It was a stereotypical Italian pizza joint, with everybody having a great time. The place had an old world atmosphere, and Kate couldn't help but smile. She had a fleeting notion that New York could become a distant memory without much difficulty.

Eve waved to the hostess, holding up two fingers. "Isn't this place great? Come on, looks like Amy found us a spot." The two friends settled into a booth with seats covered in red Naugahyde and perused the menu while waiting for the server to bring their drinks. Eve used the pause in the action to question Kate, leaning across the table and looking intently at her friend. "So, be honest with me, Kate. You've told me your impressions of the shop and you've seen the financials, so what should I do about *Potion*?"

Kate realized she wouldn't be able to stall for an answer until after their food arrived, so she decided to just come out with it.

"How long has *Potion* been open?"

"I'm starting my third year."

"How many similar shops have come and gone since you've been here?" Kate asked.

A worried look crossed Eve's face. "Four."

Unable to bear her disappointment, Kate remembered how she felt when she was standing in *Potion*—that she would do whatever she could to help the place succeed. "You need a hook. Something that makes you stand out—different from the rest. When I walked into *Potion*, I was charmed. It's quirky and inviting. Just like you." Kate squeezed Eve's hand as the server came back with their drinks.

Over pizza and cocktails, the two friends talked about ways to bring in patrons through special events, sales, and giveaways, but nothing seemed to click. The server arrived to clear the table. "Dessert and coffee, ladies? We got fresh homemade cannoli in from Boston."

"Ugh! No dessert," Eve said, patting her stomach. "But I want coffee! A double espresso for me, thanks."

"How can you drink coffee at this hour?" Kate asked. "Won't you be up all night?"

"Nope. It's never been a problem. Coffee is my magic potion." Eve waved her arms as if conjuring a spell.

Something dawned in the back of Kate's brain. "What did you say?"

"Coffee is my magic potion," Eve repeated.

"Hold up a minute. Eve, you might have come up with a solution... if you're willing to adapt *Potion* into something more than just a gift shop." Kate ran her hand over her brow and thought. "How many weeks until the tourist season kicks into high gear?"

"Well, things get cracking around Memorial Day weekend. So, I guess fourteen to sixteen weeks. What are you thinking, Kate?"

Kate tapped her finger on her chin, her jaw set in determination. "Look, occult shops are all over town. What if you turned your place into something more than just a shop? More like a place to hang out. You said coffee was your magic potion. What if you opened a coffee and tea shop? The storefront is large enough to do both retail merchandising and beverage service. You can still sell jewelry, books, and everything else, but now people can come and enjoy coffee and then stay and shop. Do you know of any other occult coffeehouse in Salem?" Kate paused, trying to gauge her friend's reaction.

Eve stared at Kate, wide eyed. "Coffee... tea...."

Kate could practically hear the wheels turning in Eve's brain. She waited. Then Eve started laughing.

"That's fucking brilliant.... Of course! *Potion* can mean different things to different people. Kate, what an incredible idea! It's a perfect solution." Eve's eyes shone with tears as she grabbed Kate's hands. "Let's do it!"

"Well, before we jump in, let's do some market research. I can do a study on tourism and foot traffic while I'm here. We need to make sure it's something the market can support, okay?" Kate looked all business as she calculated just what the options could be. "I'll work up a budget for you this week. We'll need to spend some money on renovations to the place...." Kate trailed off and looked at Eve, who was grinning from ear to ear. "What?"

"You keep saying 'we.' Does that mean you are thinking of making the move?" Eve asked, her voice filled with hope.

Kate tensed. Could she make that sort of change? Leave everything behind and try something new and untested? "Give me some time, Eve. Okay? I just got here. Let me mull this over for a bit." The last thing she wanted was to disappoint her best friend, but it was a big decision to make. Did she trust herself enough to step outside of her comfort zone?

"Got it. Sorry," she said, holding up her hands in surrender. "I promise not to push you too hard. It's just this is so exciting. I know this is an enormous step." Eve started gathering her things. "You ready to head back? I've got a twelve-year-old bottle of Jameson at home that I thought we might want to taste-test."

The restaurant had quieted, with just a few patrons hanging out at the bar. Calls of good night were heard as they stepped out into the winter landscape of falling snow. It made Kate smile. Salem was so different from New York, with its hometown feel and gentler pace. *Maybe this is what I need. A place where I can breathe and not be just another human scurrying around a big city.* The two friends crunched through the snow, both holding onto the new possibilities waiting for *Potion*.

Chapter 3

"Why don't we take a break, Katie," Eve said as they sat in the office. The two friends had been working non-stop for the last several days, putting together the new and improved plans for *Potion*. "You haven't really seen any of the town. Take a walk while I clear up some of these files, then we'll make dinner and crash for the night. Plus, you could do me a favor and stop at the market for a bottle of wine. Sound good?"

Kate looked out the shop window as sunshine tried to peek through clouds filled with snow. "Maybe I will. I'd like to look around town before the weather turns."

The smell of the ocean greeted Kate as she stood on the street, breathing in the crisp winter air that had quickly become her favorite scent. The chill invigorated her as she headed south toward the Charter Street Historic District. She imagined the streets and storefronts in summer, decked out with flowers and banners welcoming the tourists who would make Salem part of their vacation plans. She found it easy to imagine *Potion* being a part of that experience for people. As she and Eve worked through the plans for the shop, Kate kept returning to the thought that *Potion* felt like the right thing to do. Not only from a business standpoint, but from a personal one as well. The more time she spent in Salem, the more New York and Sterling Bank felt like a distant memory. The quirky shops, the friendly locals, and Eve, of course, all gave Kate a feeling of belonging—something she hadn't felt in a while. *Could this have been Eve's plan all along*, Kate thought with amusement.

As she walked along, lost in thought, Kate found herself standing at a rustic iron gate that opened into the Old Burying Point, the oldest cemetery in Salem. She hesitated for a moment, unsure if she should enter. Cemeteries always made her feel uncomfortable because they seemed to be such outward signs of grief. Turning away from the gate, she caught the scent of lavender, seeming to come from the grounds of the cemetery. *Probably just growing wild*, she reasoned. *But it's January. That's strange.* It reminded her of the scent at Eve's place on the first day she arrived. Despite her discomfort, she found herself drawn to enter, as if the lavender were pulling her in. Suddenly, she wanted to look at the old tombstones; to see and connect to those who once lived in this place so long ago. Kate unhooked the latch, opened the gate, and entered, carefully making her way across the uneven ground through centuries of human stories, all told through pieces of stone jutting up from the earth.

Wandering through the tombstones, she noted the names and dates of those who had passed, from sea captains and good Christian wives, to infants who had only lived a single day. Kate found herself moved by the inscriptions, especially that of a young man who died in 1688 whose stone read, "An aged person that had seen but nineteen winters in the world." *To die at nineteen. When all of life is ahead of you?* Kate shivered at the thought. *I'm twenty-seven. What's ahead for me?* Thinking of how her life had been so far, always reaching for something, but what? Status? Success? When she took the time for self-reflection, it didn't seem like the makings for a glorious life. Kate looked up at the gray clouds gathering and sighed, feeling tired deep down in her soul as she stood over the grave in the quiet January afternoon. With a slight hesitation, Kate reached out and put her hand on top of the cold slate marker, sending up a silent plea for the young man, a plea that he was at peace and that he was not forgotten. Lost in thought, she didn't hear running shoes stopping abruptly at the gate to the cemetery.

Pete had decided that the only cure for his writer's block was a bracing run before the snow started. What he hadn't expected to see was a vision of the Celtic goddess Áine, standing over a grave in the middle of Salem's oldest cemetery. Stopped dead in his tracks, he watched the woman looking down as if in prayer. *This can't be*, he thought, trying to process the vision of the woman, who suddenly looked up, sensing she was being watched. Pete froze, feeling like a voyeur. But when their eyes met, he lost his breath—she was a twin of the image from the manuscript. The woman turned and rushed toward the far gate, looking back once before heading down the street in the opposite direction.

He leaned on the fence, trying to get his bearings. "This is impossible. Who is she?" He looked across the cemetery, but she had already disappeared down the street. *I need to find out who she is.* He almost took off in a run after her until reason returned. "Jesus Christ! Stop it," he said, talking himself down and turning away from the cemetery. The snow began to fall as he ran down the empty street in the opposite direction. His footsteps took up a rhythm that should have cleared his mind, but all he could think about was the goddess he had just seen standing in the middle of the Old Burying Point.

As the two went their separate ways, a mist formed in the stand of barren trees on the cemetery grounds. Within moments the shape of a woman formed, dressed in Victorian clothing. She looked first after Kate, then turned and watched as Pete continued his run in the opposite direction. A slight smile crossed her face as she slowly turned and disappeared into the mist.

———◦———

As Kate hurried to the market, she turned several times to look behind her, hoping that the creeper wasn't following her. *Hey, you've lived in New York for almost two years and seen all manner of strangeness. You can handle some perv watching you in a cemetery,* she told herself. But once in the market's safety, she couldn't help thinking that from the quick look she could get, he didn't look like a typical creep. In fact, from what she could see, he was handsome. And he was wearing clean running gear—with a Harvard sweatshirt, no less—not dirty clothes and a trench coat, which was often the uniform of choice for New York City's perv-ier citizens. *Wow, girl. You're judging the hotness of a creeper? Maybe it has been too long since you've been on a date.* Kate rolled her eyes, then turned her attention to the wine aisle. Grabbing a few bottles, she reasoned that there were creeps in every town, and at least Salem had the decency to have handsome ones.

Chapter 4

K ate buttoned her coat as she came down the stairs and into the office where Eve was pouring over paperwork. "I'm heading over to the library. I've been wanting to get over there all week to gather data, and since I'm leaving tomorrow, this is my last chance."

"Okay. I hope our library won't be too disappointing. It's definitely a little old school. Oh, and don't be late. I made dinner reservations at the best seafood place in Salem. Time for one last celebration before you head back."

Kate raised her hand in salute. "Got it, Chief. I'll be back by five."

She'd located the library earlier in the week, surprised by how beautiful it was. But then, who could resist a library housed in a lovely red brick Victorian mansion built by a sea captain? She was eager to see the inside of the place, hoping she could get her hands on the tourism and commerce data she needed.

Once inside, Kate continued to be charmed by the building. As she approached the circulation desk for help, she noted the restored woodwork, glowing with a patina of well-worn care, which got her thinking about how much her father would love the place. The librarian directed Kate to the city records and left her sitting at a table with stacks of documents in front of her. *Wow. Eve was right—it is old school. No banks of computers and databases for Salem, I guess.* Taking out her laptop, Kate noted all the information she required: sales and tax forecasts, the nearest location of similar businesses, as well as tourism patterns. As hard as she was working, she couldn't help but stop to look up at the beautiful building she was in, impressed with how well maintained it was, with windows looking out onto what must be beautiful gardens in the summer.

I could live here. History, a beautiful little town, my best friend.... She thought of the cemetery and the tombstone of the young man who died. The memory of that moment stayed with her, reminding her that life was short. During the week Kate kept a list of pros and cons in her head, and it was becoming apparent that the pros of moving to Salem were winning. *Maybe it's time? Forge a fresh path and all that... what's keeping me in New York, anyway?* If she was going to be honest with herself, the only thing keeping her in New York was fear. *What if Potion doesn't work out?* Then another new thought surprised her. *But what if it does?* Smiling to herself, she realized how much of Eve's positive attitude was rubbing off on her. It was a relief to admit to herself she was going to start a new life in Salem. *Wait until I tell Eve,* she chuckled, imagining her face when she gave her the news.

Kate turned away from the window to wrap up her research when she had a feeling that someone was watching her. Across the room, she saw a handsome, dark-haired guy staring at her. She glanced behind her, thinking he had to be looking at someone else, but there was no one there. She turned to find him still staring, then realized it was the same guy who had been watching her in the cemetery. *What the fuck? Is this creep stalking me?* She looked down at her laptop, saved the file, closed her computer, and began collecting her things. With as much discretion as she could muster, she glanced at the location where the guy had been. He was gone, and she sighed in relief. Kate turned back to pack up her things and found him standing next to her. She jumped in fright.

"Sorry. Uh, sorry, I didn't mean to frighten you," the handsome creeper said, giving her a tentative smile.

She ignored him and kept packing up her things. He stood like an awkward statue, unmoving and silent—just looking at her as if he'd seen a ghost or something. With a burst of adrenaline, she pushed back her chair and stood, squaring off with the stranger. "What do you want?" she demanded in her iciest, most professional voice.

"Nothing. Umm, I'm sorry. You just resemble someone. Well, not someone, but a drawing of someone..." He trailed off.

Kate looked him square in the eyes, committing every detail to memory in case she had to pick him out of a line-up. *Damn, he's handsome.* The thought skittered through brain, before giving herself a mental shake. *Handsome, but crazy.* "Look, I don't know who you are or what you are talking about. But here is something I do know. STOP FOLLOWING ME." She grabbed her laptop bag and held it between them like a shield.

"I'm so sorry. I'm not following you. Really! I just happened to be in the library. I'm not a stalker." He looked horrified as people glanced up from their tables with interest. "Please, please.

I am so sorry." He stood as if trying to figure out what to say next.

"Yeah, right," Kate said, grabbing her coat and heading for the entrance, never looking back until she was outside. *Who was that guy?* With long, quick strides, she headed to Eve's place. *I mean, what a freak. Hot, but good god, he's obviously nuts. What did he mean by I look like someone—not someone, but a drawing of someone?* She shook her head, turned around once more to make sure he wasn't following, then hurried back to *Potion*.

You fucking idiot. Nothing like scaring the crap out of the poor woman. Pete cringed, remembering what he'd said in their brief exchange. *You resemble someone. Well, not someone, but a drawing of someone.* He sat down at the table Kate had just vacated and looked out the window. When he saw her up close, it confirmed her resemblance to Áine. Those eyes—the way they flashed at him in anger. He'd never seen a more beautiful woman in his life. *Well, you'll never see her again, that's for sure,* he thought, rubbing the back of his neck. Getting up from the table, he headed for the entrance, more than a little depressed by the idea that he'd never see the fiery redhead again.

Kate and Eve sat, looking out at the empty harbor as a full moon reflected off the winter sea. They'd finished a fabulous seafood dinner and were enjoying an after-dinner whiskey before heading out into the cold.

"So, you're heading back tomorrow." Eve stated the obvious.

Kate sensed she was on pins and needles, wondering what her decision would be. "Yeah, I'm catching an early train out of Boston. Back to the office on Monday," Kate said, swirling the glass of whiskey and grinning at Eve. She figured it was time to put her out of her misery. "So, Eve. This has been a wonderful week. Really productive. Right?"

"Yeah, I think it has been. I'm excited by what *Potion* can be in the future," she said, shifting in her seat.

"And it's been so fun hanging out with you. I love Salem, and I think we make an excellent business team."

"Uh huh," Eve said.

Kate paused for dramatic effect, lowering her glass to the table. "So, I was wondering if you'd like to hire me? I can't start until I give notice at my current job, but if you'll have me..." Kate wasn't able to get another word out because Eve jumped up from the table and hugged her.

"Oh, thank the Goddess! Kate, this is the best news I've had in years! I kept hoping.... Oh, we are going to make a great team." Tears filled her eyes. "Look, I know this has been a tough decision, but I promise, you won't regret it."

"No regrets. This is just what I need. So, let's get to work." Kate hugged her friend, feeling as if a major shift had just happened in her life.

Chapter 5

K ate arrived at her office on Monday morning, a large latte in her hand and a smile on her face. After settling in at her desk, she pulled up the resignation letter she had been working on since the night before. She made a few minor changes, then emailed it to the powers that be and waited. Within thirty minutes, Kate's supervisor called to review her exit plan. It took Kate a bit by surprise, realizing that as difficult as it had been for her to decide to leave, it took her employer less than an hour to set the plans in motion to replace her.

With her resignation in place, Kate knew there were two calls she needed to make—a call to her mother, Gale Chase, and her father, Kevin Murphy. Kate sat in the quiet of her office and looked at the phone. After a quick internal pep talk telling herself to get the tough call over with first, she picked up the phone and dialed the number. Her mother picked up on the second ring. "Mom. Hi. It's Kate," she said.

"Hello, Kate. This is a surprise," Gale said, without a hint of surprise in her well-modulated voice.

"A surprise? I call you every month," Kate said, already feeling the friction rising between them.

"Usually you call on Saturday mornings. It's a Monday afternoon. What's wrong?"

Holding the phone away from her ear, Kate sighed and looked at the ceiling. She tried to put a smile in her voice and continued the conversation. "Nothing is wrong. Can't I call you on the spur of the moment just to talk?" Kate realized, of course, that she never did anything spur of the moment, especially when it came to her mother. She looked around the office at the four stark white walls and began doodling on the notepad on her desk. "Anyway. How are you?"

"I'm fine. Jason and I are planning our spring vacation. I think we're going to Bermuda. He wants to golf with some of the partners at the firm. God knows, I find it tedious, but he's one of those lawyers who likes to socialize with his colleagues. I'll probably spend most of my time by the pool."

Kate rolled her eyes, picturing her mother standing in her opulent high-rise condo as she looked out over Lake Michigan. It was a gorgeous home, but not a place she ever felt comfortable. Too *Architectural Digest* for her taste. "That sounds nice," she said in her most non-committal voice while desperately trying to figure out how to bring up the subject of her job. *I should have thought of that before I picked up the phone.*

"How is New York?" Gale asked.

"Cold. Snowy. Pretty much how you would expect New York to be in late January. I'm sure it's the same in Chicago, right?"

"How are things at Sterling? Are you networking? Making connections? It's been what? Two years since they hired you?" she asked, the questions coming out more like an interrogation than a conversation between a mother and daughter.

"Things here are fine. Yes. About two years." Kate paused, realizing this was the moment of truth. "Actually, that's one reason I called."

"Oh?"

"Yes, umm." Kate stood up at her desk, then abruptly sat back down. She clenched her phone, taking a deep breath. "Mom, I gave notice today. I'm leaving Sterling and going into business with Eve Marsden. She has a shop in Salem, Massachusetts. I'm going to—"

"What? You cannot be serious. You are going to leave a lucrative career to work with that strange girl?" Gale asked, the well-modulated tone of her voice falling away to be replaced by that of a drill sergeant.

"Mom. Stop... please." Standing up again, Kate looked out the window at the traffic below. "Eve is my best friend. I don't appreciate your comment."

Gale's voice returned to its normal non-emotional timbre, as if trying to reason with a small child. "Look, Kathryn. You need to take time and think this through. You have everything going for you in New York. Why would you want to leave when you are just getting established in your career? Your friend can certainly hire anyone to help her out with her little shop. Really, this is a ridiculous notion. I'm disappointed in you, Kathryn. This isn't like you at all."

Using Kate's formal name made it clear they were now in battleground territory. She felt her anger prickle and before Kate could stop herself she asked, "How would you know, Mom?"

"Excuse me?"

"How would you know what I'm like? I mean, it's not like we ever talk about anything of substance. If it doesn't involve climbing the corporate ladder and making more money, you don't invest much into our conversations." Kate sat down, trying to control her bristling anger. "Look. I've made my decision. I'm sorry if that disappoints you but for once, I'm going to do something that's right for me."

"Well, that's dramatic. I spent my life making sure you had every opportunity for success. I thought a career in New York was what you wanted. Now you tell me you want some bohemian lifestyle in a little seaside town?" Gale's voice rose, her anger coming through loud and clear.

"I never said that! Who's being dramatic now? I'm using my skills to help a friend with her business, not joining some hippie commune!" Kate looked at the monitors flickering a constant stream of numbers. "Mom, I haven't been happy in New York for a while now," she said, stopping herself from adding, *not that you would know*. Her comment was met with silence. "I have to go. I'll talk to you next month." She sat down and disconnected the call, not waiting for a response.

As she looked around her office, Kate realized that everything in the room was a representation of what her mother wanted for her. The framed MBA hanging on the wall, the upscale office furnishings, the assistant sitting right outside her door. Kate rubbed her temples and did her best to get her scattered thoughts under control. *I'm doing the right thing, aren't I?* She shook off the question as she called her father.

"Hi Dad, it's Kate."

"Katie! How are you?"

"I'm doing okay Dad. How are things in Door County?"

"Ah, it's winter. Quiet in the retail shop. Which is great because I've been working on some furniture projects. A beautiful cherry wood trestle table for a customer's dining room. It's a lovely piece, some of my best work, I think. But how are you? Still enjoying New York City living?"

"Not so much. But there are some changes on the horizon. I wanted to let you know that I'm leaving Sterling Bank." Kate was far less worried about broaching the subject with her dad.

"Really? Wow. Where are you going?"

"My friend Eve, you remember her from my college days. I brought her with me one summer to visit you?"

"Oh, I remember her. Lovely girl."

She warmed at her father's kindness. "She has a retail shop in Salem, Massachusetts. I'm moving there to handle the business end of things. I should be settled in by the end of February."

"That's great, Katie. I'm sure Eve is happy that you two will be close again. And I'm sure she's going to appreciate all your expertise. It sounds like an exciting venture. I'm proud of you."

A lump rose in her throat. That was the message she needed to hear, and she was grateful for her father's understanding. "Thanks, Dad. That means a lot. I'll send you my address as soon as I get settled. But I'd better go now. I've got a lot of loose ends to tie up here at the office before I leave."

After saying their goodbyes, Kate was glad she'd called her father last. His positive outlook helped erase the negativity of her mother's comments. She looked at the calendar on her computer—four weeks and counting. Excitement surged through her as she thought about what the future might have in store.

Chapter 6

"You will reach your destination in four hours and twelve minutes," the disembodied voice of Kate's GPS informed her as she drove out of New York on I-95, heading for Salem. The roads were empty on that sunny, cold February morning as she reviewed the past twenty-four hours. The movers had finished packing up her apartment and all her material possessions were on their way except for a couple of suitcases, a few boxes with kitchen and bathroom essentials, and a blowup mattress which she'd stowed in her car. Just enough to get by until the movers delivered her furniture on Monday. Eve had called last night asking what time she would arrive, but Kate suspected her friend just wanted to confirm that she was actually coming to Salem.

As Kate drove along, she mused on how relatively easy it had been to make such a drastic change in her life. She had finished out her last month at Sterling Bank, wrapping up accounts and handing them over to her colleagues. While most of them thought she was crazy for giving up such a high paying, lucrative career, they were also envious she was striking out on her own, leaving the corporate world behind her. Subletting her tiny apartment had been easy, since the housing market was so tight in New York. Kate thought with amusement what a force of nature Eve had been, tracking down an adorable little house in

Salem, a few blocks from the ocean and a ten-minute walk to *Potion*. Eve had gone on about how the house had good energy. Ever practical, Kate was more concerned that it had two bedrooms and a reasonable rent than whether the place had good energy. But she had to admit, the photos Eve sent were charming. The dark hardwood floors gleamed, and the kitchen was cute and functional. Down a short hall was a bathroom with retro fittings, followed by two bedrooms, one of which had a door leading to a porch and garden at the back of the house. But best of all was the stone fireplace in the living room. As the miles clicked by, bringing her closer to her new life, Kate imagined sitting by the fire on a chilly night.

With the four-hour drive, Kate also had plenty of time to dwell on the one dark cloud in the transition—her mother. While she had expected her mother would not be happy, it still stung, especially when Gale had called her two weeks ago to see if she had given up the 'ridiculous' idea of leaving Sterling Bank and New York City. When Kate emphatically told her mother she made the right choice moving to Salem, the two ended up in a heated discussion. It wasn't long before Gale had thrown Kate's breakup with Michael Francisco into the mix, as well as her failed corporate career. She made it made clear to her daughter that her plans did not bear any resemblance to the roadmap Gale wanted for her. When the call was over, Kate's determination was still intact, but Gale Chase had succeeded in leaving a chink in Kate's armor of self-confidence. Gripping the steering wheel, Kate shook her head to clear the negative thoughts, noting that there was no place for that kind of thinking anymore.

Kate easily found her way to the house, thanks to both the GPS and Eve's detailed directions once she arrived in Salem. The house was an adorable gray cedar shingled cottage with white trim and an arched front door with black wrought iron fixtures. She pulled into the drive next to a white Toyota Prius, with no mistaking the car belonged to Eve, not only because it was eco-friendly but also because of the two bumper stickers—one that said COEXIST and another saying MY OTHER RIDE IS A BROOM. Her car door was barely open when Eve came bounding down the front steps and ran full speed toward her friend. She was dressed in worn jeans and a black long-sleeved tee-shirt that said GOT MAGICK? They laughed and hugged—both amazed that Kate was finally in Salem.

"You're here," Eve squealed, pulling her friend's arm toward the front door. "C'mon, let's go in the house. We can get your stuff in a minute. I want you to see the place first!" Eve bounced up and down as she handed Kate the keys. "I hope you don't mind, but I came in earlier today and *smudged* the house."

"You did what?" Kate asked, as they walked in the front door.

In a matter-of-fact, this is just common knowledge tone, Eve said, "I went from room to room and burned sage. It rids the house of bad energy and spirits."

"I thought you said the house had good energy, Eve."

"Oh, it does, but you can't be too careful!"

Kate stopped inside the front door, taking in the room with its dark hardwood floors and fireplace, just like the photos Eve had sent. By the hearth, her friend had set up two canvas lawn chairs with attached tables. "I figured you would need someplace to sit until your furniture arrived," Eve said.

Her friend's thoughtfulness touched her. "Oh Eve, thank you. The house is beautiful."

"Come on, let me show you the rest of the place." Eve took Kate through the house, extolling the charms of each room they entered. After the brief tour, they brought in the boxes. "Do you want to unpack now?" Eve asked, dusting off her hands as she put a box on the kitchen counter.

"Not really. I only have a few items for the kitchen and bath, plus my trusty air mattress and pillow. It won't take me that long to unpack. I am getting hungry though."

"Do you feel like taking a walk? There's a diner close to *Potion*."

The two set off toward Essex Street. Late February meant the tourist season was a long way off, but the sunny day brought out a lot of neighbors, many calling out their hellos as they got closer to the center of town. They passed *Potion*, popping in to say hello to Jenny before heading to the diner.

Kate noted that the streets of Salem were quiet, with almost all the shops posting signs saying either *early closing* or *closed until April*. She had a moment of panic, hearing her mother's voice telling her she was making a foolish mistake. Eve interrupted her negative thoughts, stopping in front of the diner.

Seated in a booth by the window, Kate started the to-do list for *Potion*. "We have a lot to get done in the next three months. We'll have to order equipment, furniture.... Did you find a good contractor to build the coffee bar on short notice?" Mentally, she went through a list of needed items and materials.

"Yes, I've got a great contractor, Jon Bradley. He helped me when I opened *Potion*. He does beautiful carpentry work. It's still early in the season, so he agreed to meet us tomorrow to go over measurements and the design. Oh Katie, this is just what *Potion* needs." Eve jumped up and sat next to her friend, hugging her tight.

The sun was setting as they left the diner and walked back to Kate's house, with streetlights coming on, giving the town a picture postcard glow. The two friends talked excitedly, making plans and schedules for the grand re-opening of *Potion*.

"So, Jon will meet us at noon tomorrow," Eve said as they stood in the driveway.

"Sounds good. He can give us a quote on the work, then I can start budgeting for equipment and furniture. I should have internet up and running on Monday while I'm waiting for the movers. On Tuesday I can be at *Potion* to get started." Kate looked at her friend, whose face was positively glowing with happiness. "We'll probably have to go to Boston for coffee and kitchen equipment. Do you think you could carve out time next week?"

"I'm sure Jenny can mind the shop. Probably Wednesday if that works for you."

"As of right now, I'm on the clock and my time is yours."

The two said their goodbyes, and Kate headed into the empty house. She looked around, smiled, and went into the kitchen to empty boxes, first stopping to dock her phone into the speaker she had unpacked. She thumbed through her playlist until she found her favorite Van Morrison song, *Moondance*. Kate turned up the volume and started singing along, feeling happier than she had in ages.

Chapter 7

K ate woke the next morning, cursing the air mattress that had deflated during the night. To clear the cobwebs from her brain, she made her way to the kitchen and turned on the coffeemaker, then reveled in a hot shower, washing away the grime of yesterday's travel.

Feeling much more human after her shower, Kate grabbed a cup of coffee and looked out the window to see snow falling. It was pretty, but she was ready for spring. "Well, let's make the best of this," she said, walking to the mantle. Eve had said it was a gas fireplace and within minutes, Kate had a pretty fire blazing away. She made herself comfortable in one of the lawn chairs, sipped her coffee, and took stock of all that had changed in her life.

If someone had told her that two-and-a-half years after graduate school she would live in Salem, Massachusetts helping her best friend turn around a floundering business—an occult bookstore and gift shop no less—she would have told them they were crazy. *I was so sure of myself back then.* Memories flooded back, and her mind wandered to her ex-fiancé and Chicago. Kate was surprised, thinking that her memories didn't hurt as much as they once did. In fact, if she was being honest, the breakup was probably for the best. She and Michael dated throughout undergrad and grad school, getting engaged at the end of their first year while studying for their MBA. They were so wrapped up in their plans and careers that in hindsight—she wondered if they really knew each other. Kate still missed Michael, but it felt more like she missed the idea of him rather than his actual presence. *I guess I'm making progress,* she thought, getting up for one more cup of coffee before leaving to meet Eve.

The crunch of snow under Kate's feet broke the silence on the residential street. The air was frosty, and it carried the now familiar scent of sea salt. She turned and looked at the cottage she would now call home, feeling a wave of contentment flow through her. Eve had done a magnificent job picking out the house. Across the street was a picturesque park with a swing set and a small fountain surrounded by benches. She thought about summer in Salem, and it made her smile. She and Eve had made a one-year agreement, but Kate wondered if she would want to leave when the year was up. After her visit a few weeks earlier, Kate found she loved the pace of Salem and the thought of returning to a big city didn't hold the excitement it once did.

Kate wandered through the neighborhood until she reached Essex Street, arriving outside of *Potion* fifteen minutes early. The door was locked, so she sent Eve a quick text. Moments later, Eve came bounding to the front door.

"Sorry, I'm early," Kate said.

"No worries. Come on in and warm up. Jon should be here shortly. And here, you'll need these, partner," Eve said, handing her keys to the shop. "So, how was your first night in the house? Did you sleep okay?" she asked as they headed back to the office.

"Well, I'll be glad when I don't have to sleep on an air mattress. My bed can't get here soon enough. Now I remember why I don't enjoy camping!"

"You can always stay here tonight."

"No, that's okay. The movers will be here early tomorrow morning, and so will the cable guy. I think I can survive one more night."

There was a knock at the front door, and Eve gave a nervous jump. "Oh, that will be Jon. Come on!"

Kate thought it odd that Eve was so anxious about the contractor being there. However, when she ushered him in, Kate understood why. Jon Bradley was adorable, with a neatly trimmed beard and long blonde hair he wore in a ponytail. He wore a plaid flannel shirt, worn fitted jeans, and work boots. Eve was looking at him adoringly, and he looked equally smitten with her. *Ah ha*, thought Kate.

Eve made the introductions, and Kate couldn't help but smile. She also couldn't wait to get her friend alone so that she could get the complete story of their relationship. She had never seen Eve behave like that around a guy.

"Great to meet you, Kate. Eve talks about you all the time." Jon said, extending his hand.

"Nice to meet you, too. Eve tells me you are the best in the business."

"I try to do my best. But I think Eve is too generous with her compliments." He turned to Eve and gave her a smile. She looked like she would melt into the floorboards.

Kate shot her friend a look of amusement, and Eve, clearly flustered, tried to get the conversation back on a more professional footing. "So, Jon. We've decided to change the focus of *Potion* a bit. Kate had the brilliant idea of adding a coffee bar to the place so that we can expand the business." Eve smiled at her friend. "We need a coffee bar and pastry case built, along with a few rustic tables. Oh, and a water line and sink installed too."

"That's a great idea. And you've got plenty of room. Why don't I take some measurements and draw up some plans?" he offered.

"Great! We'll be back in the office," Eve said.

The two women walked to the back and as soon as they were at the office door, Kate grabbed her friend's arm and dragged her into the room, laughing. "Okay, Eve. What is going on here? There are so many sparks flying off the two of you, you're about to start a fire."

Eve couldn't contain her excitement. "Oh, Katie, I've had a thing for Jon since I met him a year ago. But he had a live-in girlfriend, so he was off limits."

"*Had* a live-in girlfriend. Past tense?"

"Yeah. They broke up four months ago."

"Well, what are you waiting for, girl?" Kate asked. "It's not like you to pass up an opportunity!"

"I don't want to be the rebound chick," Eve wailed.

"Honey, the way he was looking at you, I don't think you have anything to worry about."

"You think so?" There was a note of hope in her voice.

"I *know* so. Go get him!"

Ten minutes later, Jon walked back to the office to find them. "I have a couple of ideas that might work. I've got the measurements and should have something on paper by the end of the day," he said.

"That's awesome. Maybe we could get together this evening and go over everything? We could meet up for dinner," Eve said, looking like she didn't have an ulterior motive, but Kate knew better.

"That would be great. How about seven o'clock?"

"Kate, are you free tonight?" Eve asked, while giving her friend a look that said she'd better say no.

"Sorry, guys. I can't. The movers are coming tomorrow morning, and I need to get some things done around the house before they arrive. I'm sure you two can handle the details." Kate gave her friend a wink. Eve and Jon seemed relieved when she declined their invitation, and Kate had to bite her lip to hold back a chuckle.

"Okay. Well, I'm sure we can figure things out," Eve said, smiling at Jon. Then as an afterthought, "Oh man, I hope the ghosts don't give us problems when we remodel."

"Excuse me," Kate said, thinking that she hadn't heard Eve correctly.

"The ghosts. When I first moved into the space, they made their presence known several times. Things have quieted down, but things go missing only to show up in a totally different room. Oh, and lights will mysteriously go off and on. But it's no big deal, really. I just think they're letting me know they're here, looking after the place."

Jon acted like this was just a normal, everyday occurrence. "I thought Pete was coming in to investigate?"

"Yeah, his schedule has been pretty busy with the spring semester underway. But I want him to come in soon to find out who or what is here."

"Uh huh," Kate said, feeling like she had just dropped into an alternative universe. "Hey Eve, can I talk to you for a minute, privately?"

"Well, hey, I'll get started on some drawings and a budget. I'll pick you up at seven o'clock, Eve." With that, Jon let himself out the front door.

Kate turned and shot her friend a skeptical look. "Ghosts? Really? You don't believe in that..." Kate was going to say crap but thought better of it. "... stuff. Do you?"

Eve took a deep breath and looked at her friend. "Yes. Yes, I do believe in that *stuff*. Look, I know you think this is crazy talk. But there are things in this world that can't be explained away as coincidence. I know you're not a believer, but all I ask is that you keep an open mind, okay?"

"Okay," Kate said, feeling sheepish. "I'm sorry. The last thing I would ever do is hurt you. I promise to keep an open mind." Kate gave Eve a hug, then in a serious tone said, "But Eve, there is one important thing we have to discuss."

"Huh?"

"What are you wearing on your date tonight?"

After spending an hour in Eve's apartment going through her closet to find the perfect outfit, Kate walked home. It was still snowing, and several inches had fallen since her arrival at the shop. She thought about Eve's revelation about *Potion* being haunted and shook her head. *Ghosts? Really?* No matter how hard Kate tried to accept the possibility of ghosts and spirits, she just couldn't believe they actually existed. But Kate reminded herself of the promise she made to Eve and focused on keeping her cynicism at bay.

On her walk, Kate stopped at the market to pick up groceries, her mind briefly flashing to the handsome-crazy-stalker-guy. *Oh please, on top of the ghosts, don't let me run into that guy.* After a tentative look down the aisle, she realized she was being silly. She pushed thoughts of the local voyeur out of head and instead made her way to the wine section, which was well stocked. She picked up a couple of bottles, thinking if she got snowed in, at least she'd have alcohol.

Carefully balancing her grocery bags while stepping through a snowdrift to her front door, Kate decided it would be a perfect night for a fire. She dropped the grocery bags on the kitchen counter and poured a glass of wine. Pulling the air mattress into the living room along with her pillow and blanket, she lit a fire, kicked off her shoes, and settled on the floor near the hearth. The house was quiet. As she watched the hypnotic flames, her thoughts drifted to Eve and Jon, heading out for their business dinner. She chuckled to herself. Kate thought about the excitement of a new relationship, which led her to memories of Michael. A wave of loneliness washed over her as she gazed out the living room window, watching the snow fall. *Maybe it's time to start dating.* Kate sipped her wine and returned her gaze to the flames. "One thing at a time, Kate. You have a lot on your plate and dating is the last thing you need right now." But saying those words did nothing to ease her loneliness.

Chapter 8

They decided *Potion* would close during remodeling, making it easier for Jon to do his work. Kate developed a rhythm of arriving at the shop around eight o'clock in the morning, and since Jon started early with construction work, the smell of fresh coffee and sawdust typically greeted her when she walked in the door. After the unique smells of New York City, she didn't think it was a bad way to start her day.

It was no surprise to Kate when Eve and Jon started dating. Apparently, the business dinner had continued into breakfast the next morning and Eve was beside herself with happiness. Thrilled to see her friend so happy, it impressed Kate that Eve could focus in on business details while Jon worked on the remodel, a mere twenty feet away. Although she had caught Eve on more than one occasion staring dreamily at Jon while he worked. Regardless of the distractions, two weeks into the renovation, the shop was looking great and Kate was confident they had a solid plan mapped out for the future. Now, all they needed were customers.

"Hey Kate," Jon said, poking his head into the office as he wrapped up work for the day. "When did they say the coffee equipment and refrigeration unit would arrive?"

"It should all be in around mid-April—another four to six weeks. Is that going to be a problem?"

"It shouldn't be, if everything arrives on time."

Kate looked at her watch. It was almost five o'clock. "I'll call them first thing on Monday and get a solid confirmation, okay?"

"Great," he said, as Eve came down the back stairs from her apartment, a strange look on her face.

"What's up, Eve? You look a little freaked out," Kate said.

"Um, yeah, well.... Ah, I went upstairs to drop off some supplies on the third floor and when I started back down to the shop, the scent of lavender overwhelmed me. When I reached the bottom of the stairs, I looked up at the landing and...." Eve rubbed her forehead, looking perplexed. "There was a woman standing at the top."

"Someone is in the building?" Kate asked, alarmed. "How did she get in here?" She stood up and headed for the stairs.

Eve took her arm, stopping her. "Katie, she's gone."

"How can she be gone? There's no other way out of here." The meaning behind Eve's comment sank in, and suddenly she didn't like where the scenario was going. "Eve, what do you mean?"

"She disappeared. I mean, she just evaporated. She wasn't solid. Uh... I could see her—she was wearing a Victorian dress with her hair put up—but she was transparent, and there was a distinct scent of lavender," Eve said, taking a shaky breath.

At the mention of lavender, the hairs on the back of Kate's neck stood up. She remembered the first time she was standing in that very stairwell with Eve and caught the fragrance—and then again in the cemetery. She pushed the thoughts away as nonsense and watched as Eve sat down, an expression of surprise on her face. After a minute of silence, she looked at her friend. "Eve, are you sure? I mean, look, you've been working so hard these past few weeks. Maybe you just *thought* you saw something."

Jon put his arm around Eve, hugging her. "You need to get in touch with Pete. Seriously, he needs to come check this out."

"Yeah, I think I'd better." Eve took out her cell phone and dialed. She made a face as the call went to voice mail. "Pete, hey, it's Eve Marsden at *Potion*. I really need to talk to you about a situation here at the shop. Can you call me as soon as possible? I'd appreciate it." She disconnected the call and looked at Jon and Kate. "Can we get out of here?" Kate had never seen her friend so freaked out—and there wasn't much that freaked Eve out.

"Sure, honey. Get your coat and let's go," Jon said. "Why don't we all go over to *Sabatino's* for pizza?"

"That sounds good. I could use a large vodka martini right about now," Eve said.

They grabbed their coats and made a quick exit. Outside, Eve exhaled, visibly relaxing as she locked the door and pocketed the keys. They walked to the restaurant in silence, which seemed to suit them all.

At Sabatino's, Jon waved to the bartender as they waited for the hostess. "I'll get the drinks if you want to grab a table. Eve, you want a Grey Goose martini?"

"A double," Eve said. Kate noticed Eve was returning to her old self.

"What are you drinking, Kate?"

"I'll have a Jameson and ginger ale, thanks Jon," Kate said, as she headed to the table, following her friend.

The two women sat down, with Eve immediately holding up her hand as if she were stopping traffic. "Look, before you say anything... I know what I saw, Kate—and smelled. The lavender fragrance was so pronounced."

Kate was out of her depth in dealing with the topic of ghosts. "I know, Eve. I'm sorry, I'm trying to understand all of this."

Before Kate could continue, Eve's phone rang. "Oh, that's Pete! I have to take this," she said, grabbing the phone. The interruption relieved Kate as she watched Eve relay the story again, growing more animated and excited as she spoke. "We're at *Sabatino's* now. Why don't you meet us for dinner, and we can talk?"

Oh great, thought Kate. *Some ghost hunting weirdo is joining us for dinner.* She suddenly wished she had asked Jon for a double on her drink, too. *I wonder if he'll show up in a tinfoil hat.* Kate nearly laughed out loud at the image in her mind of a socially awkward, middle-aged geek living in his mom's basement.

"Pete called. He's meeting us here in twenty minutes," Eve said, as Jon arrived with drinks in hand.

"Good. The sooner he can come check this out, the better," he said, draping his arm over Eve's shoulder.

"So, what do we want on our pizza?" Kate asked, before taking a sip of her cocktail. She was desperate to change the subject, even for a few minutes. The tactic worked, and after placing their order, the conversation shifted to how the remodeling was going, when they thought spring might finally arrive, and if Jon was planning to play on the local hardware store's softball team during the summer. But under the surface of their casual conversation was the fact Eve thought she had seen a ghost.

The pizza arrived, and as they were getting ready to dig in, Eve looked up. "Oh, there's Pete!" She waved him back to their table as Kate braced herself for the crazy onslaught.

Jon stood to greet him. "Hey Pete. Glad you could join us."

"Well, Eve tells me activity might be picking up at the shop, so I wanted to talk as soon as possible. Plus, I haven't seen either of you in what? Has to be three months."

"Too long," Eve chimed in. "Pete O'Brien, I'd like you to meet my best friend and business partner, Kate Murphy."

Kate looked up. No tin foil hat. No Ghostbusters tee shirt. Nope. Not one scintilla of strange about *this* guy. Instead, what she saw in that split second before her brain engaged were deep brown eyes and dark brown hair framing a face looking like someone could have chiseled it into a Roman coin. Six feet tall, high cheekbones, full lips, all wrapped in khakis, button-down shirt, and a down vest. She thought he looked familiar, and then it hit her.

"You," she said incredulously. "Are you kidding me? What the hell are you doing here?" She couldn't believe the crazy stalker guy was standing at their table, though she had to admit he looked as shocked to see her as she was to see him.

Pete made a seemingly quick recovery and smiled, extending his hand. "Nice to meet you, Kate."

"Uh," Kate stammered, at a loss for words. *Oh my god! Get your shit together, woman.* She held out her hand and shook his because she didn't know what else to do.

Eve looked totally confused, glancing from Kate to Pete. "Wait. You two know each other?"

"No!" Kate said, louder than she would have liked. She heard Pete chuckle under his breath, which made her angry. *So, this is the 'paranormal investigator' Eve was talking about. Well, doesn't it just figure? No wonder he was creeping around a freakin' cemetery!* She was about to launch into how he was really a stalker when a server appeared out of nowhere to take Pete's drink order. She looked like she was ready to take anything else he wanted to throw her way, but to his credit, he seemed oblivious as he gave his order with a distracted smile. As soon as she walked away, Pete turned his attention back to the table.

"It's a funny story." His tone was light, but he stared at her as if he'd never expected to see her again. "I was on a run about a month ago, past the Old Burying Point. I had a bit of writer's block and thought a run would clear my head. I saw Kate standing by a tombstone in the cemetery, looking very much like the Irish goddess Áine that I've been researching." As if transfixed, his gaze searched her face. "You look exactly like an illustration I found in a four-hundred-year-old manuscript." He turned back to the others. "Of course, her immediate assumption was that I was some sort of stalker—especially when I ran into her at the Salem Library a few days later." His laugh sounded awkward as the story wound down.

"Oh, that's hysterical! You? A stalker? Oh, Katie! Poor Pete," Eve said, laughing as she looked from one to the other.

Kate didn't respond, instead looking down at the pizza on her plate. The last thing she wanted to be was the butt of anyone's joke. *This guy, what was his name? Pete? What a jerk, and kind of arrogant too.*

He seemed to sense her embarrassment and changed the subject. "Okay, well, do you want to start from the beginning and fill me in on what's been happening at *Potion*? You were pretty cranked up when I talked to you on the phone, Eve." Kate noticed a dimple formed in his left cheek when he smiled, then silently berated herself for noticing. She turned her full attention to Eve. It was safer that way since, apparently, as humiliated as she was, she was having trouble keeping her hormones under control.

"Sure, Pete," Eve said. "Well, you know that I've had innocuous stuff happening since I moved in—things moving to different rooms, lights turning off and on every once in a while—but today," Eve paused, reliving the moment. "I was coming down the stairs from my apartment into the shop when the scent of lavender filled the stairwell. I got to the bottom of the stairs, turned, and there was a woman, in what appeared to be Victorian dress, looking down at me from the second-floor landing. She was transparent, almost smoky looking. After a few seconds, she turned and just disappeared."

"Uh, huh. Any sound?" Pete asked.

"No. Nothing." Eve shrugged.

"Have you ever smelled the fragrance of lavender before? You don't have perfumes at the shop, do you? Something that spilled by accident?" It relieved Kate that he was looking for practical explanations for Eve's experience. Maybe he wasn't totally insane.

"No, never," Eve said.

"Hmm. Have you seen any orbs or flashing light?"

Eve shook her head.

Okay, forget about not being totally insane. The guy is talking about orbs. What the hell is an orb? And he's dead serious! Kate wondered if maybe he wasn't some sort of charlatan or something. Kind of like those people back in the 1920s who claimed they could communicate with the dead through seances. She looked at him again. *Good looks. Charm. Yeah, he could totally be a con man.*

"Well, I think we should do an investigation. But it's going to be a couple of weeks before my calendar opens up. Can you wait?" he asked.

"I think so." Finishing her double martini, Eve appeared more at ease.

"I'll look after her," Jon said. He smiled at Eve and put his arm around her shoulder, pulling her close. "I'm working at *Potion* most days doing the remodeling, so I'll keep my eyes open."

"That would be great. But if activity really ramps up, then I'll see what I can do about rearranging my schedule," Pete said, scrolling through the calendar on his phone.

"So, what do you do when you aren't ghostbuster-ing?" Kate barely kept the snark out of her voice. She was determined to figure this guy out because there was no way he was going to take advantage of her best friend.

With a slight smile, Pete turned his attention to Kate, and she noticed that damned dimple again. "I'm an assistant professor at Harvard. I specialize in Irish history," he said, almost as if he was throwing down the gauntlet.

Harvard? He has an actual job? Well, that blew Kate's theory that he was some fly-by-night con man. "That's interesting," she said, turning back to her pizza.

"I take it you don't believe in ghosts," he said, grinning at her, clearly enjoying her discomfort. "I get that reaction a lot when I tell people I'm a paranormal investigator."

Kate's irritation grew with his condescending tone, so she turned and looked him in the eye. "No. I do not believe in ghosts," she said. She wanted to say more, but Eve was there and Kate didn't want to hurt her feelings by telling this guy he was full of shit.

"Huh," he said. The two of them stared at each other, ready to square off in an argument. But then something changed. Pete's pupils dilated, turning his eyes almost black. He looked down at her mouth, then to her eyes, as Kate held her breath, mesmerized.

"So, Pete. How have classes been going this semester?" Jon said, breaking the tension. In an effort to slow her pulse, Kate exhaled slowly and stared down at her pizza.

"Good. I'm teaching three courses this spring—one of them is a hundred-seat lecture class, so I'm staying busy. But spring break is in a few weeks, so I'll be heading down to Virginia to see my dad. Looking forward to the time off," he said.

Kate looked up to see Eve giving her a wide-eyed look. "Will you excuse me a minute? Kate, why don't you come with me," Eve said, standing.

Frustrated that she couldn't come up with a good excuse, Kate dutifully got up and joined her friend. All things considered, it was probably a good idea because she needed to put some distance between herself and the arrogant, hot professor who believed in things that went bump in the night. They wove their way through the crowded bar to the women's bathroom. It was a quiet respite from the din. As soon as they got through the door, Eve spun around to her friend, turning on the drama with a well-placed arched eyebrow. "So, what was *that* all about?"

"What do you mean?" Kate desperately tried to play dumb.

"Oh hell, you know what I mean. I have eyes. You two looked pretty damned hot out there," Eve grinned.

"Oh please, you've got to be kidding me. I just met the guy. Besides, we have nothing in common, *and* he's not my type."

"Right. I don't think it would take much for him to become your type," Eve giggled.

Kate rolled her eyes and walked into the stall. When she came out, Eve was still standing there. "You know, he's single," Eve said in a singsong voice. Kate brushed past her to the sink. "He really is a nice guy." She looked at Kate in the mirror with an encouraging smile.

"Look, Eve. I appreciate your efforts to hook me up, but please leave it alone."

"But why? You two are obviously attracted to each other."

"Eve, stop. I want nothing to do with some weirdo who stalks women in cemeteries and has a hobby hunting for ghosts on the weekend!" As the words left her mouth, she wished she could take them back, because the smile evaporating from Eve's face was evidence of her insensitive comment.

"I see," she said, turning to leave the close confines of the room.

Kate grabbed Eve's arm before she reached the door. "No, wait. Please.... I'm really trying to understand all this. It's new to me. I do believe you think you saw something. And I don't think you're crazy! I'm sorry. Just give me time to adjust to this, okay? I can't give you a guarantee that I'll end up a believer, but I can promise that I won't be such an ass with hurtful comments, alright?"

Eve was quiet for a long time, then looked up at Kate. "Okay. Apology accepted. But girl, you need to lighten up. Not everything in the universe can be explained. And Pete isn't a stalker either!" She reached for the door, then delivered a good-natured parting shot. "I still think the two of you looked hot together." Laughing, she headed back into the noisy bar, with Kate trailing behind, shaking her head in exasperation.

When they returned to the table, Jon and Pete were discussing the Red Sox and whether they had a shot at a World Series win. Pete turned to Eve. "So, when did you and Jon start dating?"

Eve and Jon looked at each other, radiating happiness. "It's been two weeks," she said, as Jon took her hand. "What about you, Pete? Are you dating anyone?" Eve asked, looking like the picture of innocence, but Kate knew better and inwardly groaned.

"No, not right now. Things have been busy at work. I'm wrapping up research on a book project that I'm working on with some colleagues at Trinity College in Dublin. So, no time for dating right now."

Eve shot a look at Kate that made her want to kick Eve under the table. Instead, she sat there, silently eating her pizza and counting the minutes until she could go home while the others chatted away about Pete's research and the upcoming tourist season.

As dinner plates were cleared away, Pete turned to Kate. "So, when did you move to Salem?"

"Two weeks ago." She offered no more than that.

"Well, what did you do before you came to Salem?" It was clear her chilly, brief responses did not deter him.

"I worked in New York City for Sterling Bank." She glanced at him briefly, then looked down at the table.

"Kate was the shining star in grad school," Eve said, unable to contain the pride she had in her best friend. "She had a lucrative career in private banking—I'm lucky that she gave it all up to come here and help me get *Potion* moving in the right direction. It was Katie's idea to branch out into a coffee and tea shop. Brilliant, right?"

Kate couldn't help smiling at her friend. "Eve is too kind. I'm just happy to help. She's the creative fire, I'm just offering practical advice to help her out."

"Practical." Pete chuckled, giving her an appraising look.

"Why the laugh?" Kate asked, working hard to tamp down her irritation.

"I just think practical is an understatement." He obviously thought he was funny, but it came out condescending.

To control her anger, Kate took a deep breath and turned, giving him a chilly smile. "Well, I've always believed that practicality is a valuable personality trait. You should try it for yourself some time." With that, Kate took her wallet out of her purse, grabbed some cash, then turned and looked Pete in the eye. "I'm so glad that you have me figured out. Considering I've only met you an hour ago." She said with as much ice in her voice as she could muster. She turned to Eve, who had a look somewhere between shock and amusement. "I'm going to head home now. I'll talk to you later. Jon, I'll confirm delivery of the coffee equipment on Monday morning." Kate put the money on the table and stood up. Pete stood as well.

"It was nice to meet you, Practical Kate," he grinned, holding out his hand.

Kate rolled her eyes and took his hand. "You too, ghostbuster." With that, she attempted to leave, but Pete held onto her hand for a split second longer than necessary. She felt a frisson of electricity and broke the contact, hearing him chuckle as she walked away.

Pretty boy, ghost busting, jerk! She opened the door and headed into the chilly night. Walking down the street toward home, she stopped in front of *Potion* and looked in the window. "Ghosts. Really, this is just silly," she muttered to herself. After a minute of looking in the window, Kate turned to head home. As she walked away, a mist formed inside the shop, morphing into a woman in Victorian dress. She watched as Kate headed down the empty street.

Chapter 9

The rolling hills of Virginia were just what Pete needed to relax. In fact, he could feel the muscles in his shoulders loosening the closer he got to home—to Capall Farms. It had been a stressful year for Pete, working to finish his manuscript and dividing his time between Harvard and Trinity College. But there was finally a light at the end of the tunnel. The manuscript was almost complete, and in a few years he would be up for tenure at one of the most prestigious institutions of higher learning in the country. All he needed to do was stay focused.

So why did he feel so unfulfilled? He shook his head to clear the cloud of dissatisfaction from his brain and looked for the turnoff into the farm. A list of things he should be grateful for ran through his head, starting with his dad and ending with the fact that he had an outstanding job and a roof over his head in a nice New England town. Which then brought his thoughts to Kate Murphy. Pete had been thinking about her ever since they met at *Sabatino's* and she'd called him ghostbuster. He laughed at the memory. *She was so prickly*, he thought. But damn, she was beautiful with those green eyes and long red hair that he couldn't get out of his mind.

The line of white wooden fencing told him he was home. He pulled the Subaru off the main road and headed back through a grove of trees to the white farmhouse and stables beyond. As he exited the car, Pete inhaled the familiar scents of earth, grass, and horse, and felt at peace. All the stress and worry he was carrying about his job and research melted at that moment. He was walking toward the stable when a wiry, gray-haired man in worn jeans, plaid shirt, and work boots came around the corner.

"Ah, there he is," the man beamed. "I've been waiting for you all morning. I've got plenty of chores just waiting for you to get started on!"

"Hey, Dad," Pete grinned, greeting his father with a hug. "Don't I have time to say hello and grab my bags before you put me to work? And I'd like to remind you I'm on spring break!"

Jacob O'Brien looked up at his son with pride and amusement. "You've been in the city for too long. Spring break? We don't celebrate that holiday here!" He slapped Pete on the back and gave him another hug. "I've missed you, son. Come on, let's go up to the house. Mae has been baking up a storm, and I'm thinking we'll find some fresh scones and tea in the kitchen."

The two men strolled to the house, stopping only for Pete to grab his duffle bag and laptop. "Did you bring work?" Jacob asked. "I thought it was your spring break."

"No rest for the wicked, Dad. I have student essays to grade and some writing to do on my manuscript. But I promise I'll keep up with my chores," Pete teased.

"You work so hard. I think you deserve a bit of a break."

"Maybe next year, Dad. Once I finish this book, then I can take a break. Working toward tenure isn't easy."

They went in the house through the side door and there was Mae, a plump, brown-haired woman, standing at the sink in the big farm kitchen, brushing flour from her hands. "Pete, you're here! I thought I heard a car pull in." She gave him a hug and a kiss on the cheek, then ordered both men to sit down. "I've got a pot of tea on and scones fresh out of the oven."

Pete knew better than to refuse Mae, as they sat down while she bustled around the kitchen. Within minutes mugs were on the table with a big plate of warm scones, jam, and clotted cream. "Oh, how I've missed your baking, Mae," Pete said around a mouthful of scone. "These really are the best."

Mae beamed at Pete. "We're just so glad you could come and visit. Now, after you two finish, take your bags up to your room. We'll have a nice relaxing evening once Jacob gets done putting you to work."

The afternoon passed quickly, with Pete working alongside his father, repairing stall doors, and hauling hay to the loft. By the end of the day, his muscles ached, but his mind felt a lot clearer. On the walk back to the house, he commented on how great the farm looked.

Jacob stopped at the fence, looking out over the rolling hills as horses grazed quietly in the late afternoon sunshine. "It's a beautiful place, and this is where I was meant to be," he said, growing nostalgic. "You know, when your mother died, this place kept me going. First, just throwing myself into the work helped keep my mind busy. But after a while I realized this is my life. When I left Ireland, I had nothing. But your mother and I built this place up from a rundown old farm. My soul is here," he said with a soft smile. "And I'm grateful God sent me Mae. Before your mother passed, she made me promise I would find someone.... I didn't want to even consider it. But life has a funny way of working out, doesn't it?"

"Well, I only hope that I can find that kind of happiness one day."

"Are you seeing anyone, lad?"

Kate's image flashed in his mind. "No.... Well, I met this woman a few weeks ago. But I'm not sure she's interested. A fiery, Irish redhead, Dad." A look of admiration crossed his face as he remembered her.

Jacob caught his son's look and laughed. "Uh, oh! Look out, son."

Pete laughed along with his father, then grew thoughtful. "She seems pretty guarded. But there is something there, Dad. And she's so beautiful. I can't seem to stop thinking about her." He shrugged. "So, what should I do?"

"Seriously? My highly educated, Harvard professor son doesn't know what he should do? Ask her out, man! For goodness' sake!"

Pete laughed and tried to appease his father. "Okay, Dad. Okay. Maybe I will."

Chapter 10

"What do you mean, it's going to be another month before they deliver the equipment?" Kate asked the customer service rep. "They gave me a guarantee the espresso and refrigeration equipment would be here by now." From the other end of the phone, the representative explained they had pushed deliveries back because of a trucking strike in Italy. That meant the espresso equipment wouldn't be leaving the country for another two weeks. There would then be a delay with customs. A month. "Well, can you at least ship out the refrigeration unit?" After going back and forth for twenty minutes, they agreed they would deliver in two shipments. While it was a solution, it meant they wouldn't get around to installing, testing, and training until early May. They had hoped for a soft opening at the first of May, but now that was in jeopardy. Kate sighed, hanging up the phone and dropping the file folder with the invoice and materials on the desk. She then headed out to the shop to give Eve and Jon an update.

The two were standing by the almost finished coffee bar, discussing the materials for the top. "What do you think of black granite?" Eve asked.

"Too expensive. I'm thinking you need a quartz stone composite material. Easier to maintain and they work better in commercial applications," Jon said. "Plus, you can design just about any color you want. We'll need to go to the showroom today to get an order placed."

Kate joined them. "Hey guys. I've got some bad news on the espresso machine delivery." After telling them about the transportation strike in Italy and giving them the new delivery information, Jon thought for a minute.

"Well, we should still be okay. I have the dimensions on all the equipment and where it's going to be placed. If the refrigeration unit arrives on time, then we should be fine," he said.

"But what about training on the new equipment?" Eve asked.

"That's what I was worried about, too," Kate said. "We'll just have to make the best of it. If you and I know how to use everything, then we can train Jenny and anyone else we decide to bring on."

"Alright.... What else can we do?" Eve shrugged. "Hey, Jon and I are going to go to the showroom to choose the countertop materials. Do you want to come with us?"

"No. I'll stay here for a couple of hours and wrap up some files and work on the new financial software. You two go ahead," Kate said.

Kate watched as they headed out to Jon's truck, leaving her in the peace and quiet of the shop. Locking the front door, she went back to the office, turned on some music, and settled at the desk, ready to get back to work. Reaching absently for the file she had left there, Kate realized it was gone. "What the heck? It was here ten minutes ago," she said, looking around the office. "What did I do with it?" She headed back out to the front of the shop, thinking she might have left it on the coffee bar. It wasn't there. Aggravated, she went back to the office, where she found the missing file sitting in the middle of the desk. "What the f— am I losing my mind?" She sat down, feeling unsettled, but shook it off and got back down to work.

An hour passed without incident, and by that time she'd forgotten about the missing file. She was getting up to stretch when a blast of cold air came through the office. Wondering if Eve and Jon had returned, she went out into the shop. But the front door was shut tight. "Weird," she muttered, returning to the office.

"Might as well look at the financial software," she said, logging into the computer. As she waited for the data to load, she thought she heard someone faintly calling her name. She turned around quickly, but no one was there. "Okay, what the hell is going on?" She got up and walked to the front of the shop again. Nothing. On her way back, she caught the scent of lavender.

"That's it. I'm leaving. I'm tired and stressed and I know this is just my imagination." She shut off the computer, grabbed her coat and purse, and practically ran to the front door.

Once outside, she locked the door and took a deep breath to calm herself. *Katie, there is a perfectly good explanation for all of this. There are no ghosts! You just let yourself get spooked.* That made her feel a bit better, but she vowed there was no way she would mention any of what happened to Eve. The last thing she needed to do was stoke her belief that *Potion* was haunted.

She stopped at the market on the way home, feeling that if she did something 'normal' it would bring everything back into perspective. She wandered down the aisles and with each step she felt better—until, turning a corner, she almost collided with Pete O'Brien.

"Well, if it isn't Practical Kate," he grinned.

"Oh boy, it's the local ghostbuster," she deadpanned. He laughed, clearly delighted with their sparring. She noted his laugh, warm and resonant—and she wanted to kick herself for letting her mind go there. "Shouldn't you be at Harvard teaching a class or something?"

"I didn't know you were so interested in my schedule. I'm flattered," he teased. Kate scowled. "Actually, I finished my last class an hour ago. Thought I'd hit the market before I went home. How are things at *Potion*? Any activity since the last time we met?"

Kate stiffened, thinking of what just occurred at the shop. "Of course not."

"So that's a hard no?" He was smiling at her.

That damned dimple. A flame of anger and self-preservation lit up within her. "Look, I know you and apparently everybody else in this town believes in ghosts, witches, and things that go bump in the night. I do not. My best friend is working hard to make her business successful, and I'm here to help her make that happen. Now she tells me she's seeing women in Victorian dress wandering around her shop. I don't want *anyone* messing up our hard work by feeding her a line about the place being haunted. Got it?" She thought about Eve and how everything was riding on the changes they were making to *Potion*. The last thing Kate wanted was her friend worrying about ghosts.

"I got it," Pete said, no longer smiling. "But if Eve wants me to investigate, I will. I appreciate you are her friend and business partner, but it is *her* decision." He paused, as if in thought. "And for the record? I don't feed anyone a *line*. You would do well to learn to respect other people's beliefs. Not everything in life is black and white with sharply drawn edges. Got it?"

Kate blushed with embarrassment at having her words thrown back at her. "Got it." She turned on her heel and retreated down the aisle to the checkout.

"Well, that went well," Pete muttered, watching Kate storm out of the grocery store. The happy, surprised feeling of seeing her evaporated as quickly as her exit, to be replaced, first with confusion, then exasperation. He laughed without humor, thinking that their fortuitous meeting should have been a chance to get better acquainted. What he hadn't expected was the fury she'd unloaded on him. Pete returned to his shopping but became increasingly pissed off as he paced the aisles, throwing items into his cart with more force than necessary.

I don't need this kind of crap in my life. What the hell does she think I am, some sort of snake oil salesman? Jesus! She's impossible. He paused, taking a deep breath to tamp down his growing anger. *I've got too much going on right now—how did I ever think that she would be a person I'd want to go out with? What did I ever do to this woman? And why is she so freaked out?* He stopped, realizing that on a certain level she seemed almost scared. *Well, you were staring at her in a cemetery. And don't forget your smooth moves at the library.* He groaned, realizing she had every right to think he was—well—if not a stalker, a weirdo. And he had to give her credit, she certainly was loyal to her friend. He shook his head in frustration as he moved to the check-out line. *Stop making excuses for her, Pete.... But damn, she's hot when she gets mad.* That thought startled him as he fantasized about her in the middle of the grocery store— wondering if that passion continued in the bedroom.

He paid for his groceries and threw the bags in the back of his car. On the drive home, he couldn't get the beautiful, practical, frustrating Kate Murphy out of his head. By the time he walked in the front door, Pete had convinced himself it had been a momentary lapse in sanity to be attracted to the prickly redhead and decided what he needed was a drink. Juggling groceries and shutting the door, he turned to see his cat, Finn, sitting at the top of the second-floor landing, giving him the stink-eye. "Yes, I got cat food. God forbid you have to wait a few hours to be fed," he said with exasperated affection. The cat padded down the stairs and gave a plaintive meow in Pete's general direction. "Oh, come on! I don't need you bitching at me." Walking into the kitchen, he continued his conversation with the cat. "Did a certain redheaded goddess call and tell you to tear into me, too?" Pete filled the cat's bowl and put it down on the kitchen floor. Finn turned, swished his tail, and proceeded to eat his dinner. After putting away the groceries, Pete poured himself a whiskey and went into his study, firing up his computer and kicking off his shoes.

At his desk, he replayed the whole grocery store episode. "I shouldn't have lost my temper. Why let her get under your skin like that?" But he knew the reason she was getting under his skin. It was her fiery independence, that long red hair he wanted to touch, those bright green eyes that flashed when she challenged him. He sipped his whiskey and took a deep breath. As much as he tried to talk himself down, Pete found himself more and more frustrated by her behavior. "I'm a nice guy, aren't I?" he asked Finn, who had finished eating and sauntered into the study. Finn blinked at him. "Thanks. You're no help at all."

He opened the browser on his laptop, deciding to research Eve Marsden's building, hoping to find some history that would give him clues about the apparition that had appeared. He also hoped it would take his mind off a certain redhead. Within an hour he had some interesting details on the place and hoped they might answer some of Eve's questions regarding whoever was haunting her shop. Pete looked at his calendar to confirm the date of the *Potion* investigation. Three weeks. Kate probably wouldn't be at the investigation anyway, since she obviously didn't believe in ghosts. But all the same, Pete planned to ask Eve if she would be there. Just so he could be prepared for her angry outbursts. It had nothing to do with getting a chance to see her again. Not at all.

Chapter 11

K ate hadn't seen or heard anything about Pete in weeks. Eve had carefully kept conversations about the resident ghost between herself and Jon, which suited Kate just fine. The incident in *Potion* three weeks ago was fading, and Kate had convinced herself it was all in her imagination. With things moving full speed ahead, there was barely a free minute to think about anything else other than getting ready for their soft opening. It seemed she was constantly reviewing checklists in her head, doing everything she could do to make sure they stayed on schedule.

Much to everyone's relief, the espresso equipment arrived a week early, giving them one less thing to worry about. Kate admired the machine gleaming in the light, sitting in pride of place on the bar as Jon and Eve carefully connected the water lines. Correction, Jon connected the water lines while Eve handed him tools and supervised.

As Kate looked around the room, she couldn't be more pleased. A few simple changes had transformed the place. The sign painter had arrived a few days prior to paint the new *Potion* logo on the window and the front door. The shop had an airy feel to it, with white stucco walls accented with heavy timber beams, with the coffee bar and display case taking up the back wall and blending in as if it had always been there. Jon had created beautiful rustic tables and Eve had picked up mix and match chairs at an estate sale, which gave the place a funky, comfortable feel. To finish the decor, Eve hung cool antique coffee posters on the walls surrounding the seating area. Kate noticed people would stop and look in the windows to see what was going on. It gave her hope they could draw in a mix of locals and tourists when they re-opened.

"Beautiful," Kate said, walking up to Eve.

Eve leaned into her friend, her voice filled with emotion. "I couldn't have done this without you, Katie. Thank you. This is going to change everything—I'm sure of it. I can feel an energy shift in the place."

"It's me who should thank you. I've never felt so happy. You saved me from a workaholic, empty life. I love it here."

Jon stood behind the counter, wiping his hands on his jeans. "Water lines are all hooked up. Do we want to test it out now or wait until tomorrow?"

"Let's turn the water back on and make sure we don't have any leaks," Eve said. "But why don't we wait until tomorrow to test out the gear and make our first cup of espresso."

"Good idea. I want to sleep tonight—last thing I need right now is espresso," Kate said.

"Okay, cross your fingers." Jon ran to the back of the building and turned on the water. They waited. "Any leaks?" he shouted.

"No, we're good," Eve said.

Jon walked back with a grin, "Do it right the first time, every time."

"Oh, you always do it right," Eve said, wrapping her arms around him.

"Hey, do you two need some privacy," Kate said.

Eve grinned, "No, I think we can contain ourselves, for a few hours at least."

"So, what's left on the *Potion* to do list?" Jon asked, giving Eve's ass an affectionate pat.

Eve rattled off the list. "We have to bring in the sofa and upholstered chairs for the corner. Then, set up the storage pantry and work up an inventory system for the coffee and supplies." It impressed Kate how quickly Eve was embracing the business aspects of running the place.

"No problem. I can stop on the way in tomorrow and pick up the furniture with the truck. I'll leave the computer inventory fun for the two of you," Jon said.

"Thanks, honey. Are you heading out soon?"

"Where are you off to?" Kate asked.

"Home opener at Fenway. Meeting my brother Jim in town." Jon packed up his tools and kissed Eve goodbye.

"I'll see you in the morning, love," Eve called as he left.

"Why don't you come over for dinner if Jon's going to be out tonight," Kate asked.

"Yes! We've been so busy we haven't had five minutes to catch up. What can I bring?"

"How about a bottle of white wine? I'll make a salad with some fresh bread. Then after dinner we can have some girl talk!"

On the street heading home, Kate could feel the change of season. A warm breeze rustled the bright green leaves in the trees as she walked along. *How can you not feel happy and hopeful on days like this?* She unlocked the front door, dropped her keys on the hallway table, then docked her phone on the speaker as jazz flooded the room. After adjusting the volume, she headed for the kitchen to start dinner, looking forward to spending an evening with Eve.

"So, tomorrow night Pete O'Brien is going to do a preliminary investigation at *Potion*." Eve casually dropped the comment into the conversation after dinner as she was clearing the table. "I wanted to give you a heads up. I hope you'll stick around for it."

Kate froze, thinking about what had happened a few weeks ago. She brushed it aside, telling herself there weren't any such things as ghosts. "I don't know, Eve. You know it's not my thing," she said, being careful of her feelings. Besides, she didn't need the complication of seeing Pete again. Between the embarrassment of their last meeting, plus the effect he had on her, Kate wanted to keep as much distance between them as possible.

"Well, I just thought it would give you a chance to see that it's not as crazy as it might sound. It's actually an interesting process. Plus, it will give you a chance to see Pete again."

"I don't really care if I ever see Pete O'Brien again. Last time I ran into him, it didn't go so well."

"When did you see him?"

"It was about three weeks ago. The day you and Jon went to pick out the countertop for the coffee bar. I saw him at the market. We had a bit of an argu... discussion," Kate looked away, trying to hide her embarrassment, remembering the tone of their conversation.

"Huh, he didn't say anything to me. In fact, yesterday he asked if you were going to be at the investigation."

"Yeah, probably so he can be ready with more sarcastic comments," Kate said bitterly.

"Hey, to be fair, you were pretty snarky to him from the get-go," Eve pointed out.

Kate thought about it and had to admit that Eve was right. "I guess so." She bit her lip. "But I was worried. I didn't know how well you knew him, and I was afraid he was some sort of charlatan or something. *You* never told me he was a professor at Harvard!"

Eve laughed and waved off her comment. "Well, jeez. That's not the first thing you say when you're making introductions. Come on, Katie. You should check it out. I promise I won't try to push the two of you together. Although I can't for the life of me understand what you are running away from. He is smokin' hot."

"I'm not ready to get involved. Breaking up with Michael was enough pain for a lifetime. Sometimes I think it just might be easier to give up on romantic relationships. I'm not sure there is anyone out there for me anyway," Kate said, moving into the living room.

Eve settled on the sofa next to Kate. "Oh honey, why would you say that?"

"Because I'm too rigid! And always so responsible. How boring is that?" Visions of Pete calling her Practical Kate made her cringe.

"Maybe it's time to change things up then," Eve said. "Maybe you need to do something a little bit different—get out of your comfort zone. What better way than coming on a ghost investigation," she grinned, daring her friend.

Kate shook her finger at Eve. "Oh, you're good. Sneaky, but good. Alright. I'll expand my horizons and come on this ghost hunt. But you have to promise me something."

Eve clapped her hands, delighted. "Anything! What do I need to promise?"

"That you will not try to fix me up with Mr. Ghostbuster, okay?"

Eve sighed, "Okay. I promise. We'll take this in baby steps."

"There will be no baby steps. I have nothing in common with him. I'll do my thing and he can do his," Kate said.

"Yeah, but what if the thing he wants to do is you," Eve said sweetly. She then broke into raucous laughter, and Kate couldn't help but join in.

Chapter 12

Kate went into *Potion* the next day, feeling more than a little anxious. The thought of seeing Pete after their last run-in made her nervous, but she promised Eve she would try moving out of her comfort zone by joining in on the ghost investigation. To continue the trend toward exorcising her more practical side, Kate stopped in a souvenir shop, and as a joke bought a black v neck tee shirt that said BOO across the front. She was exiting the bathroom after changing into the shirt when Eve walked around the corner.

Eve let out a low whistle. "Damn, girl!"

"Yeah, it's too tight. I'm need to change."

"What are you, nuts? It looks fantastic! You just aren't used to wearing things that *fit* you."

Biting her lip, Kate inspected the neckline and her cleavage in the mirror. "I don't know. Is it too slutty?"

Eve smacked her arm. "No! You look amazing! And it's so cute. Pete will love it."

Kate shot a warning look at her friend. "Eve, what did I say about all that? Do *not*, under any circumstance, do *anything* that even looks like matchmaking. Okay?"

"Right. Okay. Got it. Anyway, once he gets a look at you, I probably won't have to do a damned thing." She tossed the comment over her shoulder as she sauntered out to the front of the shop.

Another look in the mirror, and Kate thought about changing clothes. But after careful consideration, she smiled. *Oh, why not! Let's give the ghostbuster a thrill.*

Pete hurried down Essex Street, hoping to beat the thunderstorm that had been threatening for the last hour. Shifting the heavy duffle bag on his shoulder, he mentally reviewed the contents. *Night vision cameras, EVP recorders, motion detectors, spirit box.... I think that's everything we'll need tonight.* He checked his watch and attempted to reign in his anxiety—anxiety having everything to do with a certain fiery redhead. *Chill, dude. She may decide not to show up,* he thought, remembering their last run-in at the grocery store.

As he approached the storefront, he noticed Eve and Jon sitting at one of the newly installed tables, finishing their dinner. *Okay. She's not here. Now relax.* Knocking on the door, he watched as Eve ran to let him in. He entered on a gust of wind and rumble of thunder. "Hey, how's it going? Looks like we're in for a thunderstorm tonight. That should set up some great conditions."

"Hi, Pete. C'mon in and set your stuff over there." Eve pointed to the table. "Did you eat dinner?"

"Yeah, I grabbed something before I left home, thanks." He busied himself unloading the gear and didn't notice Kate walking out of the office on to the shop floor. "Wow, you've really made progress in the shop. Will you be ready..." He stopped mid-sentence as soon as Kate entered the room, struck dumb momentarily as he glanced down at the shirt molded to her curves. *Sweet Jesus...* "Nice shirt," he said when his brain finally engaged. *Really? That's your smooth response? She already thinks you're a stalker. Get a grip.* He wanted to sink into the floor. Instead, he turned back to the bag of gear.

"Thank you," she said, crossing her arms over her chest as she hurried to the other side of the room.

Within minutes, Pete filled the table with all sorts of electronic gear. Eve and Jon stepped closer, picking up pieces of equipment and asking questions, while Kate hung back and busied herself with cleaning up the paper plates from dinner. Pete noticed she would look at the equipment incredulously every time she passed. When she came back in the room and settled in a chair, doing her best impression of someone who couldn't care less about what was going on, he called her on her attitude. "What?" He practically dared her to make a sarcastic comment.

"Nothing," she said, fixing her face in a bored expression.

"You'll never be a poker player, Practical Kate." He knew he was goading her, but if he was being honest, he was looking forward to seeing her eyes flash at him.

Instead of flashing eyes, Kate gave him a saccharine smile. "I was just thinking, it can't be *that* difficult to track down Casper that you would need all of this stuff. Makes me wonder if you are as good as everyone says you are."

Pete gave her a long look that seemed to dare her to find out. "Well, I haven't heard any complaints," he said, just loud enough for her to hear. He watched her blush and hurry to the window. *Well, I won the first round. Tonight might be more fun than I thought.* "Why don't we all sit down and I'll fill you in on the research I've been doing," Pete suggested, reminding himself he was there to do a job, not flirt with the beautiful woman who had been haunting his daily thoughts. Once everyone settled, he started on the history. "So, they built the building in 1880, during the Victorian period."

"The woman I saw was in Victorian dress," Eve said, excitement in her voice.

"Right. The building was owned by an Abigale Hastings," Pete said.

"A woman owned this place? How cool is that?" Eve's eyes shone.

"Yeah, she was a shop owner—had a business selling textiles. She was incredibly successful."

"Was she married?" Jon asked. "I mean, wasn't it kind of unusual for a woman to have her own business back then?"

"Apparently, Abigale Hastings was a spinster. She grew up the daughter of a sea captain who instilled independence in Abigale. She was an only child and her father's heir, since her mother died in childbirth. When he died, he left her everything. So, she started her own business." Pete noticed Kate's growing interest. She sat forward, listening intently to his report. "In 1890 there was an accident; a team of horses were pulling a flatbed wagon filled with textiles to be delivered to the shop. Abigale went out to meet the driver and something spooked the horses. Abigale was trampled. They brought her into the building, and she died hours later from her injuries."

"Oh, that's horrible," gasped Eve.

"The shop closed, but apparently Abigale felt tied to the place. Townspeople reported seeing her wandering the second and third floors of the building late at night," Pete said.

"So, you're saying it's Abigale Hastings who is haunting the building?" Jon asked.

"I'm not sure, but it's a good place to start, don't you think?" Pete replied.

"Poor Abigale. It's just so incredibly sad," Eve sighed.

Pete saw a skeptical look cross Kate's face. He had her attention with the independent businesswoman, but the minute it crossed over to something paranormal, she shut down. He wondered if there was anything he could say to change her opinion. *Maybe the ghost can do the talking*, he thought, hoping Abigale or whoever was there wouldn't be shy. "Well then, let's get to it. I thought we would start with some EVP work here on the first floor to see if we get any responses."

"EV what?" Kate asked.

"EVP. Electronic voice phenomena," he said patiently, as if he were talking to a child.

Kate crossed her arms, clearly irritated with him. "How does that work?"

Seeing his tone had rankled her, he changed his tack and went into professor mode. At least she seemed interested. He picked up a gadget off the table. "I have a recorder here that can pick up what the human ear often misses or can't hear at all. We'll ask a few questions and wait. Then we play back the recording to see if we get any kind of response. It's important to be quiet and not move around while doing this, so we don't pick up extraneous sounds on the recording. Okay?" Everyone nodded. "Let's get started then."

Eve turned off the lights as they moved to the center of the room. Pete turned on the recorder, noting the date, time, and location. There was an ominous rumble of thunder, which he noted on the recording. Then he began. "Hello. We are here to talk to you and mean you no harm. We think you might have shown yourself to Eve. Can you please tell us your name?" He paused for a moment, then continued. "Are you Abigale Hastings? Did you own this building?" He waited about twenty seconds and turned off the recorder. "Okay, let's play it back and see if we got anything."

The recorder replayed the one-sided conversation, since there were no responses to the questions being asked. "So, does that mean no one is here?" Eve asked.

"No, not necessarily. Why don't we go upstairs and split up into teams?" He went to the duffle bag and pulled out another recording device, plus a night vision camera. With a flash of inspiration, he said, "Eve and Jon, why don't you go to the second floor, and Kate and I will take the third."

"Sounds good," Eve said, grinning at Kate.

On the second floor landing, they stopped. "Just go from room to room asking questions. I know I don't have to tell you, but I say it all the same. You are dealing with people—they just happen to be dead. Be kind and considerate," Pete reminded them. "Eve, what's on the third floor?"

"Most of the floor is empty. I keep inventory stored in the two back rooms—otherwise it's pretty bare."

"Okay. Try not to use your flashlights unless absolutely necessary. Use the night vision camera view finder. But be careful." Pete turned to Kate and gestured toward the stairs, handing her the recorder. "I'll go first, if that's okay with you?"

"Fine."

Pete could feel Kate's silent judgment filling the staircase as they climbed to the third floor. He knew he shouldn't care what she thought, but he couldn't help it. Her opinion of him now seemed to be all he could focus on. At the top of the stairs, he stopped abruptly as Kate bumped into him with a muffled *oomph*.

"Where do you want to go first?" she asked, sarcasm in her voice.

He gave her a clipped response, suggesting they start in one of the rooms used for storage. *Okay. Just get through this. You've done hundreds of investigations—focus on that—not the obstinate redhead.* He opened the door, where they were greeted by neatly stacked boxes against the wall, along with the smell of dust. "Alright. Why don't you turn on the recorder and ask some questions?"

"Be happy to," she grumbled, fiddling with the machine while trying to find the record button.

Pete watched her struggle with the buttons for a minute before taking the recorder out of her hand. When they touched, he noticed Kate stepped back, as if jolted by an electrical current. *Well, well.* Pressing the record button, he handed the device back to her. "You ready now, PK?" he asked with a smirk.

"PK? Oh, hilarious. You're also a stand-up comedian? Let's just get this over with," she said, shooting him a look and sticking her tongue out at him.

He raised his eyebrows in mock surprise. "Oh, that's mature."

Kate ignored him and started the questions, only pausing to await replies. "What is your name? Are you a woman? Is your name Abigale? Why are you here? Are you looking for something?" After a few seconds, she handed the recorder back to Pete.

"Let's see if we got anything," he said, starting the playback. There was nothing on the recording except their verbal sparring and Kate's unenthusiastic questions. "Let's move on to the front of the building, by the windows."

"Fine," she said, following him like a petulant child. The large front room was dark except for the faint illumination from the streetlights and flashes of lightning from the epic storm ramping up outside.

Once they settled on a location in the room, Pete handed the recorder back to Kate. This time she flipped it on to record with ease and gave him a look of mocking triumph. She repeated the series of questions, waiting dutifully for a response, then turned it off and handed it back to Pete, who was watching her closely. As with the first session, it was a one-sided conversation. Kate sighed with exasperation. "Gee, it seems like Abigale, or Casper, or whoever you are looking for has decided not to show up."

Pete ignored her sarcasm. "Well, it often takes a few nights of investigating to gain their trust."

"Oh please," Kate snorted.

Pete's eyes narrowed. "What *is* your problem?"

"I don't have a problem. I just think this is ridiculous. There are no such things as ghosts. Frankly, I'm getting pretty pissed off being treated like *I'm* the one with the problem. You walk in here with your bag of techno-crap and expect it will impress everyone, and think this is all very scientific. Sorry, but I'm not impressed with a digital recorder and a night vision camera." Kate was on a roll. "You can waste your evening spinning ghost stories and walking around a dark building throwing questions into the air. I've got better things to do."

With a massive clap of thunder and a flash of lightning, the streetlights went out, leaving them in total darkness. "Damn it," she muttered, pulling her phone out of her pocket and turning on the flashlight app.

Pete had reached his limit. After an evening filled with a litany of Kate's sarcastic comments and incredulous looks, he wanted nothing more than to be done with the investigation and her. But watching her, aglow in the light of her phone, her red hair a halo around her face like an avenging goddess, his pulse quickened. Suddenly, he wanted nothing more than to touch her, kiss her, make her see the magic in the world around her. As she turned to leave, he reached out, taking her arm, spinning her around. He opened his mouth as if to say something. Instead, he pulled her close and lowered his head. He could smell the scent of lavender and sea air as he lifted his hand to her hair, murmuring her name.

Kate stared up at him, wide-eyed. Pete's lips touched hers, tentatively at first. But when she didn't protest or pull away, the kiss deepened as he pulled her into his arms. *Home,* he thought, caressing the side of her face as his tongue parted her lips. He heard her sounds of pleasure as she pulled herself tight against him, returning his kiss with equal passion, heating his blood.

"Hey, you guys, that lightning was something else! Are you okay up there?" Eve yelled from the second-floor landing.

The two jumped apart as if jolted by an electrical current, both breathing hard from the effects of their physical contact. Pete ran his hand through his hair. "Yeah, we're fine. Just getting ready to wrap things up. Meet you on the first floor," he said, never breaking eye contact with Kate.

"Okay," Eve said, oblivious to what had been happening one floor above her.

"Kate," he whispered, taking a step toward her.

"No," she whimpered, brushing back her hair while stepping away from him. "I have to go." She turned, holding her phone with shaking hands as she worked her way down the stairs, with Pete right behind her.

Eve and Jon were in the middle of the shop, looking out at the darkened street, when Kate and Pete joined them. "Did you see something, Kate? You look pretty shook up?" Jon asked.

"No. No, Casper tonight. I've got to go." Kate rushed to the door as Pete looked on in disbelief.

"Are you okay, Kate?" Eve's eyes narrowed as she searched Kate's face in the dim light.

"Fine. I have a headache. I'll see you tomorrow." Kate headed into the storm before anyone could say another word. Pete watched her run off in the darkness, powerless to stop her.

Chapter 13

K ate stepped out of the shower, put on a pair of sweatpants and her favorite tee shirt, then went to the kitchen to put on the kettle for tea. She just wanted to sit in the dark and cry as her phone rang. It was Eve.

"Katie, are you okay? You left in such a hurry. I'm worried about you," Eve fretted.

"I'm fine. Really. Just a headache." A wave of guilt washed over her for lying to her best friend.

"Are you sure? Pete seemed really upset when you left. Did something happen between you two?" As always, Eve zeroed in on the actual issue. There was a long pause on the other end of the phone. "Kate?"

Kate knew she couldn't keep anything from Eve. And besides, she really needed to talk to her best friend. "Yes," she whispered.

"What?"

"Oh Eve, Pete kissed me," Kate admitted, confused and embarrassed.

"Oh, praise the Goddess! That's awesome!" Eve practically jumped through the phone.

"No, it's not! Look, I'm just not ready. There are hundreds of reasons it would never work." She had a litany of excuses at the ready.

"I'm coming over."

"No! Really, I'm okay."

"No, you're not okay. I'll be there in fifteen minutes." Eve hung up before Kate could protest any further.

Kate put down the phone and got another teacup from the cupboard. Within fifteen minutes there was a knock, and she opened the door to find Eve holding up a bottle of Jameson. Kate's laughter quickly turned to tears.

"Oh sweetie, talk to me," Eve said, shutting the door against the storm and hugging her.

"What is there to talk about? I just made a huge, idiotic mistake," she said, looking at her friend with a watery smile. "C'mon. Let me get some glasses and ice. That Jameson will not drink itself."

After pouring two generous glasses, they settled in the darkened living room, watching the lightning from their cozy vantage point on the overstuffed sofa. Kate clinked her friend's glass. "Sláinte."

"Cheers." After a few minutes of watching the storm in silence, Eve turned to her friend. "So, are you going to tell me what happened?"

"I told you. We were upstairs and started arguing about the whole ghost investigation thing." Kate looked at her friend guiltily. "Sorry." Eve waved it off good-naturedly and sat back on the sofa, tucking her feet underneath her. "I was getting ready to walk out when that huge lightning strike took out the streetlights. I reached in my pocket for my phone to turn on the flashlight app...." Kate stopped and took a healthy sip of her drink, giving herself a moment to relive the mind-blowing moment. "Well, I started to walk away, then Pete took my arm and the next thing I knew, he was kissing me."

"And...."

"And what?"

Eve gave an exasperated sigh. "And how was it?"

"It was fine... good...."

Eve arched an eyebrow. "Fine? Good? Do I have to drag this out of you? Drink up! Your expression when you came downstairs, it looked as if you had seen a ghost—absolutely stunned. So, I'll ask you again, my dear. How was it?"

Kate took another long drink of her whiskey. She was beginning to relax, thanks to the amber liquid warming her up. "Okay, okay. It was amazing. A-one, first class. Panty-melting, even. There, does that make you happy?" As much as she hated the admission, it brought relief.

"Yes, it makes me happy." Eve grabbed the bottle and poured them both another round. "And it should make you happy. Katie, why are you so dead set against getting involved with Pete?"

The storm was moving out to sea, leaving only the distant rumble of thunder and the occasional flash of lightning. Kate was caught in an emotional tug of war, and she realized that as much as she disliked sharing any sort of personal drama, she needed to confide in her friend. After a long pause, she finally spoke. "You know my parents divorced when I was thirteen."

"I know," Eve said, moving closer.

"The reason they divorced was... complicated. They were remarkably successful—a real power couple." She laughed without humor. "You know my mom left my dad. She spent her entire life pushing his career, making sure he would be a success —because that would mean *she* was a success. You've met Gale, you know what she's like." Eve nodded, but didn't say a word.

"I used to hear them fighting after I went to bed at night. My mother complaining that my father wasn't moving fast enough up the corporate ladder. Grousing about money, the house, getting the prime invitations to all the right parties and telling my father to network more. It was never enough for her. For my dad's part, he stayed quiet most of the time—only raising his voice when he couldn't tolerate her constant complaining." Kate stopped for a moment, reliving those nights when she would lie in bed, wishing they could be happy. "It came crashing down when Dad had his heart attack. I think that was his wake-up call. I remember the day he came home from the hospital. He looked worn-out but resolved, you know?" Kate took another sip of her drink. "From that point on, he spent a lot of time in the garage. That's when he took up woodworking. He would come home from the office, change clothes, have dinner with Mom and me, then head out to the garage. He would be out there until late at night. Mom was furious."

Kate looked out the window and took a shaky breath. "One day, Dad came home from the office and told my mother he'd quit his job and was going to open a woodworking shop. He said working with his hands made him happy, and he was sick of being unhappy. The next thing I knew, Mom was packing a suitcase and shuttling me off to a hotel. God, it was horrible."

Eve put her arm around her. "I'm so sorry, Katie."

"You know, from the time I was thirteen years old, living with my mother, all I ever heard from her was if or when I ever married, I needed to find a successful, practical man. Someone who wasn't prone to flights of fancy or dreams. Since she couldn't push my father anymore, she pushed me. 'Get into the best school. Only date the most successful men. Work your way up the corporate ladder—be the best,'" Kate's voice broke on a sob. "When I met Michael, it seemed like the perfect fit. He was driven to succeed. He was wealthy and handsome. I thought we'd make the perfect power couple. My mother was thrilled. Funny thing is, I've spent the last few months realizing that when Michael and I broke up, I wasn't so much missing Michael, but missing that *goal*—you know?" She put her head in her hands, "I am so fucked up."

"Hey, don't talk like that. You got by doing what you had to do. That was your life then. You have the power to rewrite how this story goes, Kate." Eve looked at her with the intensity of a laser beam.

"Oh Eve, I'm not you," Kate whispered.

"Well, thank the Goddess for that," she laughed. "Can you imagine two of me?" She hugged Kate tightly. "So, what about Pete?"

"How am I supposed to feel about a guy who the first time I meet him, after realizing he was staring at me in a cemetery, mind you, calls me Practical Kate? Talk about pushing my buttons. Plus, he hunts ghosts as a hobby. Sorry, but there is no way around that. He is everything I don't need in my life."

"But what about what you *want* in your life?"

That pulled Kate up short. "Want?"

"What do you want in your life? Put it out there. Claim it! What do you want?"

"I've always thought need and want were the same thing."

"Well, they're not. Need is about the basics—food, water, a roof over your head. Want is about your dreams, what's in your heart. Those intangible things that make you happy, that lift your soul." Eve sat forward on the sofa, urging Kate to push herself beyond the boundaries she had set up for herself.

Kate thought for a moment, taking an unsteady breath. "I guess, well, I've always wanted to travel." Eve nodded, rolling her hand to continue. "And I want to be happy in my work, to feel like I'm making a difference."

"You can have those things, Kate. Are you happy working here?"

"Of course! This is the best decision I've ever made. I love it here. I love what is happening at *Potion*, and I love being close to you again."

Eve smiled. "See, you've already checked one thing off the list. Travel you can do too. Plan that trip to Europe, or South America, or wherever! You don't need anyone's permission to do those things." Kate nodded, taking it all in. "But there is one thing you haven't mentioned, Katie."

"What?"

"Do you want love?"

Kate's face crumpled as the tears fell. "I don't know. I think about my parents' divorce, my breakup with Michael. Sometimes I just think I'm better off without it."

"Really? Do you *really* feel that way?"

Waves of sadness and fear of admitting what she truly felt washed over Kate. "I'm so damned lonely, Eve. It's not that I *must* have a man in my life. But other than you, I have no one to talk to, share experiences with, and frankly, I don't want to sleep with you." She smiled faintly and shook her head.

"You are skirting the question, Katie. Do you want love?" Eve clearly wasn't going to let her off the hook.

Rain falling on the roof broke the silence. "Yes," Kate finally whispered. "I don't want to spend the rest of my life alone, regardless of the risks."

"Okay. You've done the hard part. Now, you just need to put yourself out there. And you might want to start with Pete." Kate protested, but Eve cut her off. "Kate, it's time to let go of those old messages holding you back. Pete is a professor at Harvard. He's gorgeous, kind, cares about his community. And apparently, he's got the hots for you. Not too shabby in my book. If the only thing holding you back is that he believes in the afterlife, then I think you have a pretty lame excuse." Eve sat back, as if expecting Kate to give her another reason it wasn't possible. It didn't come.

After a long pause, Kate sighed with a note of surrender. "*If* I pursue something with Pete, and that's a big *if*, I'm not interested in starting anything until after we get *Potion* up and running for the season. There is too much riding on this to lose focus, okay?" Kate was in negotiating mode.

Eve raised her glass and clinked it against Kate's. "Okay. Wait until the summer gets rolling, then you better jump his bones."

———◆———

Pete sat in the darkness of his study, sipping his whiskey. Outside, the rain came down in sheets while the wind rattled the windowpane. Finn padded into the room and jumped into his lap, purring softly. "You always know when I need you, don't you buddy," he said, stroking the cat. "I think I made a big mistake tonight." In response, Finn yawned and blinked his green-gold eyes at Pete, as if waiting for him to continue his tale of woe. "I kissed her, Finn. It was... incredible." He closed his eyes, reliving those few moments thinking that mistake or not, he was damned glad it happened. He could still feel her lips, the softness of her body, the scent of her hair. And nothing had surprised him more than when she reached for him and pulled herself tight against him. He sighed in frustration. *So why did she run away?*

That kiss—she wanted it as much as he did. It was like nothing he'd experienced before, and he thought about why that was. He'd kissed plenty of women, but Pete couldn't remember ever having that kind of reaction. It was a feeling of passion and coming home—a feeling so simple and yet so complex. Even with his ex-wife Jeanine, he'd never had that sort of feeling or connection. He groaned in frustration and Finn, just drifting off to sleep, meowed in protest. "Sorry, buddy," Pete apologized, scratching him behind the ears. Appeased, Finn promptly fell asleep.

So now what? he wondered. *I can't just call her up and ask her on a date. She was so freaked out tonight.* The lights flickered as the electricity came back on in the neighborhood. He looked at his watch—one o'clock. He gently picked up Finn and headed to bed, hoping he might get a certain redhead off his mind, even if it was only for a few hours.

Chapter 14

The physical transformation of *Potion* was almost complete, leaving Kate with plenty of time to do other things—mainly worry about the business plan and think about Pete O'Brien. From a practical standpoint, she knew they had done everything they could to make the business successful. Now, all they had to do was wait for the start of tourist season, which would arrive in a matter of days. But with Pete O'Brien? Well, Kate found herself reliving the kiss they'd shared weeks ago. Never one to be a mooning, lovesick kind of person, the fact he was on her mind so much drove her crazy. She was sitting in the office one day staring at the wall, remembering how his lips felt, how hard he was against her. *Enough! I need a distraction.* To break her wayward thoughts, she walked out to the floor of the shop to find Eve rearranging a book display. "Hey, I'm going to take a walk. I need a little exercise. I'll be back in a bit," Kate said, as she headed for the door.

It seemed as if overnight Mother Nature had flipped a switch. The trees were bright green with young leaves and the storefronts along Essex were sprucing up with fresh coats of paint and colorful blooms in the planters and flower boxes. Everyone, it seemed, was prepping for the tourist season. Kate waved to shop owners as she passed, thinking that the community was all in this together, which lifted her spirits. *Such a difference from the big city.*

Before long she found herself in front of the library, which wasn't a surprise, since it was one of her favorite buildings in Salem. It stood so proudly, its red brick Victorian façade practically glowing in the spring sunshine, while all around it, flowers bloomed in beautiful, manicured beds. She walked in and found herself drawn to the genealogy section. The library had yet to upgrade to an online genealogy service, so she perused the shelves until she found a book specifically about Salem's founding families. Sitting at one of the old wooden tables, she started her research. As embarrassing as it was to admit it, she was searching for information on Abigale Hastings—the ghost of *Potion*—because it felt like a connection to Pete. But, she reasoned, she might as well try to understand the history of the place where they were doing business. It wasn't a difficult search because the Hastings family was well-to-do in Salem, and within minutes Kate found a written history—of the captain, at least.

As Pete had pointed out, the patriarch of the family was John Hastings, a sea captain who married Sarah Parker in 1848. They settled in a lovely Federal period row house on Chestnut Street and soon after, Sarah found she was pregnant. However, the pregnancy was hard for Sarah, and she died in childbirth, leaving Captain Hastings to raise an infant daughter on his own. *That must be Abigale.* The historical narrative stated that Captain Hastings' mother moved into the home to help raise his daughter. The balance of the history outlined the captain's death in 1879, leaving his vast wealth to his spinster daughter, Abigale.

That's it? Nothing more about his daughter? The heir to his fortune? Kate was more than a little miffed that women got such short shrift back then. She closed the book and moved to the microfiche, determined to find more information.

It wasn't difficult to find the obituary for Abigale, which repeated the story Pete had told them. Although there was one more bit of information in the clipping that Pete hadn't told them—Abigale was buried at the Old Burying Point—where Kate first saw Pete. A shiver went down her spine; she could have passed right by the woman's grave. The obituary left Kate wanting to know more, and after an hour of digging through films of old newspaper clippings, she found an engagement notice between a young Abigale Hastings, daughter of Captain John Hastings, to a young sailor, Andrew Michaelson. She had been nineteen years old at the time of the notice. *Wait! She wasn't a spinster?* Kate then searched for Andrew Michaelson and was shocked to find an article six months later announcing he had died at sea on his way to the West Indies. For reasons she couldn't explain, Kate was heartbroken by the news. *Poor Abigale, losing her fiancé at sea.*

Kate turned off the machine and sat for a few moments, thinking about the sad history of a woman whom she didn't know, but for some odd reason felt so close to. The more she thought about Abigale, the more she filled in her history. A marriage that never was must have left the young girl heartbroken. But she was still young, she could have married someone else in time. Surely Andrew Michaelson must have been the love of her life? Maybe that's why she focused her energies on business—something not typical for women of her time. *Unlucky in love, lucky in business. I can relate to that*, Kate thought. She left the library, heading to the Old Burying Point, determined to find Abigale Hastings' grave.

———◦———

This place sure looks different in the springtime. The sun was shining, and the trees were leafing out, giving the cemetery a much more welcoming feel than it had in January. She pulled the piece of paper out of her pocket, listing Abigale Hastings' final resting place. After searching for what seemed like forever, she found the gravesite. It was a small family plot holding headstones for the captain and his young wife Sarah. Next to their graves was Abigale's. A statue of a weeping angel, bent over in grief, guarded the grave, and a wave of emotion washed over Kate.

She stood for a moment in silence, listening to the wind and the distant sounds of traffic and people going about their day. Kate looked around the empty cemetery and after an awkward moment said, "Hello, Abigale." She felt like a complete fool. *Geez, Kate. Seriously, get a grip. She can't hear you.* Kate shook her head, amused by her reaction. But after a few minutes, she felt the urge to talk to Abigale. She sheepishly took another look around to make sure no one was there. "So, I've been reading about you. From what I can tell, you led quite a life. It's nice to know even back then there were independent women making their way in the world. Well done, you."

She was warming up to her one-sided conversation. "Everybody seems to think you're hanging out at Eve's place. Well, it was your place originally, I guess. Right?" With a self-conscious laugh, she realized she was asking a question of a headstone. "Yeah, this isn't too weird. Anyway, your history has a few gaps in it. Plenty of stuff about your dad, but you are still a bit of a mystery. What happened to your engagement? Your fiancé died...." Kate trailed off, wondering what the etiquette was for conveying sympathy in this situation.

In awkward silence she stood, not sure what she was waiting for. She looked around the grounds. "This is a pretty place. If you're going to be laid to rest, this is a prime spot for it.... Sorry, is that a rude thing to say?" Kate threw up her hands, realizing she had utterly lost her senses. "What is it about Salem? It makes people act strange. Anyway, I just wanted to see where you were and, I guess, well, pay my respects?" Kate moved to leave when she smelled lavender. She turned, sensing that Abigale was standing right next to her. "I wish I knew more about you." Kate hesitated. "Well, goodbye." With a self-conscious wave she left the cemetery, feeling a little foolish, but also happy to have found Abigale.

Abigale watched Kate exit the cemetery and smiled. It was nice to be remembered. Being dead all these years, there were no distant family members who ever visited her grave. And Kate's questions brought back so many memories, some good and some painful. *What had she said? That I lived quite a life. Well, that certainly was true.* Abigale had been proud of what she had accomplished with her business and what she had done for the community. She reflected on her past and how it must have looked to someone living one hundred and thirty years in the future. *Had it been that long? My goodness!* She moved to a stone bench under an old elm tree and sat down.

Kate's question about her fiancé sent a flood of regret through Abigale. *Oh, Andrew,* she sighed, stirring the flowers growing around the bench. *If there was one thing I would have done differently, it would have been saying yes to Andrew.* She remembered that day so clearly. Andrew had proposed and Abigale said yes. They set a wedding date for early August, and the two counted down the days with anticipation. But then one day Andrew arrived at her home, bursting with news. He had been given a captain's position aboard a ship heading for the West Indies. Andrew begged Abigale to marry him then and there and travel with him to the Caribbean. But she refused. As much as she loved hearing tales of the sea from her father growing up, she had no intention of uprooting her life and living aboard a ship.

And Abigale had an excuse for every point Andrew tried to make: her grandmother's failing health, her work in the community with the children's orphanage. She couldn't leave when these people needed her. But what she couldn't admit was that she was afraid. Afraid to leave what was familiar, even if it was for the man she loved. As independent as people perceived her to be, the truth was she only felt secure within the confines of Salem. Losing her mother—never knowing her—reminded her of how tenuous life could be. Because of that loss, Abigale would do anything she could to control the outcomes in her life. Going to sea, stepping into the unknown, would fly in the face of every fear she had.

The discussion between the young lovers ended in an impasse and the engagement was called off. On the day Andrew was to set sail, he called on Abigale to say goodbye. They sat in the parlor on the loveseat by the picture window, and he begged her one last time to join him. And one last time she said no. She told him she loved him but could not leave. Before parting, Andrew gave her a gold locket with a lock of his hair inside as a remembrance. Abigale, at his request, gave him a lock of her own. As he turned to leave, he promised to return one day and ask her to marry him again. Then he kissed her one last time and departed.

So stubborn! So afraid! I should have gone with him. Instead, she waited at home every day for word of his travels. One snowy January afternoon she received a letter notifying her of his passing from scarlet fever. They had buried him at sea and every time Abigale thought of it, her heart broke all over again. Even now, Abigale realized not even her own death could soften the pain of that memory. In life she used that pain to drive her success, because through her success she could help others. *But now who can I help?* Her thoughts went to Kate Murphy. *Such a determined young woman. Intelligent and driven. Not unlike me.* Abigale smiled.

She's afraid too. She runs away from that handsome young man, Pete O'Brien. But it's obvious to anyone with sense they were meant for each other, Abigale thought with frustration. She recognized Kate could easily fall into the same trap she had all those years ago—saying no to love out of fear of the unknown. *Well, I certainly cannot let that happen. I will need to keep an eye on those two and do what I can to bring them together.* Pleased with her decision, Abigale moved away from the gravesite, ready to lend a ghostly hand where it was most needed—bringing two modern, stubborn people together.

Chapter 15

*P*otion was a smashing success. Since the opening, they hit all their sales goals, and as summer arrived and tourists flooded the town, it seemed every one of them made a point of stopping at *Potion*. They even wrote about the shop in the travel section of the *Boston Globe* as one of the top ten places for coffee in the greater Boston area. They put the ghost investigations on hold since Pete, after wrapping up his semester, was busy working on his manuscript. He had stopped in on opening day, but they were so busy there wasn't a chance to talk. Kate couldn't help but notice while he was there that day, that on more than one occasion, she found him staring at at her. She hadn't seen him since then, which she told herself was fine, but she couldn't help wondering just where he had gone.

Kate sat in the office and gazed intently at the monitor as Eve came down the stairs from her apartment. "You've been working non-stop since the opening. Take the afternoon off! It's a glorious summer day. Go on. We've got plenty of coverage here," she said, shooing her like a chick in a farmyard.

"I've got to get these reports pulled together before the end of next week. But I'll compromise. I'll work from home this afternoon. Deal?"

"Okay, but I still say you are working too hard."

"Hey, look at what our hard work has brought to us." The two of them looked out at the coffee bar to see people reading, chatting, and buying coffee. "We've done well, my friend." After making sure the shop had staff coverage, Kate grabbed her purse and a couple of files and headed out into the street, enjoying the sun and the early summer breeze blowing in off the ocean.

Once at home, she dropped everything in the guest bedroom, doubling as an office, fired up her computer, and went to change into shorts and a tank top, stopping on the way to release her hair from the ponytail she always wore. *It feels good to let my hair down*, she thought, imagining Eve telling her how she should really let her hair down.

She'd been working for an hour when she realized she'd left a flash drive sitting on the desk back at the office. She picked up the phone and called Eve to ask if it was there.

"Yep. It's right here."

"Do you think you could take a break and run it over to me? I really need it to finish this report I'm working on."

"Sure. I'll get it to you within the hour, okay?"

"Great. Thanks, I'll see you then."

While she waited for Eve to show up, Kate listened to some music. She chose some classic David Bowie, and within minutes was dancing around to *Suffragette City* until she heard a knock at the door. She flung it open, singing at the top of her lungs.

"Now that's one hell of a way to answer the door." Pete O'Brien stood on her front step, lips twitching, gaze roving over Kate in all her wild glory. "Sorry to interrupt your performance, but Eve asked me to deliver this," he said, handing her the flash drive and her favorite Italian soda.

"Umm, yeah, sorry about that." She bit her lip, trying to tamp down her mortification. "Would you like to come in?"

"Thanks," he said, as she ushered him into the living room.

"I'll be right back." Kate pointed at the sofa, and without waiting for a response headed back to her bedroom to change, thinking about the different ways she would kill her meddling match-making business partner. She looked at herself in the mirror. *Oh my god, Kate, you look like a wild woman.* Her hair was down around her shoulders in untamed curls, and her face was flushed from dancing and embarrassment. Throwing on a pair of jeans and pulling her hair back into a ponytail, Kate took a deep breath and headed back to the living room. "Thanks for bringing the drive over. You didn't have to do that."

"No trouble. Eve looked like she was busy. Besides, I would have missed your performance," he grinned.

Mortified, she sank into a chair across from him. "I am so sorry. I had no idea."

"Kate, it's okay. Nice to see that you let your hair down once in a while. Just sorry you decided to put it back up. So, it looks like *Potion* is a gigantic success."

"Yes!" She was happy to have a topic of conversation. "We've exceeded our expectations as far as sales. I couldn't be happier with how things are going. I'm glad to see a lot of locals are making *Potion* their new hangout. We knew getting the locals to buy in would help in our success, especially in the off season." Kate wound down and looked at the floor, feeling totally unprepared to have him sitting in her living room. *You are such a dork. Find something else to talk about.*

There was silence until Pete cleared his throat. "So, do you enjoy living in Salem? You've been here, what? Three months?"

"Yes, a little over three months. I love it here. I feel like I've landed in the right place. And it's great working with Eve."

"You don't miss New York City?"

Kate rolled her eyes. "Not at all. It loses its sparkle after about a year."

"Well, Salem is not without its quirks, but it's a great place to live, especially if you like history. Actually, the entire east coast is almost like a museum with all the historical sites."

Kate settled back into her chair. "It's great. I grew up in the Midwest and it lacks a lot of history. I should say that history isn't as easy to find in the Midwest. You need to look a little harder for it. Did you grow up on the east coast?"

"Sort of. Southeast. In Virginia. I grew up on a horse farm."

"Wow, that had to be an incredible experience."

"It was pretty incredible." He sat back, bringing one long leg up and propping one ankle on the other knee. "My dad still has the farm and I go to see him as often as I can."

"That's nice. I think once everything gets on an even keel at *Potion*, I'll have some time to get out and do a little sight-seeing. Maybe head north up the coast and visit some small towns," Kate mused.

He nodded. "You should. Definitely. I'd be happy to show you some places of interest around here."

"That would be great, thanks." On the outside, Kate was calm, while inside, she was doing cartwheels. They fell into silence again, but this time it was much more comfortable.

Pete stood up. "Well, I guess I'd better let you get back to work."

"Thanks again for bringing the flash drive over, and the soda," she said as they walked to the entry hall.

In the doorway, Pete turned abruptly, looking into her eyes. "Kate, I wanted to apologize about that night in *Potion*. I was out of line—I let my emotions get the better of me. I'm sorry."

"Apology accepted. But really, don't give it another thought," she said, looking up at him, her breath catching.

"Well, see, that's the problem. I can't seem to forget it." His gaze slid down to her mouth, then back up to her eyes. "I'll see you around, Kate," he said, stepping out into the sunshine.

She watched him walk down the front path, then closed the door and leaned against it. "I can't forget it either."

Chapter 16

I t was a few days after Pete's visit when Kate got the phone call. She'd arrived home from the shop, looking forward to Netflix and an enormous glass of wine. Things had been so busy at *Potion*, but now it seemed they were settling into a rhythm and the days were far less hectic. Her phone rang, and she practically dropped it when she saw Michael Francisco's number on the screen. For a moment she freaked out—debating if she should pick up. On the third ring, she answered, trying her best to sound casual. "Hello, this is Kate Murphy."

"Katie! It's Michael."

"Michael, how are you?" She thought she sounded calm, but inside her mind was racing. "To what do I owe the honor of this call?"

"I wanted to catch up. I heard a rumor you left Sterling and moved to Salem, Massachusetts. Is that true?"

"Yes, it is. I came in to help Eve with her retail shop. It was time to get out of New York City. But how are things in Chicago? Are you making millions in the Windy City?"

"Chicago is awesome. But I'm in Boston for a conference until Sunday and I was wondering, since you're so close, if we couldn't meet up for a drink. There is so much I need to tell you."

Kate's brain started working overtime, trying to fill in the meaning of *so much I need to tell you.* "Well, I could probably meet you on Friday afternoon, if that fits your schedule? I can meet you in Boston, there is a great little bar by the harbor."

"That will work. How does four o'clock sound?"

Kate agreed and gave him the details on where to meet. She sat down on the sofa, disconnecting the call, and wondered what had just happened. Then she called Eve.

"What the hell? What does he mean by *so much he needs to tell you*? Kate, how do you feel about this?"

"I don't know. I mean, it's just so out of the blue. I guess I'll find out when I see him."

"Well, it seems weird to me. I don't know. Katie, you don't still have feelings for him, do you?"

"God, no! Not like that. Enough time has gone by that I think I'm okay. I'm more curious than anything else."

"When are you meeting him?"

"Friday."

"Oh good. That gives us time!"

"Huh? Time for what?"

"Shopping! You need to show off the new Kate—let him know you've moved on with your life. Tomorrow we'll stop at that cute little boutique down the street from the shop. I saw some great sundresses in there that would look adorable on you."

"Eve, I don't need new clothes. I'll wear khakis and a shirt, no big deal."

Eve was in planning mode, and she was not about to be deterred. "Absolutely not! Didn't we talk about you making some changes? This is a perfect opportunity! Oh, and before I forget—now that things are less hectic at work, Pete is going to do an investigation on Saturday night. You'll be there, right?"

Without stopping to give it a thought, Kate said yes, her pulse kicking up at the thought of seeing Pete. She could hear Eve giggle on the other end of the line. "You are a force to be reckoned with, Ms. Marsden. What would you do if I said no?"

"Oh, I have my ways of wearing you down, Ms. Murphy. It's settled then. Clothes shopping tomorrow, seeing Michael on Friday, and ghost hunting with your hottie on Saturday night." With that, Eve hung up and Kate settled in for the night, wondering what Michael Francisco needed to tell her.

By the time Friday arrived, Kate had worked herself into a frenzy of nervous energy. Her competitive side wanted to show Michael she could be a success anywhere and didn't need to be in New York City to do so. But outside of those competitive feelings, Kate wanted him to know she had moved on, happy at last with where her life was heading. "I can do this," she said, looking in the bedroom mirror and giving herself a pep-talk. The new sundress she'd bought at Eve's urging fell around her bare legs in a swirl of pale blues, purples, and greens. "Not too bad," she said, braiding her hair loosely, until it fell like a silky auburn rope down her back. She looked at her reflection, surprised at the woman looking back at her. For the first time in her life, she felt happy in her skin—she was okay, just the way she was. She smiled at her image, grabbed her purse, and headed out the door.

Because it was such a glorious summer day, Kate took the ferry to Boston, arriving at the dock with a few minutes to spare. It was fun watching the families hustle on with kids, happy to be going out on the water for a trip into the city. Once on board, she headed up the stairs to the outside deck and sat down, enjoying the warmth of the sun on her skin. Inhaling the sea air, she relaxed and gave in to the enjoyment of being on the water. The engines revved, and the kids talked excitedly as the ferry pulled out of Salem Harbor. The sun flashed off the ocean as they passed Marblehead and the beautiful mansions on the bluff as the boat sped up, while Kate closed her eyes, enjoying the physical sensation of flying across the water.

It was a quick trip to Boston, and as the boat docked, passengers started gathering their belongings. Kate hung back from the crowd, waiting for the boat to clear out. She wanted to give herself a moment to collect her thoughts and settle her nerves. Once off the boat, she headed toward the park filled with tourists who were taking photos and admiring the beauty of Boston's historical harbor. Within minutes she arrived at the bar, and taking a deep breath, opened the door into the cool, dim interior.

Michael was sitting at the bar, and Kate had a moment to study him before he saw her. He hadn't changed a bit. Still handsome, with a relaxed air about him that always seemed to draw people in. His blonde hair was shorter, cut in a business appropriate style, but he still looked like he was in grad school— wearing khakis and a polo shirt. Kate smiled as memories flooded back to her. As if sensing her presence, he turned.

"Katie!" He jumped up, hugging her. "It's so good to see you. You look fantastic. Salem must really agree with you. Wow, really, you look great. Still drinking Jameson and ginger ale?" he asked, getting the bartender's attention.

"Still my drink of choice," she said, settling next to him at the bar as her nervousness disappeared. "It's good to see you, Michael." Kate gave his arm a squeeze. "I want to hear all about what's happening in Chicago. How do you like the city? The job?"

"It's great, Kate. The job is intense, but I love it. I've gotten an opportunity to travel to various clients around the US. I might do some international travel next year. But I want to hear about why you left Sterling." The bartender returned with her cocktail, as Kate shared the reasons she left New York and why she was so happy to be in Salem, starting a new life with a new business.

"Weren't you concerned about the financial risk of jumping into an unknown venture?" Michael asked, turning on his practical business mind.

That is so like Michael. Her attitude had changed so much since moving—she was beginning to realize personal happiness was a far greater measure of success. She assured him her happiness and sanity were worth the risk and watched him sit and process the idea as if it were something foreign to him.

"Well, you sound happy, Kate. You look happy too. You look beautiful."

Kate blushed. "So, tell me about Chicago," she said, eager to shift the subject away from herself.

They talked about work, Chicago, and about where classmates had ended up after graduate school. Their banter was light and flirtatious, revealing a certain conversational short-hand often shared between old lovers who had known each other for years. It was around six o'clock when Michael looked at his watch. "I'm going to have to go soon. I'm meeting colleagues for dinner."

"Oh, sure. I understand. It's been wonderful catching up with you."

"I know! I've missed talking to you, Katie." Michael paused, looking as if he needed to say something, but not entirely sure how to go about it. "Before you go though, I wanted to tell you something."

"Sure...." Kate waited.

"Katie, I'm getting married," he said, then rushed on with a touch of nervousness. "We met when I was out in California on business. Her name is Stephanie. We've been traveling back and forth between Chicago and Southern California for the past six months. She put in for a transfer to Chicago and we're getting married in September."

What? Married? But.... "Michael, that's wonderful news. Congratulations." She hugged him and picked up her purse, feeling like she was having an out-of-body experience. "I wish you both the very best."

Michael had a look of relief. "We had a long history, Katie. I just wanted to let you know."

Kate leaned in and kissed his cheek, "Take care of yourself, Michael." With that, she turned and walked out into the early evening, making her way to the dock. *Married? Long-distance relationship? Only six months?* She boarded the ferry in a daze and moved to the bow of the boat where she could have a bit more privacy. Hundreds of thoughts and memories floated to the surface of her mind. She was happy for him, certainly. But she couldn't help thinking that he hadn't wanted to put in the effort of having a long-distance relationship with her. *What's wrong with me? Why wasn't I worth the effort?* Hot tears pricked her eyes. *Don't cry, Kate,* she admonished herself, desperately blinking to hold back the tears. She moved to the railing as the ferry pulled out of the harbor, unable to stop the tears from falling down her cheeks.

"Kate? Is that you?"

Kate quickly wiped her eyes, trying to compose herself as Pete joined her at the railing. "Hi Pete," she said, clearing her throat.

"Hey, what's wrong? Are you alright?" Concern etched his face, and as much as she tried to contain her emotions, at the sound of his voice Kate burst into tears. Pete put his arm around her, "Come with me, let's sit down." He gently guided her to a seat away from the other riders.

"I'm fine. Really. Just had a strange day," she said, trying once again to regain her composure.

"Okay. Well, how about we sit here and if you want to talk, I'm here to listen?" With a gentle smile, he sat back and looked out as they headed into open water.

The warm breeze and the rhythm of the waves quieted Kate's emotions. She felt her breathing slow and allowed herself to relax in the moment. They sat watching the water in silence for a long while, until Kate turned to Pete. "What are you doing here?"

"I was at my office doing some research. It was such a beautiful evening, I thought I would take the ferry back to Salem instead of the T. Nothing better than being out on the water, right?" He nudged her shoulder with his own. "Can I ask what you're doing here?"

"It's a long story."

"Well, we have about another half hour on this boat. If you're not done by then, I'll take you to dinner so you can finish the story."

"You don't have to do that."

"I know I don't *have* to. Maybe I'd like to. If you don't want to have dinner with me, either talk fast or just tell me you don't want to go." He grinned, and Kate couldn't help noticing the dimple in his left cheek.

She looked down at her hands. In her head she heard Eve's voice saying, *what do you want?* She looked up at him, eyes bright from her tears, "I'd like to have dinner with you."

His grin turned into a warm smile. "Well, good. It would be a shame to just go home when you look so beautiful in that dress."

Kate blushed. "Thank you. Eve picked it out. She's got an expert eye." She looked down at the summery fabric and smoothed it with shaking hands.

"Remind me to thank Eve. So, about that long story...."

Kate started from the beginning. About how she dated Michael for five years, meeting in undergrad and getting engaged in grad school. She talked about the plans they had to move to

New York, get married, and set the financial world on fire, and how it all ended when Michael took a job in Chicago. She paused for a minute before admitting that after just a few months of a long-distance relationship, Michael broke off their engagement. Pete took it all in, not speaking.

The ferry arrived in Salem as the sun was setting. "There is a great seafood place down off the wharf, if that's okay?" he asked when they reached the dock.

"Sure."

They walked quietly toward the small waterfront restaurant. Occasionally Kate would steal a glance at him, taking in his strong profile and easy, open manner. When they arrived, Pete held the door for her, putting his hand momentarily at the small of her back. Kate felt that now familiar buzz of electricity at his touch.

The hostess showed them to a table by the window facing the harbor. Kate sat down and looked out at the water, turning inky black as the sun sank lower in the sky. She turned her attention back to the table where Pete was gazing at her with warm eyes. Kate smiled shyly. After a few moments, he broke the silence. "So, do you want to finish telling me what happened when I found you on the ferry?"

"Okay.... I got a call from Michael the day before yesterday, telling me he was going to be in Boston. He asked if I wanted to meet him, and I thought it would be nice seeing him again to catch up." She paused for a minute. "It was a great reunion until I was getting ready to leave and he told me he was getting married."

"Ah," said Pete, looking a little crestfallen.

Kate saw his look and quickly corrected his impression of the situation. "I'm happy for him. I have no romantic feelings toward him at all. That ended a long time ago. I guess what upset me was...." She stopped, trying to control her emotions. "Well, I thought the reason Michael broke up with me was because of distance. But he didn't have a problem jumping the distance hurdle with his new fiancée. All I could think was... it must have been me. What's wrong with me? I had to be the reason we broke up. Maybe I just wasn't enough for him, and the distance scenario was a good way out. After five years...." Kate stared sightlessly at her hands resting on the table, feeling equal parts miserable and mortified that she had shared such a personal bit of information about herself.

Pete grasped her hands. "There is nothing wrong with you, Kate Murphy. You are strong, intelligent, and beautiful. You are perfect, just as you are." Kate looked up at him and he smiled. She blushed. "And when you blush, you drive me to distraction," he said, squeezing her hand.

"Can I ask you a question?" Kate asked after the server had taken their dinner order.

"Ask me anything."

"Why do you believe in ghosts?"

He sipped his wine, looking lost in thought. "It's a long story," he said, echoing Kate's words from earlier in the evening.

Kate tipped her head to catch his eye and smiled. "I've got all night."

He gave her a long look and for a moment she thought he wouldn't answer. "I believe because I've seen them," he said. "The first time it happened, I was thirteen years old. I'm an only child and close to my parents. When I was eleven, my mom, Helen, was diagnosed with cancer. She was a trooper through it all and fought hard for two years."

"Oh, Pete. I'm so sorry," Kate said, putting the pieces together as the server returned with their food.

"Thank you. Like I said, she was a trooper and tried to never let me see how much pain she was in or how sick she was. I'd get home from school and she'd want to hear all about what was going on, making sure she stayed present in what was happening in my life. I knew she was sick, but I thought she was going to be okay. That she would be the one to beat the odds. One day, like most others, I got up, got dressed, made myself some breakfast while Dad was out at the stables, and hurried off to the bus. I was late, so I didn't have time to check in and say good morning to Mom. A couple of hours later at school, the principal's secretary came to my classroom looking for me. I followed her out into the hallway to find my dad standing there, looking like his world had collapsed." Pete stopped, as if once again he could see the scene unfolding before him. "Mom died. The one thing I never allowed myself to believe was that someday she wouldn't be there. I didn't get to say good morning to her, let alone say goodbye." Kate reached across the table and took his hand. He stroked his thumb across her knuckles.

"The next few days were a blur of people and events. At the funeral, I couldn't cry. I felt numb. I watched my father fall apart and all I could do was stand there, still not believing it was really happening to us. Later that night, after everyone had left, I went to bed, exhausted. But I couldn't sleep. I laid there thinking and remembering, and finally the tears came. I asked God why this had to happen. Why didn't I get to see her, to at least say goodbye? Then it happened. I saw her standing next to my bed. I sat up. She smiled at me. I talked to her, telling her I loved her and that I didn't want her to go. She must have stood there silently looking at me for a minute or two, then she disappeared." Pete shrugged. "That's why I believe."

Tears filled her eyes. "I had no idea. When I think of how dismissive and downright nasty I was to you...."

"It's okay, Kate. You couldn't have known. There have been a few times in my life when she has come back, in much the same way as she did that night when I was thirteen. Usually, when I'm facing a big decision or difficulty. It's like she is still with me, looking after me."

When Pete finished his story, there was a shift in their conversation. It became more relaxed and open. Pete shared stories about working at Harvard and his research, and Kate told him about settling into life in Salem. They finished their meal and left the restaurant, walking outside to a perfect summer night. The full moon hung low over the harbor, and a light breeze rustled the leaves in the trees. "Thank you so much, Pete. This really has been a lovely evening."

"My pleasure. I couldn't have asked for a better spur-of-the-moment date."

Kate couldn't help but flirt with him. "Date? Is that what this is?"

"A delicious dinner with a beautiful woman on a Friday night. That sounds like a date to me."

"Well, far be it from me to disagree with that definition."

"Good. I'm glad we've reached a meeting of the minds." Pete took her hand as they walked to Kate's house.

Their route took them past the Old Burying Point. As they passed the cemetery gate, Pete looked down at Kate and grinned. A breeze stirred the leaves, casting moonlit shadows across the grounds and headstones. Within a stand of trees, the figure of Abigale Hastings appeared. She watched as they walked by, hand in hand, and she raised her hands to her heart, happy to see romance blossoming for the couple.

Chapter 17

Date! We're on a date! Kate worked hard to keep a lid on her excitement as they passed the Old Burying Point. But no matter how much she tried to stay calm, her mind raced through every scenario about what would happen when they got to her house. *Should I invite him in? Will he think I'm too forward?* she wondered, as Pete turned and smiled at her. She gazed up at him, her heart fluttering in her chest. *Who cares, this is happening!*

She was so wrapped up in her inner monologue it surprised her when they were standing at her front door. In the halo-glow of the porch light, Pete took her hand. "I'm glad our paths crossed today," he said, his eyes dark.

"I am too," Kate said, a little more breathless than she expected. They stood in silence, staring at one another. "Well, I guess I should be...." But she didn't finish. Pete leaned over and kissed her, his free hand gently cupping her face. He pulled back and waited a moment, looking down into her eyes, as if he were trying to commit the moment to memory. It was then that she reached up, pulled his head down, and kissed him with all she had. Within moments he had her against the front door, kissing her mouth, her neck, nuzzling her ear. She thought she would faint from wanting him. "Pete, wait," she gasped. He stopped immediately, looking down at her, his breath ragged. "Not sure I want to give the neighbors a show. Why don't you come in for a nightcap?" He nodded in agreement, never taking his eyes off her.

Fishing her keys out of her bag, she unlocked the door. She took Pete's arm, guided him into the house, and shut the door on the rest of the world. "Why don't you sit down, and I'll get us a drink. Whiskey on ice okay with you?"

"Sure," he said.

She turned on some classical music on her way to the kitchen, then did her best to relax, as she filled two glasses with ice and a generous pour of whiskey. She looked down at her slightly shaking hands. *Breathe, Kate,* she reminded herself. But all she could think of was Pete sitting in her living room, and she had a fairly good idea of where the evening was heading. *Stop thinking, just be.* Picking up the drinks, she walked back to the living room. Pete stood and took the glasses, placing them on the coffee table. Then he sat back down on the sofa, taking Kate's hand and pulling her down next to him. She giggled softly.

"I like your laugh," he said in her ear, putting his arm around her. She snuggled into his embrace.

"I like the dimple in your left cheek."

He grinned down at her, his dimple on full display. "Do you now?"

"Oh yes, it's one of the first things I noticed about you."

"So, not my intelligence or charm?" he asked, raising an eyebrow in mock surprise.

"No. It was pretty much just your dimple."

With that, Pete pulled her closer. "Kate...." He kissed her, gently at first, then with growing passion. Pausing, he looked down as she sighed with pleasure, running her hands down his back, pulling him closer until he was almost lying on top of her. His hands moving over her, molding the softness of her body, as he murmured his desire between each kiss and stroke of his tongue against hers.

For Kate, it felt as if everything was in hyper-reality. Pete's whispers as he kissed her mouth and neck sent her spiraling into a vortex of lust. She could feel the muscles in his back—his hardness pressed against her as she ran her hands down to his ass and pulled him closer. She was hungry for him.

Pete groaned, pulling back a fraction. "Wait. I need to ask you something."

"What?" she breathed.

"Well, I wasn't expecting, uh... this situation tonight," he said, looking somewhat embarrassed. "I didn't bring condoms."

Through her haze of raging hormones, Kate remembered the speed dating attempt a few months ago. She'd bought condoms as a 'just in case' scenario. Now she was glad they were sitting in her medicine cabinet. "Oh, right. Don't worry. I have that covered." As soon as she said it, she giggled. "Well, that seems an appropriate thing to say, right?"

Pete whispered her name, then kissed her, biting softly on her lower lip until she moaned with pleasure. His tongue found hers as they devoured each other, kissing each other breathless. He moved to trail featherlight kisses on her neck, moving up to her ear, nibbling on her lobe. "I want you, Kate."

Who doesn't want to hear that? she thought, feeling the heat building between them. She broke their embrace and took Pete's hand, pulling him from the sofa and down the hall, stopping in the bathroom to grab the condoms. He followed her in and when she closed the cabinet door they were face to face with their reflection in the mirror. Kate's skin was flushed, her lips swollen from his kisses.

Pete pulled her back against his chest and smiled against her neck, breathing in her scent. "Katie," he said, his voice rough as he skimmed his hands up her sides to her breasts, teasing her nipples through the thin sundress, watching her reaction in the mirror.

Kate was so turned on, watching herself panting with need, lost in the sensation of his hands on her breasts and his cock pressing against her back through his jeans. "Pete, oh Pete...." She trailed off, her head falling to one side. With access to her neck, he kissed and licked at the place where her pulse thrummed.

She took his hand to lead him to the bedroom. "Wait," he said as he took her hair in his hands and loosened the braid. He ran his hands through her hair, spreading it in a curtain across her shoulders and breasts. "You look so wild, so beautiful." He turned her around, pulling her against him so she could feel his need. "This is what you do to me—what you've done to me for weeks."

They made their way to the bedroom, dark except for the glow of a soft light in the corner of the room. Pete moved Kate to the bed, and taking the hem of her dress, gently pulled it up over her thighs, to her waist, and then over her head. She stood before him in lavender lace. "My god, Kate... so beautiful." He ran his fingers down the edge of lace on the cup of her bra as her nipples reacted to his touch. She shivered. "Are you cold, Kate?" he asked with a sly grin.

"No...."

He slipped his fingers underneath the lace, freeing her breast and rolling her nipple between his fingers. Kate felt as if her skin was on fire. She was burning and aching for him. "Let's see how you taste," he murmured, taking her in his mouth, sucking and gently biting her nipple, bringing her close to climax. She didn't know when her bra came off because she was mindless from his touch. He drifted his hands down her sides to her hips and over the edge of her panties. "I think these have to go too, don't you?" he asked, his voice a hoarse growl. All Kate could do was nod in agreement. Pete knelt in front of her, peeling the scrap of lace down her body. She stepped out of her panties and for a moment he knelt before her, gazing up into her eyes, almost in worship. She felt like a goddess, powerful and potent. Then he kissed her at the juncture of her thighs, stood up, and gently but insistently ran his fingers over her sex. "Kate... God, you are so wet. I... God, I need to be inside you."

"Please, I can't wait," she pleaded.

"What do you want?" he asked, trailing his lips from her neck to her collarbone.

"Ah... you... I...." She was incoherent, feeling his hands and mouth on her body, leaving a feverish trail on her skin.

Pete gently laid her on the bed and quickly stripped, never breaking eye contact as she lay with her hair like a cloud on the pillow. Everything became a series of images and sensations. The coolness of the sheets against her skin. Pete in all his beautiful nakedness, parting her thighs and kneeling between them, his large cock rock hard. She felt as if all her nerve endings were hypersensitive as Pete ran his hands down her body to her sex. Slowly, he moved his fingers inside of her. Picking up a rhythm, he rubbed her clit with his thumb, holding off her climax as he watched her. Her moans became wanton as she matched the rhythm of his fingers, pushing against his hand, wanting him deeper inside her. When he could no longer hold back, Pete put on a condom and moved to enter her. She wrapped her legs around him, pulling him to her, desperate to have him. Slowly, he pushed into her hot, wet softness. He moaned as she tightened around his cock, her body hungry for him. With agonizing slowness, he pulled out slightly, teasing her, and then once again slowly pushed in to the hilt, while his thumb continued to massage her clit. She let out a howl of pleasure. "Oh, my god. Faster. Harder."

When he heard her say those words, Pete lost control, picking up a hard and furious rhythm. "Katie, you're so tight... hot..." he muttered, his jaw clenching.

"That's it, yes. Fuck me, Pete. I. Want. It. Everything you have. Yes!" Kate came with a moan. He thrust into her, calling her name as he joined her, arching his back as he released.

For minutes they lay there, bodies vibrating. Eventually, Pete moved, pulling out of Kate as she practically purred like a kitten. He pulled her close so they were nose to nose. "Wow," he said, tucking her hair behind her ear and kissing her gently. She looked at him and sighed. "Well, one thing is for certain," he murmured against her hair. "Never again will I refer to you as 'Practical Kate.'"

Kate blushed, then ran her fingers lightly down his back, hearing his breath catch as she reached for his ass and squeezed. She threw her leg over him, sighing with satisfaction. "Never, *ever* judge a book by its cover, Mr. O'Brien."

"No, indeed," he said, looking into her eyes. After a few minutes, he pulled away from her, taking off the condom. "I'll be right back. Don't go anywhere."

"Wouldn't dream of it." Kate watched him, beautiful and naked, crossing down the hallway to the bathroom. She sighed and burrowed into the blankets, feeling happy and satisfied. Within minutes, she was asleep.

Chapter 18

K ate woke, thinking she'd experienced the best dream ever, until she felt the warmth of an arm wrapped around her waist and realized it wasn't a dream at all. Shifting on the bed, she turned to see Pete's face, then gave herself a mental high-five. *Damn, girl. He is fine.* She got out of bed and, as quietly as she could, headed for the bathroom. Looking in the mirror, she smiled at her reflection. Her hair fell around her shoulders in a mass of messy curls, her lips full and her face flushed. About to tie her hair back, she stopped herself. *He said you look beautiful and wild with your hair down.*

She returned to the bedroom as quietly as she could, carefully avoiding the one creaky floorboard. Pete looked to be sound asleep as Kate slipped into bed and rolled onto her side so that she could look at him to her heart's content. She took in his profile, the beard stubble on his chiseled jaw. She imagined him rubbing that stubble on various parts of her body, and she squeezed her thighs together. *He really has that effect on me*, she thought, chuckling to herself.

"What are you laughing at?" Pete said, opening one eye at her.

"Oh, nothing," she said, her lust spiking with his look.

He rolled toward her, pulling her close. "Why do I think you might be telling a fib? Remember when I said you wouldn't make a good poker player? Well, that assessment still stands."

"Well, I was laughing because you make me think all kinds of wicked thoughts." She kissed and nipped his neck.

"Mmm, what kind of wicked thoughts? Maybe we could make some of them a reality." He moved his hand to her breast and gently teased her nipple.

Kate rubbed the stubble on his jawline. "I was wondering what this would feel like rubbing against me," she said, giving him a sly smile.

"Why, Ms. Murphy, you are full of surprises. And since you graciously allowed me to spend the night, I think I can arrange exactly what you are looking for." With that, he grabbed Kate and flipped her on to her back. He leaned over her with a sexy glint in his eyes as Kate giggled. "I don't think I'll ever tire of hearing that laugh," he said, positioning himself between her legs. He kissed her lips softly, his tongue probing, then continued his way down her neck, kissing and rubbing his jaw against her soft skin.

"Mmm, that's nice," she breathed.

"Oh, I'm not done yet," he growled, moving to her breasts—alternately kissing and licking, then rubbing his stubble across her sensitive nipples. From there he moved further down her body until he was between her legs, kissing the inside of her thighs, "Oh, Kate." He parted her sex and slowly ran his tongue over her, only stopping to rub his chin gently where his tongue had been, sending Kate into a vortex of sensations as she grabbed onto the sheets underneath her.

"Pete," she groaned. "Oh, yes.... More, baby."

He growled low and deep, "Greedy girl, I'll give you more." Pete kissed her sex, rubbing, licking, blowing gently, paying attention to the way her body responded to him, bringing her close to climax and then holding back. He was playing with her, reveling in her uninhibited response to him.

"Please, oh god. So good..." she whimpered.

She watched him through half-closed eyes as he reared above her. "What do you want, Kate?"

"You know what I want." Her voice was husky and breathless.

He grabbed a condom off the nightstand and slowly rolled it on to his cock, gritting his teeth. "Turn over." Kate rolled on to her stomach. Pete ran his hands down the cheeks of her ass, squeezing and massaging, as she gloried in the feel of his hands on her skin. He grabbed her hips, lifting her onto her knees and elbows. "So beautiful," he said, parting her legs and running his fingers down her ass and between her legs until he reached her clit, feeling her slick and ready for him. Her back arched as he stroked. She watched over her shoulder as he entered her, pumping furiously as she tightened around his cock. "You are so fucking hot. You feel so good." Within minutes he came, moaning his release. His moans echoing in her ears, and knowing she had given him pleasure, sent Kate over the edge as she came, sighing his name.

Pete spooned Kate as they lay on the bed bathed in sweat, waiting for their bodies to come back to earth. Turning with a sigh of satisfaction, Kate ran her hand gently down his chest. "Wow. Bravo. Well done, sir."

Pulling her to him, he gently brushed back her hair. "Well done you, madam."

Kate stretched and kissed his neck, loving the taste of him. "Would you like some coffee?"

"Coffee would be great, but why don't we take a shower first," he said, giving her a look that made her heart skip.

"That sounds like an excellent idea." Taking his hand, she pulled him from the bed. "You can't stay in bed all day."

"If you're there I can," he grinned, following her into the bathroom.

Kate was standing in the kitchen making coffee and reading her texts, feeling a bit guilty at the number from Eve the night before, asking where the hell she was and why she hadn't responded. She was just sending her a text saying everything was fine and not to worry when Pete walked into the kitchen, his hair still damp from their shower.

"Everything okay?" he asked, moving behind her and wrapping his arms around her waist.

"Yeah, I had a bunch of texts from Eve. She knew I was going to Boston yesterday. I think she was a bit freaked out that I hadn't responded. I just wanted to let her know I was okay," she said, stepping out of his embrace to hand him a cup of coffee. "Do you want to sit out in the backyard?" At that moment, she got another text from Eve and started laughing.

"What's so funny?"

"She wants to know what happened last night that was so important I couldn't answer a text."

"What are you going to tell her?"

"Well, she *is* my best friend. But I think I'll wait and give her the news in person. I want to see her reaction. Come on, let's go out to the porch. It looks like it's going to be a lovely day." With that, the two of them walked down the hall and back into the bedroom. Kate felt herself blush as they walked past the bed to the back door leading to the garden.

"Are you blushing, Ms. Murphy? You know you drive me to distraction when you do that."

Her pulse raced at his look. "I'm not doing it intentionally."

"I know. That's what makes it so charming." She opened the door, and they stepped onto the porch. "Wow, this is great," Pete said, taking in the table and chairs, hanging lanterns, and a small backyard landscaped with beautiful flowers and trees.

"Isn't it? I swear, when I got here in February, I didn't know the backyard would look like this. It's been nice watching it develop as the seasons progress. The owner of the property has a yard service that comes once a week to cut the grass and manage the front and back garden. Thank goodness too, because I don't know beans about gardening, and I don't have a lot of time."

They sat in comfortable silence, listening to the birds calling to each other on the early morning breeze while they sipped their coffee. "Are you going into the shop today? And were you planning to be at the investigation tonight?" Pete asked.

"I thought I'd go in later and then hang around for the investigation." Sharing a smile, they sat enjoying their newfound intimacy. With her knowledge of Pete's history surrounding the paranormal, Kate told him what happened the day she was alone in the shop. "I should probably tell you something I haven't told anyone else about the haunting at *Potion*."

Pete looked at her quizzically. "Okay."

"One day, this was before *Potion* opened, I was alone in the building while Eve and Jon went out shopping for materials. Within the span of maybe two hours, I had several things happen. A folder disappeared and then showed up back on my desk. I felt a chilly breeze and a sound like someone was calling my name. Then the capper was I caught a faint scent of lavender. After that, I bolted out of the shop, telling myself the entire time it was my imagination. That's the day I saw you in the market. When you asked if there had been anymore activity—well, that's when I blew up at you," Kate said, mortified by her past behavior.

"Ah ha, that explains a lot! Boy, you really let me have it that day," Pete grinned.

Kate put her hands over her eyes at the memory. "God, I was such a bitch."

"Hey, don't say that," Pete said, taking her hands from her face and holding them. "It freaked you out, and you were only being protective of your friend. Which, by the way, are you going to tell Eve about what happened?"

"Yes. I'll tell her before tonight's investigation. I'm still wrapping my head around all of this paranormal stuff, but hearing the story about your mom... well, it changes your perspective on things." She shrugged. "Oh, something else too! I did a bit of research on Abigale Hastings."

"Oh yeah? What did you find?"

"Did you know she's buried at the Old Burying Point? I found her grave. And I smelled lavender while I was there."

"I didn't know that's where she was buried. But it makes sense. I'll have to check it out if you'll come with me," he said. Then he leaned across the table and gave her a kiss. "Hey, what time is it?"

"Time for breakfast."

"Great idea. Why don't we go into town and get something at the diner, and then I can drop you off at *Potion*? I've got a conference call with colleagues in Dublin at noon, so I'll need to be home by then."

"Let me just grab a couple of things and then we can go." She rose from her chair and went back into the house, stopping in her office to grab a few files she had been working on. When she got to the living room, Pete was sitting on the sofa, looking at a magazine, and her heart flipped. He looked so at ease, and she wondered if she might be dreaming. But then he looked up at her and smiled, and she knew it was mind-blowingly real. Getting up, he walked over, took her in his arms, and practically kissed the breath out of her. When they parted, she thought she wouldn't be able to stand on her own. "Are you sure you don't just want to stay here?"

Pete groaned, "Don't tempt me, woman. Come on, let's get out of here before I change my mind."

Chapter 19

The look on Eve's face when the two of them walked hand in hand into *Potion* was something Kate would never forget. Eve looked from Kate to Pete, to their hands, then back at Kate. If her jaw could have hit the floor, it would have. "Kate? Pete? Good morning..."

Kate couldn't stifle a giggle. "Oh hey, Eve. How's it going this morning?"

"Uh, good. Busy...." Eve shot them a wicked grin, "Now I understand why you didn't answer my texts last night."

Pete put his arm around Kate. "Sorry to have worried you, Eve."

"No problem. I'm just happy to see you two together—finally. There was a full moon last night. That must have helped move things along," Eve said with an air of certainty as she went behind the bar. "Can I get you two some coffee?"

"I've got work I've got to get to, so I'll take a pass on the coffee for now. I'll be back around six for the investigation, okay?" Pete looked down at Kate. "I'll see *you* later." He kissed her gently, resting his hand on the side of her face.

She looked up at him with a dazed grin. "Don't be late," she said as he walked to the door and waved goodbye. As soon as he was out of sight, Eve let out a whoop of joy, causing a few of the patrons to turn around and look at her quizzically. Blushing to the roots of her hair, Kate grabbed Eve's arm and pulled her back to the office.

Once they were safely out of earshot of the curious customers, Eve grabbed Kate in a bear hug and hammered her with non-stop questions, all of them boiling down to a final, "Tell me EVERYTHING!"

Kate sat down at the desk and looked up at her friend. "Well, it's a long story, so for now I'll give you the short version. I ran into Pete on the ferry, coming home from Boston. We went to dinner and well... I guess, things just clicked."

"Whoa, I guess you clicked is right! You are positively glowing, girl," Eve said, grinning from ear to ear and sitting on the edge of the desk. "I have to say, I'm in shock. I thought it would take another month of throwing you two together before anything might happen."

"Well, in this case, I think it's safe to say that fate brought us together last night," Kate said, recalling how everything just seemed to fall into place the night before.

"Kate Murphy using the word *fate*? What the heck happened to you—besides the obvious? And what happened with Michael?"

"Oh, Eve. Everything started off okay, but then, well.... Michael asked why I came to Salem and we talked about our jobs, life, and all that stuff. When I was getting ready to leave, he told me he was getting married—to a woman in Southern California who he'd been seeing long distance for six months."

"Oh, Katie. That had to hurt."

"Right? I congratulated him, left the bar, got to the dock and bam! The full force of my insecurities hit me once I got on the ferry. I was crying, and that's how Pete found me. Oh Eve, he was so thoughtful and caring. He made me feel like I could tell him everything that had happened. So, I did." Kate paused, remembering how considerate he had been. "We ended up at dinner and I asked him why he believed in ghosts. Did you know about his mom?" She looked up at her friend. Eve nodded. "Why didn't you tell me?"

"You were so set on not believing. I didn't think it would change your feelings—plus it's not my story to tell—it's Pete's. I'm glad he told you about Helen," Eve said, touching her arm.

"Well, I've got an open mind now—once he told me about his mom, I knew he was sincere. I've spent my entire life being a skeptic. It's going to take me a while to get past that, but I'm looking forward to tonight's investigation." Pausing, she thought for a minute. "Thanks for your patience with me. I know I've been more than a little rigid in my opinions on the paranormal. You're a good friend... my best friend...."

Eve jumped off the desk and hugged her. "Our friendship is rock-solid and that will never change. But now, I'm going to get us some coffee and you are going to fill me in on all of last night's epic details." She walked to the door then turned, wiggling her eyebrows at Kate. "Prepare to tell all!"

The rest of the day flew by, with the usual Saturday crush of tourists stopping in to shop and sip coffee. Kate worked at the counter with Eve for a few hours while the baristas took their lunch breaks. She loved watching customers walk in for the first time and see the delight on their faces as they took in the merchandise and the welcoming coffee bar. They had created a location that drew people in—almost like magic, as Eve was fond of saying.

They ushered out the last of the customers at five o'clock and put the closed sign on the door. Kate changed out of her work clothes and into shorts and her *BOO* t-shirt. Eve shook her head. "You are a born flirt, girl." Jon arrived with a pizza from *Sabatino's* as Eve grabbed a bottle of Lambrusco from the fridge. Shortly thereafter, Pete knocked on the door, duffle bags in hand. Kate ran to let him in and greeted him with a quick kiss. The four gathered around one of the big wooden tables and shared pizza and wine before the start of the investigation.

"Were you busy today?" Jon asked.

"Crazy busy! Kate and I worked the counter for a while and it was non-stop customers," Eve said.

"It was fun. I love watching people walk in here for the first time. They always look so happy," Kate said.

"I'd be happy too if I saw you standing behind the coffee bar." Pete winked at her as Kate blushed and took his hand.

"How was your conference call today?"

"Great! Actually, I have some news. I'm going to Dublin in mid-August to meet with my history colleagues at Trinity College. We need to finish up some odds and ends on the manuscript. Timing worked out great—right before classes begin."

"Cool! Ireland is so beautiful—and the people are amazing." Eve's eyes sparkled.

"Lucky you," Kate said. "Is it really as green and lush as it seems in every travel photo?"

"You've never been? A Murphy and you've never been back to the old sod," Pete teased.

She shook her head. "Nope. Never left North America. Been to Canada, but that's it."

"Well, it really is that green. It takes your breath away—it's so beautiful. And Eve is right—the people are just the best."

"When will your book come out?" Kate asked.

"Next May is the launch. Of course, it's an academic text, but I think it will be well received. I've been working on this history of ancient Celtic deities for two years. It's about time it's finally getting published. We're just finishing up a few research elements and presenting some details to the faculty at Trinity, so I need to be there."

"I can't wait to read it," Kate said, feeling proud of his accomplishments.

After finishing their meal, Pete opened the two duffle bags filled with gear and started handing out EVP recorders. Kate felt a twinge of embarrassment when she remembered the last investigation and how nasty she had been to him. Lust followed embarrassment when she relived the kiss they'd shared later that night.

"Okay. Why don't we start like we did the last time? Get some baseline readings and hopefully get some responses." Pete handed Eve the EVP recorder as they gathered in the center of the room. "Eve, do you want to do the honors?"

"Sure!" She flipped on the EVP recorder and noted the day and time. "Hello. Can you please make yourself known to us? We only want to talk with you and mean no harm. If you come close and talk into this device, we might hear you. Don't be afraid. Is this Abigale Hastings?" Eve paused. "Are you the woman I saw on the landing? What do you want?" Eve turned off the recorder and handed it back to Pete. "Well, let's see if we got anything."

Pete hit playback, and they listened intently. There was no response. "Let's move back to the office near the stairs and see if we get results." He handed the recorder to Kate. "Do you want to try it?"

"Okay," she said, taking the recorder and flipping it on like an expert. "Can you please let us know you are here? Is there a message we can relay to anyone? Are you looking for someone or something?" Kate turned off the recorder. "Well, let's see if we get anything." She handed the recorder back to Pete with a wink.

Pete started the playback, and this time there was a response. When Kate asked if there was a message to relay, a disembodied female voice said *yes*. More shocking was when asked if they were looking for someone, the same voice responded with the name *Kate*.

"Whoa," Eve said, watching the color drain from Kate's face. Eve touched her arm. "You okay?"

"What could she possibly want with me?" Kate squeaked. She looked at the group, feeling more than a brief panic. *Out of all the people to want to communicate with, it... she... wants to talk to me.* She tried hard not to freak out and run out of the shop.

Pete put his arm around her. "It's okay. Take a deep breath." His touch brought her out of her panic, and she inhaled deeply. "There you go," he said, pulling her closer. "Okay?"

"Yeah. But now what do I do?" she asked, out of her depth at being called out by name—by a ghost.

"We keep going. But only if you want to?" Kate nodded in agreement. "Okay then. We'll set up equipment on the second and third floors and then split up like we did on the last investigation," he said, handing out night vision cameras and motion detectors.

The four of them headed up to the second-floor landing, with Pete and Jon leading the way. Eve watched Kate with a worried expression, as if assessing her level of anxiety. "Hey, Katie. We can stop right now if you want to."

"No, I'm in this now. Who would have thought, huh?" Kate said, feeling unsure but smiling at her friend. "I just can't understand why this... person... is looking for me."

"Well, I guess we'll try to find out." Eve gave her a quick hug.

At the second-floor landing they split up, with Pete and Kate moving to the third floor. They stood in the dark, and he reached for her hand. "Sure you're okay?"

"Yeah, let's see what she wants to tell me." Pete took a motion detector and set it up at the end of the hallway, leaving Kate alone in the darkness. Everything was fine until she suddenly felt a chill. "Hey, Pete. Are you almost done down there?" she asked, trying to keep the fear out of her voice.

"Be right there," he called.

"Hurry up, okay?"

"Everything alright?" There was a note of concern in his voice.

"Umm, I think so. Just a little spooked." She stood in the darkness, scared and unsure until Pete walked back down the hallway to her.

"Wow, it's cold right here. Get the EVP recorder and let's see if we get anything," Pete said excitedly. She handed him the equipment, her hands shaking, and he stopped, looking into her eyes. "Katie, it's okay. I won't let anything happen to you," he said, and then kissed her. Kate relaxed as he flipped on the recorder. "We know you are here—we've heard you—thank you. Can you tell us who you are? Are you Abigale Hastings? What do you need from us?" He stopped and hit play. This time the disembodied voice said *yes* when he asked if she was Abigale Hastings. Pete and Kate stared at each other in surprise.

"Well, we know who it is, at least." Suddenly, the motion detector went off in the hallway.

"Come on!" Pete grabbed her hand as they headed toward the sound. Out of the darkness, the apparition of a woman in a long dress floated down the hallway, turned, looked at them with a smile, then disappeared, like smoke dissipating on a breeze.

"Did you see that? I'm not seeing things, right?" She looked up at Pete with eyes filled with wonder.

"Yep, I saw it too. Pretty amazing, huh," he said. "You okay?"

"That was amazing! I can't believe it—I mean, I *do* believe it," she said, eyes wide with excitement. "Let's tell Eve and Jon." They raced downstairs, excited to share their discovery.

Eve and Jon met them at the second-floor landing. "Did you see anything?" Eve asked.

Kate was about ready to burst. "Yes! Oh my gosh, yes! Eve, we saw the woman—and it is Abigale—she told us!"

"Kate's right," Pete said, taking her hand and watching her excitement. "She told us who she is. I'll play you the recording when we get back downstairs. Right now, why don't we turn the lights back on and I'll collect the equipment. Jon, you want to give me a hand?"

They headed back to the third floor to collect the gear while Eve and Kate went downstairs. Kate couldn't help feeling she'd stepped into an alternative universe, where everything she'd believed in the past had suddenly slipped into something totally new and unexpected. A bit unsettling, it was also exciting, and she wondered what Abigale wanted to tell her. She walked into the office, followed by Eve, and sat down at the desk, shaking her head.

Kate looked at Eve in wonder and more than a little confusion. "If anyone would have told me the ghost of a Victorian woman would appear before my eyes, I never would have believed them. Strange. And the fact she mentioned me by name is even stranger."

Eve patted her on the shoulder. "When it rains, it pours. What do you think Abigale wants to tell you?"

"How should I know!" Kate said, thinking about it for a minute. "I guess I'll find out eventually, huh?"

"Well, keep your mind open—your eyes and ears too," Eve said as the guys came down the stairs with the last of the equipment.

"Interesting evening, huh," Pete said, looking at Kate.

"Just a bit. Never expected this to happen."

"You handled it like a pro, Kate. I think I would have freaked out if I heard someone call me by name like that," Jon leaned against the doorway, shaking his head.

"Who said I'm *not* freaked out?" Kate asked, a shiver running down her spine.

After packing up the gear and stowing it in the office closet, Pete turned to Kate when Eve and Jon were out of earshot. "Would you like to come over to my place? I thought I could return the hospitality you showed me last night."

"What a considerate guy," she teased. "Where do you live, anyway?"

"Not far from here. I'm renting a place in the McIntire Historic District on Chestnut St. So, is that a yes?" He pulled her close.

"It's a yes," she said, standing on tiptoes for a kiss, which Pete quickly delivered.

"Alright, you two! Time to take that somewhere else," Eve said, delighted to see her friend so happy.

"Well, if we must..." Kate said, when they finally parted.

Taking her hand, Pete led her out into the warm evening. It was only a few minutes' walk to his house—a charming Georgian townhouse with a beautiful deep blue front door with a leaded glass fan light overhead—typical of the style. The red brick steps to the front door were lined with large pottery urns spilling over with petunias in deep purples, whites, and pinks.

Underneath the first-floor windows were hydrangeas, loaded with heavy purple blossoms.

"How pretty," Kate said, as Pete pulled his keys out of his pocket.

"Thanks. Petunias were my mom's favorite flower, so I always make sure I plant them in the summer. Come on in," he said, holding the door open for her.

Inside the house, a large gray tabby cat sat just inside the door. "Oh, who are you?" She bent down to scratch the cat behind the ears.

"This is my boy, Finn." Pete picked up the cat, stroking his head affectionately as the cat purred.

"He's huge," Kate said, rubbing Finn under his chin. He closed his green-gold eyes blissfully and pushed his head against her hand when she stopped. "What a handsome boy—friendly too."

"And spoiled," Pete said, as he put Finn back on the floor. The cat meowed, sauntering off to find something more interesting to occupy his time. "Come on, let me show you around."

"This place is beautiful." She looked to her left and saw a cozy living room, complete with a fireplace. Off the hallway to her right was a study, with books from floor to ceiling. "So, this must be where you do your research." A large oak desk sat in front of the window, and on it was a laptop computer, along with stacks of handwritten notes. There were also two overstuffed chairs with an antique floor lamp between them. "How long have you lived here?"

"Well, it's been two years. I moved here when I started working at Harvard. Come on, I'll show you the kitchen." Pete led her past the beautiful staircase toward the back of the house, where there was a bright and modern kitchen.

"Nice! This is incredible," she said, looking around the room.

"Can I get you a drink?"

"Please. Whiskey on ice if you have it," she said, as Pete moved around the kitchen, making their drinks.

"Sláinte," he said, raising his glass to her.

She smiled. "That's what I always say."

He ushered her back to the living room, and they sat down on the comfortable sofa. Pulling her close, he looked at her and smiled. "Well, you've had quite the evening, Ms. Murphy."

"That I have." She snuggled into his side. "It's so weird. I mean, I was the biggest skeptic and now this... ghost... calls me out by name. What could she possibly want with me?"

"I have no idea. Personally, I think she'll let you know in time. The theory is that it takes a lot of energy for spirits to manifest, so she may need to 'charge up' her batteries in order to communicate again. I wouldn't dwell on it—and there is nothing to be afraid of either." Finn jumped on the sofa and curled up next to Kate, purring loudly. "He likes you. You have excellent taste in women, Finn," he said, leaning over to look at the big gray ball of fur who had a look somewhere between superiority and contentment.

"He's very handsome—just like his owner." Kate rested her hand on Pete's thigh, looking up to give him a sultry smile. "Friendly like his owner, too."

Gazing at her mouth, his eyes darkened. "You haven't seen just how friendly I can be. Why don't I give you a tour of the rest of the house? We'll start in the bedroom."

Chapter 20

July arrived with long, hot days and record numbers of customers. *Potion* was always busy, but Eve and Kate had worked through most of the operational obstacles of a new business, so they were now working smarter, not harder. Their success thrilled Kate, and Eve—for the first time since she opened *Potion*—felt she could relax and enjoy her creation without the threat of financial chaos. In fact, as the financial worries subsided, Eve started planning events at the shop with music, book readings, panel discussions, and an occasional tarot card reader or psychic in the evenings.

Potion quickly became *the* hangout in Salem, not only for the events and great coffee, but because the place made people feel welcome. Kate often wondered if it was because Abigale Hastings was watching over the place. Since their June investigation, Abigale had gone silent, making Kate wonder if she would ever find out what she wanted with her. But those thoughts faded to the background as she and Eve tended to their growing business.

It wasn't all work for the business partners. Jon and Eve were happier than ever. Kate and Pete were still in the early stages of their relationship, and though Pete was busy wrapping up the work on his book, the two spent at least three nights a week together. Often, he would stop by *Potion* in the afternoons and the two would head out to the beach or take a drive along the coast.

On a well-deserved day off after working long hours, they drove up the coast toward Rockport. Once at the harbor, they headed out to Ship's Mast Light, hand in hand, where they walked along the rocky outcropping to the farthest point, looking east out to sea. "This is one of my favorite spots. It's about three thousand miles from here to Ireland, but sometimes I feel like I could just reach out and touch it from here," Pete said.

"You really love it there, don't you?"

"I do. My dad was born there. The first time he took my mom and me over, I fell in love with the place. History seems to be in the air there. It's magical and beautiful, sad and joyful in equal measures.... Sorry, I tend to wax on about the place."

"It sounds incredible."

Pete seemed lost in thought for a few minutes, just looking out to sea. Then he turned to Kate. "You know, I've been thinking. Why don't you come with me to Ireland in August?"

"What?" The invitation startled Kate.

"Come with me to Ireland. It will be fun! I can meet with my colleagues in Dublin and then we can spend some time seeing the country. Come on, say you'll go." He grabbed her hand, pulling her close. "You said you've always wanted to see Ireland. Added bonus, you get to go with me! Say you'll go."

"Really? I... well, I guess I could talk with Eve and carve out some time." Kate shook her head, "Wow, Ireland...."

"So, is that a yes?"

"Umm, yeah! Let's go to Ireland," she said, feeling a sense of joy that made her heart light.

Pete looked like a kid on Christmas morning. "Great! I'll make the arrangements. I'll have to meet with the faculty for a few days, but after that, we can be tourists. We could go for a week. Would that work for you?"

"I think so. Let me text Eve and see if that is going to be a problem." With that, she pulled out her phone and sent off a message. Eve responded immediately. *Go for it!*

For the next four weeks Kate would wake up every morning, her excitement growing as she mentally checked off the days on the calendar. Now it was here. Pete had handled all the planning, and whenever she asked what she could do to help he would say, "All you have to do is show up at the airport with your luggage and passport. I'll take care of everything else."

Now Kate was standing in her bedroom, trying to figure out what she was going to pack. Sitting on the bed with a beer in her hand, surrounded by clothes, Eve gave suggestions. "Sexy lingerie. Really, that's all you need. Although, I know you are going to want to *see* the country, so better make sure you take *some* clothing," Eve offered, giving Kate a wink. "So, has he told you anything about what he has planned?"

"No. Just to make sure that I bring something for a couple of dinners 'out' and then casual clothes for the rest of the time. I looked at the weather forecast. Looks like it is going to be low 70s during the day with occasional rain. Hey, I packed a travel umbrella in my carry-on, so that's one thing done," Kate laughed.

"Well, best advice I can give is to dress in layers. Sometimes the weather changes on a dime and it can get chilly pretty quick—even in August."

Kate glanced at the clock on her nightstand. "Well, he's going to be here in forty-five minutes, so I better finish this up." With that, she grabbed a little black dress out of the closet, along with a pair of heels. Everything else, she pulled off the bed and quickly folded into the small suitcase. Within half an hour she had finished up and put everything by the front door.

Eve grinned from her vantage point on the sofa. "Who would have thought, huh? Katie is going to Ireland—with a hot man!"

Kate blushed. "I'm nervous."

"For heaven's sake, why?"

"Well, what if we don't travel well together?"

"Seriously? You will find absolutely *anything* to worry about. Everything will be fine. Just have fun." Eve looked closely at Kate, who looked as if she were strung up on wires. "What's really going on here," she asked, as always, lasering in on the real issue.

Kate bit her lip. "I love him," she said, almost afraid to say it out loud.

"Have you told him, yet?"

"No. What if he doesn't feel the same?"

"Oh, Katie! When are you going to trust yourself? First, he is taking you to Ireland! Second, I see the way he looks at you. He's got it bad." Eve got up from the sofa and gave her a hug. "No one deserves happiness more than you, friend. Don't run away from it." There was a knock at the door. Eve elbowed Kate in the ribs. "Hope you packed plenty of birth control."

"I went on the pill six weeks ago, so no more condoms. That's my present to him on this trip." Kate grinned and headed to the door.

Pete stood in the doorway, smiling. "Hi. Are you ready?"

"I think so. Let me check and make sure I've got my passport," she said, rifling through her purse.

"Hey, Eve. Here's the extra key to my place. I appreciate you checking in on Finn while we're gone."

"No problem—happy to spend quality time with my favorite feline."

They said their goodbyes, with Eve promising to look in on Kate's house as well. Pete grabbed Kate's bag and headed out the door to a black stretch limo.

"What's this?" she squeaked, taking in their transportation.

"It's your first transatlantic trip, so we are going in style," he grinned, handing off the luggage to the driver.

"You are something else, Pete O'Brien." Kate turned to Eve, "Hold down the fort, girlfriend. I'll see you in a week."

"Have a great time." Eve gave her friend a long look. "Trust yourself, okay."

They got in the limo and were enveloped in hushed, cool comfort with classical music playing on the sound system. "You sure know how to impress a girl," she said as the car pulled away from the curb.

"You're not just any girl." Pete said as he took her in his arms, kissing her deeply. Kate sighed, losing herself in the feel of his mouth on hers, his tongue, his hand sliding up to her breast, the heat radiating from his body.

"Whoa," she sighed, pulling back slightly.

They both looked at the darkened glass partition separating them from the driver. Pete arched an eyebrow. "He would probably never know. Do you know what you do to me? I could take you in the back of this limo right now."

"You are very, very naughty," Kate murmured, holding his face in her hands. Then she pushed against him, practically climbing into his lap, kissing him, touching him, until they both knew they had to stop before they reached the point of no return.

Pete was breathing heavily. "Have you ever heard of the mile-high club?"

"Yes, I have. But no. You'll have to wait until we reach Dublin."

"Sometimes being a gentleman has its disadvantages," he grumbled.

"Oh, but a gentleman ultimately gets what he wants," she said with a wicked glint in her eyes.

Leaning close, he growled, "Good. I know what I want." Kate blinked, her lips slightly parted, and blushed. He gave her a long look that spoke volumes as to what he was thinking. "You know what you do to me when you blush, Ms. Murphy." She settled into his arms as they watched the traffic heading into Boston.

Like most airports, Logan was hectic and crowded. The limo deposited them at the international terminal, and Pete wheeled their luggage inside. After finding the airline counter, he ushered Kate to the business class line, where the agent whisked away their luggage and directed them to the private lounge. "Business class?" she asked as they walked away with their boarding passes.

"Like I said, it's your first trip across the pond, so we're going in style. And, I admit, I had tons of mileage points from all the trips I've made, so I thought we'd splurge." He took her hand as they headed to security.

After working their way through the long lines, they found the lounge. It was restful and plush, decorated in soft grays, taupes, and blues, and was a big change from the controlled chaos in the main terminal. Pete led Kate to two overstuffed chairs in a secluded alcove and then went to the bar to get drinks. She sunk into the chair and exhaled with satisfaction. *I could get used to this.* Looking out at the tarmac, dusk was settling in, turning the late summer sky a beautiful, hazy purple with shots of red and deep blue. Planes of all sizes paraded by the window, leaving Kate to imagine where everyone was going. *Ireland,* she thought excitedly. *I can't believe I'm going to see the country of my ancestors.* Kate imagined what it might look like as Pete arrived with two glasses of wine.

"Here you go, world traveler," he winked, handing her a glass.

"Thanks," she said, sipping the cool, crisp wine. "It's excellent." She sat back in the overstuffed chair and sighed. Pete paused, looking at her. "What?" she asked.

"You look so happy. That makes me happy," he said, taking her hand, stroking his thumb over her knuckles.

Kate leaned in for a brief kiss. "Are you going to tell me what you have planned for me in Ireland?"

"Well, besides the obvious..." he grinned, his eyes dark with promise. "We should arrive in Dublin around nine o'clock in the morning. I have a meeting at Trinity around two, so that will give us time to check in to the hotel and relax for a bit. If you want to come with me to the campus, you could wander around for a couple of hours until my meeting is over. Then I can show you Dublin. Oh, there's a dinner later in the evening with my colleagues close to our hotel. After Thursday morning's meeting I'm all yours," he said, giving her a look that made her squeeze her thighs together.

"All mine," she whispered with a glint in her eye, rubbing her hands together.

"You are a dangerous woman, Kate Murphy," he said, a note of lust in his voice.

They sipped their wine and talked about the places he wanted to show her in the countryside. Pete's words painted a picture of beauty, and Kate couldn't wait to get there. After about an hour of chatting and observing their fellow travelers, an attendant informed them that their flight was ready for boarding.

As they walked to the gate, the butterflies in Kate's stomach kicked into high gear. She was going to have Pete all to herself for an entire week, and while she was over the moon happy about it, she also remembered her conversation with Eve. Should she tell Pete that she loved him? Was it too soon? *Trust yourself,* she heard Eve's voice in her head. She gave herself a mental shake, told herself to put on her big girl panties, and decided to go with the flow. Kate smiled, thinking Eve would be proud.

Chapter 21

Pete closed his laptop as the captain announced their approach into Dublin. Turning, he looked at Kate, who stretched like a contented kitten. Her blouse had shifted during the night, revealing a tempting view of her cleavage, causing his pulse to quicken. "Did you have a good nap?" he asked, doing his best to tamp down his lust.

"Mmm, I did," she said, sleep still in her voice. She sat up and adjusted her blouse, much to Pete's disappointment. "Surprising, because I usually have a hard time sleeping on airplanes. Have you been working the whole time?" she asked, pointing to the laptop.

"Yeah. I wanted to polish up a couple of items for my meeting. You look like you could use some coffee." He motioned to the flight attendant. "Do we have time for a coffee?"

"Of course, sir," he said in his rich Irish accent.

After the attendant left, Pete turned and pointed over Kate's shoulder to the window. As the plane crossed the coastline on the western side of Ireland, the terrain below changed from rocky outcroppings to rolling green hills. "We're here," he said, affection in his voice. "I never get tired of this view."

"It's beautiful," she said. "Are those sheep I see down there?"

Pete leaned in close and peered out the window. Being in close proximity to her warmth made him dizzy. "I think so," he said, running his fingers down the arm of her silk blouse. He whispered in her ear. "You know, I haven't received my good morning kiss." Without hesitation, she happily obliged him, kissing him with passion. They only parted when the flight attendant returned, politely clearing his throat.

"Oh. Sorry. Umm, thank you," she said as they settled back in their seats, taking the proffered cup.

"Not at all," grinned the attendant. "Would this be your honeymoon?"

Pete watched as Kate blushed. "No. No. But it is my first trip to Ireland."

"Well, I hope you enjoy it. Welcome."

Kate watched the flight attendant walk away, then quickly turned to face the window, leaving Pete to wonder why she was so skittish at the honest mistake. There had to be more than a break-up with a long-term fiancé to make her so wary of relationships. His heart went out to her, still so guarded in so many ways. *I'll never hurt you, Kate.* He sipped his coffee and watched as she focused on the changing terrain below them. *This must be a big step for her—making this trip. Well, I'll make it memorable for her. I want her to love this land as much as I do.* She shifted in her seat and smiled, as if she could read his mind. "Excellent coffee, isn't it," he said, breaking the silence.

Before he could say anything else, the cabin was buzzing with activity as the flight attendants began preparing for landing.

Their cups were whisked away as they began their descent. He pointed out the window. "The Irish Sea. Excited?"

"Yes," she said as the plane banked to the left, giving them a view straight down to the water. She let out a nervous laugh. "Yikes! This is the part that always makes me nervous. It looks like our wings could touch the water." Sailboats glided effortlessly beneath them. Along the shore were a series of squat, stone towers. "What are those?" she asked.

"Those are Martello towers. They were built around 1804 as fortifications. The Brits were concerned about a French invasion by Napoleon, so there are around twenty-six towers along the coastline protecting Dublin. They can also be found on the west coast. Now they are great backdrops for photos, and some have been turned into living quarters—many quite luxurious. In fact, James Joyce referenced them in the opening of his novel *Ulysses*." He stopped. "Sorry, I went into lecture mode there for a minute."

"Don't apologize. I want to hear everything. It's so cool! I'd love to see them up close," she said, touching his arm.

"We can take a drive down the coast when we leave Dublin, so you can get a closer look. It's a beautiful drive." The sound of landing gear lowering and flaps moving signaled their final approach as they crossed from ocean to land and the suburbs of Dublin. Within minutes, they were at the gate. "Ready?" he asked, gathering their carry-on bags.

Like most airports, it was controlled chaos, with people rushing to their destinations. As they walked down the bustling concourse, Pete tried to see it all through Kate's eyes. After making their way through immigration and baggage claim, he pointed to the exit, where they joined the queue at the taxi stand. "Now, I know an airport isn't the best indicator of a place, but what do you think so far?" he asked, anxious for her positive opinion.

"I love the accents! I know, I know, I sound like a tourist, but it's so charming!" She hugged him. "I'm so excited! How long will it take to get into the city?"

"Not long. About half an hour, depending on the traffic," he said, holding her close. "And wait until you see the barely contained chaos of Dublin streets. They did not design the city for twenty-first century traffic."

"Can't be worse than New York. If I had a dollar for every time I was stuck in traffic."

"True. Not the same scale as New York, but Dubliners will give them a run for their money."

A taxi pulled up and a slightly balding middle-aged man jumped out of the driver's seat, popping open the trunk. He beamed at them. "Good morning! And where can I take you this fine morning?" he asked while stowing their luggage in the trunk. Pete gave him the name and address of the hotel. "A lovely place," the driver said. "Is this your first trip to Ireland?"

"Not for me, but it is for my girlfriend," Pete said as they climbed into the back seat. He caught Kate's smile when he called her his girlfriend. They took off for the city, as he took her hand and pulled her close.

Kate peppered him with non-stop questions as they drove along, with Pete giving her a running commentary on the various neighborhoods and landmarks they passed. Their driver looked at him in the rear-view mirror. "You know your stuff about Dublin. Do you come over often?"

"I'm a history professor. I work with a lot of the faculty at Trinity, so I come over a lot."

"You teach Irish history?" he mused.

"I do. I'm first generation. My father came over to America when he was a boy."

"Ah, I knew you had to be Irish. And you, lass?" he asked, looking at Kate. "With that red hair and those beautiful green eyes, you are definitely Irish."

"That I am," she said, raising her hand. "I'm a Murphy. Second generation."

The car wove through traffic at breakneck speed. "And what do you think of the old country so far?" He was watching her in the rearview mirror, and for a second Kate wished he would pay more attention to the road.

She leaned forward, smiling. "I'm totally charmed. The countryside as we were flying in was just beautiful. And the people are so friendly."

"That's true. And we're especially friendly when someone else is buying a round at the pub!" He guffawed at his own joke, then continued the hair-raising drive through Dublin's traffic and narrow streets, until he pulled up to a quaint row of Georgian townhouses, similar to Pete's home in Salem. Pete took Kate's hand to help her out while the driver grabbed their luggage and handed it over to the doorman. "It was a pleasure meeting you both, and I hope you have a wonderful time," he said, shaking their hands before he hopped back in his taxi and trundled off down the narrow street.

"I don't think I could ever drive here." Kate shuddered. "Between the narrow streets, crazy traffic, and driving on the other side of the road—I'd be a mess!"

"It definitely takes some getting used to. I had to steel my nerves the first time I drove in the city. Motorways and the countryside are much less stressful—although the country roads can sometimes seem like nothing more than a walking path," he said, taking her hand as they entered the lobby.

The hotel was a study in Georgian elegance. A beautiful crystal chandelier caught the light, giving the entrance hall a warm, welcoming glow. In the lobby was a small fireplace with beautiful period furniture surrounding it, and beyond the lobby was a cozy dining area, where guests were currently enjoying a proper Irish breakfast. To the left of the dining room was a door leading to a pub with a gleaming, dark wood bar.

A young woman greeted them warmly at the reception desk. "We have a reservation for O'Brien," Pete said, showing her the confirmation on his phone. The woman entered a few keystrokes on the computer, verifying their departure date and giving them details about breakfast, the pub, and check-out times. After handing them the keycard, she directed them to the elevator off the lobby.

The elevator was small, and as the door closed, Pete turned to Kate, his eyes darkening as he licked his lips. She blushed as he let out a sound that was a cross between a growl and a sigh. "I've spent the last ten hours thinking only of being inside you." He watched Kate's eye grow wide as he placed his hands on the wall on either side of her head. "I've been a gentleman, haven't I, Kate?" She nodded, as if in a daze. "What did you tell me in the limo about gentlemen?"

Kate's breath was rapid and shallow as she watched his mouth. Placing her hand on his chest, she slowly trailed her fingers down until they were resting lightly on his fly and his impressive erection. Pete gritted his teeth, her touch multiplying his desire. "Gentlemen ultimately get what they want," she said, giving him a wicked smile.

The elevator shuddered to a stop, and they parted as the door opened. The hallway was empty as Pete grabbed the luggage and strode down the hall to their room, with Kate sprinting to keep up with him. Once inside, he dropped the bags, took Kate's hand, and pulled her into the room, the door closing behind them with a click. He looked her up and down as if she were his prey, then pinned her arms at her sides as he slowly pushed up against her, his cock straining for release. He heard her soft moan.

"Not sure you're behaving like a gentleman right now," she said, heat in her voice.With one quick movement, he unzipped her skirt. "No, I'm not. Because right now all I want to do is strip you down and bury myself in you." He took her hand and led her to the bed, pulling back the bedspread as Kate quickly removed her top. Pete stripped off his clothes and grabbed the condoms from his overnight bag, turning to see her sitting on the edge of the bed, naked and waiting. He pushed her back onto the pillows with barely contained lust and a muttered expletive.

"You don't need that. I'm on the pill," she said, breathless with want.

"Oh, Kate," he said. "God, yes. To feel you...." He drew in a shaky breath. "Do you know what I'm going to do to you?"

"I have an idea it won't be very gentlemanly." Kate gave him a sly smile, running her hands down to cup his ass.

With a roguish grin, he traced a finger down her body, until he was sliding it into her hot, wet, center. "You're ready for me, aren't you? When you were sleeping this morning, your shirt was open, and I just wanted to touch you. Mmm, these luscious tits of yours." He chuckled before taking a nipple between his lips.

Kate arched her back, moaning. "Oh God, I'm always ready for you. I love the feeling when you first enter me. The fullness, the heat... riding your cock." She spread her legs further and took his cock in her hand, gently squeezing, then running her thumb over the head, which was slick and hot.

He looked deep into her eyes; his mouth slightly open as he licked his bottom lip. The anticipation was driving him beyond comprehension as he put his hands under her knees and moved in closer. Everything centered on that moment, those sensations, as he nudged the head of his cock against her, rubbing against her clit as Kate grabbed at the sheets. He knew just what she liked, what she needed, and he wanted to give it all to her. Slowly, unbearably slowly, Pete pushed into her, reveling in her heat as he growled with pleasure. She tightened around him and for a moment he thought he would come. The need had been building up in him for hours and feeling her against him, skin on skin, left him aching for release. He pulled back momentarily, looking down at her, her hair shimmering on the pillow like a halo of fire. Leaning over, he kissed her, moving his hips as he slid his tongue into her mouth, mimicking the movement of his cock.

She matched his rhythm, whispering between kisses. "Yes. That's what I want. Give me everything. Your cock feels so good. Pete...." She came with a cry of pleasure. At the sound of his name on her lips, Pete came with a shudder.

They lay quietly for several minutes, intimately joined, each of them coming down from their lovemaking. "Mmm.... Lovely," Kate said, rolling onto her side, running her fingers down his back.

Pete trailed kisses from her mouth to her collarbone as she hugged him close and breathed in his scent. "Welcome to Ireland," he said against her milky white skin that was hot and flushed.

"Had I known this was the official welcome, I would have visited a lot sooner."

"Sleepy?"

"Maybe a little," she said, stretching like a cat that had been lying in the sun.

"Why don't we take a nap before heading over to Trinity?" Kate nodded, and within minutes, was fast asleep. He drew her close and pulled the covers over them, smiling at the woman who had changed his life for the better.

Chapter 22

People filled the streets of Dublin—with locals going about their daily lives while tourists stopped to gape at their guidebooks. The sun had finally come out, and the temperature was pleasant and warm, with a touch of a cool breeze. On their walk to Trinity, Pete and Kate passed St. Stephen's Green filled with Dubliners, enjoying the fine weather. "The Irish can't resist a sunny day," Pete said. "I wonder how many of these folks called off sick today in order to enjoy this?"

"I can understand why. It's absolutely gorgeous," Kate said, taking in all the sights and sounds as they stood at a corner waiting to cross the street.

Pete stood behind her, kissing her neck. "You're absolutely gorgeous."

She rolled her eyes at his compliment. "Flatterer!" But as they crossed the street, Kate couldn't keep the bubble of happiness from welling up inside her as she thought about how much she loved the man walking by her side. They walked hand in hand through the front gates of Trinity, which opened into a large common green with stone buildings surrounding them.

"Okay. Directly in front of us is the Campanile and Library Square. To the right is the old library with the Long Hall and the Book of Kells." Pete pointed to the various buildings. "There is also a gift shop if you want to look around. I'll text you when my meeting is through. Just let me know where you are and I'll come and get you, okay?" Pete looked at his watch. "It shouldn't take over two hours, tops." He kissed her and headed off.

Kate wandered the campus, taking in the history of the place. Students were returning for the fall semester, and she enjoyed hearing them talk about their classes or setting up dates with friends to meet at a pub. Eventually she found herself at the Book of Kells exhibit, the 7th century illuminated manuscript of the Gospel, where she bought a ticket, and made her way through the crowded, darkened room. She gazed at the ancient, illuminated pages and was in awe of the intricate drawings of decorated initials—swirling with Celtic knots and beautiful color. She thought of the monk who had sat in a room, probably with little light, producing this beautiful work of art. *You did not toil in vain,* she thought, moved by the beauty of the work. She followed the flow of the crowds and found herself in the Long Hall—a cavernous library stacked from floor to ceiling with books. At each group of stacks on the ground floor was a bust of a famous author. From there she was conveniently guided to the gift shop, where she bought a pretty scarf for Eve and a magazine on the history of Trinity College. Checking her watch, she headed outside where the weather had turned and rain looked imminent. She studied the map she had picked up in the gift shop, then headed over to the Arts Café for a soft drink to kill time. Within twenty minutes, she received a text from Pete. Letting him know where she was, she leafed through the magazine and waited.

"Hey, you," Pete said, sitting down next to her, kissing her cheek.

"Hi. How was your meeting?"

He rolled his eyes at the memory of the meeting. "It was interesting. Academics get together and it can turn into a real geek-fest. There were a couple of questions on specific citations, but overall, I think we are ready to wrap it up. Tomorrow's meeting is really going to be a quick review of today's discussion. Sort of like a 'punch list' for the manuscript."

"Glad it went well."

"What did you do this afternoon?"

She lifted the magazine. "I went to the gift shop, then the Book of Kells and the Long Hall. It was incredible... the details and the color. But it gets a bit crowded in there. I wish I could see it without all the humanity around!"

"I can always arrange an off-hours tour if you want to go back," Pete offered, looking at his watch. "Why don't we head back to the hotel for afternoon tea. Then we'll meet some of my colleagues for dinner around 7:30. Okay?"

"Sounds great—and a real Irish tea sounds perfect," she said, her stomach rumbling in hunger. "Where are we meeting for dinner?"

"Not too far from our hotel, on the north side of the River Liffey. It's a great pub with a wonderful chef. I think you'll like it," he said, taking her hand as they headed back to the hotel.

Afternoon tea was a casually elegant affair, as they sat in a beautiful study, surrounded by antiques. The table was set with a pretty tea service, and a generous plate of scones, cakes, and various biscuits were brought to their table.

Kate sipped the fragrant tea, thinking that there was something incredibly civilized about afternoon tea. "Who are we meeting tonight?" She put down her cup and picked up a slice of sponge cake, topped with strawberries.

"I think there will be four. The chair of the History department, Declan Smithson. Then three of the faculty, one of whom is my co-author and good friend, Rob Mahoney. The other two faculty members are Sean Arbus and Morganne Callaghan. They've been invaluable in getting this manuscript completed. I promise we won't talk too much shop tonight."

"Oh, don't worry about that. I'm interested in hearing more about your research. After spending my academic life studying business, this is a breath of fresh air. I find it all fascinating," she said, excited to meet his colleagues. "How did you meet Rob?"

Over tea and sweets, Pete shared his story about meeting Rob in graduate school where they were both studying for their PhDs, with a shared interest in ancient Irish history and mysticism. Once they graduated, Rob returned to Ireland and a post at Trinity, while Pete stayed on at Harvard to teach. They remained friends and at a conference in New York, met up and talked about their interest in co-writing a manuscript. "In academia, it's publish or perish. We were both newly minted assistant professors, vying for tenure, so we joined forces on this text." Pete sat back, remembering. "It's been hard work, but Rob and I have gotten incredible support from both of our universities, so we've had access to some incredible resources.

And having the ability to pick the brains of some of Ireland's top scholars has been a godsend. Both Sean and Morganne are the cream of the crop."

"I can't wait to meet them. To have that kind of support doing something you love... it's priceless."

Chapter 23

T he pub was all dark wood and brass fittings, with groups of friends sitting and laughing, some cuddled up in the snugs—the small private rooms along the wall that accommodated more intimate conversation. Kate and Pete had just walked through the door when they heard someone calling to them. Turning, a short, red-haired man with a neatly trimmed beard greeted them. "Rob," Pete called, taking Kate's hand and drawing her toward the group of people sitting in the dining room.

Introductions, as well as first impressions, were made. Rob Mahoney charmed Kate, and she understood why he and Pete were such close friends. Declan Smithson was the picture of what a department chair should be—an older gentleman with a dry sense of humor. Sean Arbus was most likely around the same age as Declan. Quiet and observant, Kate figured there was little that got past Professor Arbus. At the end of the table were two young women—a petite blonde and a tall brunette. The blonde had an open and friendly manner, but the brunette seemed cold and standoffish. That is until Pete got close to her. Kate's radar went up immediately. Rob turned to Kate to finish the introductions.

"This is Morganne Callaghan, an esteemed colleague who has been offering valuable assistance on our book, along with Sean, who is also an expert in Irish mysticism." Morganne gave Kate an icy half smile and a slight nod of her head. Rob turned and beamed at the blonde. "And this is my wife, Sarah." She greeted Kate warmly, drawing her into the circle of people.

She settled into a chair next to Sarah. "It's a pleasure to meet you all. Pete has told me so much about all of you—it's nice to put faces with names." The only other seat available was next to Morganne, and if Kate were a gambler, she would have put money down that the woman had orchestrated the move on purpose as she watched the brunette pull Pete down next to her at the table. Kate did her best to tamp down the jealousy flaring up as she watched the woman move in on her boyfriend.

The look on Kate's face must have spoken volumes because Sarah leaned over, whispering, "That one's a piece of work."

"I can see that." Kate chuckled and turned to Sarah. "Something tells me you and I are going to be good friends," she said with a wink.

"How long have you and Pete been dating?" Sarah asked.

"Not long, a little over two months. But we met back in March. How long have you and Rob been married?"

"Two years in October. Did you know Pete was best man at our wedding? Those two are as close as brothers," Sarah said, giving the two men an affectionate glance. She then gave Kate a conspiratorial look. "Dating a little over two months, eh? Pete's never brought anyone over to visit, and he's been traveling back and forth to Ireland for the last two years. Must be serious between you two."

"Well, it is still early days. I will say, he's the kindest, most thoughtful man I've ever met." Kate looked over at Pete to find him staring at her and she blushed. His eyes went dark as he held her gaze for a lingering moment.

Sarah caught the look between the couple and laughed. "Aye, well, I think it's serious for him."

The rest of the evening went by in a blur of great conversation, wonderful food, and delicious whiskeys for every course. Kate had to admit that the whiskey took the edge off her occasional spikes of jealousy whenever she looked over to see Morganne putting her hand on Pete's arm, or leaning in to whisper something in his ear. Sarah was a help too, keeping her occupied with all sorts of stories about Rob and Pete, as well as life in Dublin.

After dinner was cleared away, the servers brought another round of whiskey to the table, and after her second glass, Kate was feeling more than slightly buzzed. She excused herself and headed to the ladies' room. She stood at the mirror, holding on to the edge of the sink to steady herself, and scrutinized her reflection. A rosy-cheeked, redheaded Irish girl looked back at her. *Not a tall brunette, but I can hold my own.* A spark of jealousy flamed in her eyes as she thought of Morganne sitting in the dining room, pawing at her boyfriend. *Well, that bitch had better not have her hands on Pete when I get back to the table.* She couldn't control her giggles as she imagined a scenario where she was telling Morganne Callaghan to go straight to hell. When she stepped out of the bathroom, she found Pete leaning up against the wall, waiting for her in the dimly lit hallway.

"Are you okay?"

"I am *great*," she said with a slight slur.

Taking her hands, he pulled her to him. "Looks to me like you've had one over the limit."

"Surprised you noticed," she said archly, looking up at him with an unfocused smirk.

"Ah, I notice everything about you," he said, his warm breath against her ear, making her shiver.

"Oh, really? I thought Morganne was doing a fantastic job of keeping you occupied," she said, punctuated with a hiccup and a giggle.

"Morganne is a colleague—nothing more than that. Is it possible I sense a little jealously, Ms. Murphy?"

"Me? Jealous? Why would I be jealous?" She weaved slightly. "Just because some dark-haired Irish Amazon is putting the moves on *my* man." She took him by the collar and pulled him down to eye level.

Pete looked at her, working hard to stifle a laugh. "Well, you have one thing right, I am your man."

Kate shook her head like a bobblehead doll. "Damn right. So, she better steer clear because I love you." Even through her alcohol-infused brain, Kate realized her admission. She looked up at him, eyes wide. There was a beat where neither of them said a word, they just stared at each other. Kate took a deep breath, pulled herself together as much as she could, and took the bull by the horns. "Look, I... I know I've had a few, but I'm not so drunk that I don't know what I'm saying. Maybe I needed a little liquid courage, I don't know. I *do* know that I love you,

Pete O'Brien. You don't have to say anything. I just wanted you to know how I feel." She focused on the buttons on his shirt and patted his chest. "Okay. Well, that's it..." She started to walk away, but Pete stopped her, taking her arm.

"Come on. Let's go back to the hotel," he said, a note of finality in his voice.

The goodbyes were a blur, but Kate remembered telling Sarah she hoped they'd see each other again as they exchanged emails to keep in touch. Pete navigated them out to the street, where a heavy downpour greeted them. He cursed under his breath and moved her under the awning in front of the pub to stay dry. "You stay right here, I'm going to get us a taxi."

Kate watched him standing at the curb, soaking wet in the rain. *He didn't say I love you back.* She was miserable, wondering how they would handle the rest of their trip after her confession. Within a few minutes, a taxi pulled up, and Pete turned and waved to her. Making her way to the curb with a sinking feeling in her stomach, she got in the taxi and they headed back to the hotel. Pete held her hand, but the silence was oppressive and Kate felt more uncertain with every click of the taximeter. To calm herself, she focused on the raindrops pelting against the window, but it only made her feel like crying. By the time they were pulling up to the hotel, Kate felt like she was having an out-of-body experience. She watched as they moved through the lobby and thought back to earlier in the day when they arrived and what had happened in the elevator. The door slid shut, and she looked at the floor, concentrating on the pattern in the carpet and wishing it would swallow her up. They stepped out onto the third floor and walked down the hall to their room. All the while, Kate prayed they would get the looming conversation over with quickly.

When the door clicked shut behind them, Kate made her way into the room and looked at Pete for the first time since they had gotten in the taxi. "Your hair is wet. Let me get you a towel," she said, turning for the bathroom.

"It can wait." Pete walked toward her, never breaking eye contact, until he was standing inches away from her. He wrapped his arms around her, holding her until the tension left her body. She wrapped her arms around his waist and lowered her head to his chest as they stood in the silence for several minutes. "Let's sit down," he said, guiding her to the foot of the bed. He scanned her face, his eyes glowing and dark, and cupped her face in his hands. "I've never met anyone like you, Kate Murphy. Ever since the night I met you at *Sabatino's* and you called me ghostbuster, I couldn't stop thinking about you. And every time after that, when we would meet, it strengthened the belief that you and I would be together. I love you, Kate. I think I've loved you since the night you tore into me on the ghost investigation." He gave her a lingering kiss.

"You had me worried there for a while. That was one long taxi ride back here," she said after the kiss, running her hands up and down his back.

He shifted Kate onto his lap. "Sorry. I just wanted to make sure we could be alone. I didn't want to lose control in the pub with my colleagues thirty feet away."

"Lose control?"

"You know what you do to me. When I heard you say that you loved me... what I wanted.... I couldn't trust myself to not kiss you senseless right there in the pub." Pete grinned as she blushed at his comment. "I want you so much, Kate. Your heart, your soul, your body...."

"I'm yours, Pete," she said simply. "I've been yours since that night on the ferry from Boston. Your thoughtfulness, kindness... your dimple." She pulled him down onto the bed with a sultry laugh.

"Ah yes, my dimple. Who knew I'd fall in love with a woman with a dimple fetish," he said, holding her close.

"Oh, it's more than the dimple. It's the entire package. Now, you mentioned something about kissing me senseless a little earlier."

"I did." Eyes flashing, he cradled her face in his hands and made good on his promise.

Chapter 24

Activity filled the days that followed, from visiting the prehistoric burial site at Newgrange, to the hauntingly beautiful ruins at the Rock of Cashel. It was at Cashel that Kate lost her heart to Ireland. As they stood on the large rock outcropping with a gentle rain falling, surrounded by the ruins and cemetery, she understood what Pete meant when he said Ireland was magical and beautiful, sad and joyful. She was overcome with a feeling of belonging, knowing that her family once lived on this beautiful island. From this spot she could feel the history of the country and its people through every stone wall and rolling green hill surrounding them. Overcome with emotions, Kate closed her eyes, allowing herself to feel everything—the ground beneath her feet, the rain on her face, Pete's warm hand in hers. In the distance she heard birds cawing and sheep bleating. She inhaled the scents of rain and stone and earth. Standing in this place steeped in ancient history, absorbing the sensations all around her, Kate heard a woman's voice say, *Here, Kate... home.* She opened her eyes and looked around, but there was no one else other than Pete. He gave her a quizzical look. "What's the matter?"

"Oh, uh, nothing. I think the beauty of this place just overwhelmed me for a minute," she said, still a bit startled by what she heard. She tried to find an explanation for the voice.

There is a lot of echo in this old ruin... and the birds.... Could that be what I heard? But Kate was losing her ability to be a skeptic after what she had been through during the past few months. Instead, she put the incident off to the side for the moment. *It's so beautiful here... no wonder you think someone is telling you this is home,* she thought, turning her focus to Pete. "It's so beautiful here... magical, really."

"It's amazing, isn't it?" He looked out over the misty valley. "I've got someplace else I want to show you. I think you'll like it. Are you ready to go?"

"Sure. Where are we going?"

"Well, that would ruin the surprise, wouldn't it," he winked. "Come on, it's not far from here."

They drove along the narrow country roads until Pete stopped at a crossroad clearing and pulled the car off onto a grassy spot. Kate gave him a quizzical look, but he just smiled and hopped out of the car. "Where are we?" she asked, joining him at the base of a hill covered in lush grass and trees, with a few cows grazing in the distance.

"This is Cnoc Áine."

"What is it?"

"It is the sacred hill of the goddess Áine."

"Wait a minute. Isn't that the goddess you mentioned when we first met?"

"The very same." Pete nodded, taking her hand and leading her to a broken-down gate. "Áine was the goddess associated with fertility, agriculture, sovereignty, and love. This hill is where the community would gather on mid-summer eve and celebrate her, praying she would bless their crops. They would walk around the hill with torches at nightfall. It must have been quite a sight. Come on, I want to show you something," he said, pulling her through the gate and up the grassy path to the crest of the hill.

At the top was a small standing stone, aged with lichen and pitted by the weather from a thousand years of wind, rain, and sun. Kate took in the 360º view of the surrounding countryside as the sun broke through the departing rain, highlighting the hills and valleys beyond. She remembered the voice at Cashel, whispering the word "home" and she couldn't help but feel a resonance with this place, that maybe there was a greater truth in the message than she realized. For the first time in her life, Kate felt anchored, secure, and at peace within herself.

She felt Pete watching her and turned to catch his warm gaze. "You look as if you belong here. Maybe you are the incarnation of Áine. All you need is a long gown and a sheaf of wheat in your arms. The locals will come running, thinking the goddess has returned."

Kate laughed at the thought of being a goddess and moved toward Pete, pulling him close. "Hmm, that would make you a god then, wouldn't it?"

"Not necessarily. Áine was known in some legends to be very friendly with the local human gentlemen."

"So, she was a bit of a free spirit, eh?"

"Oh yeah," Pete said, kissing her hair.

"Well, play your cards right and we'll see what this goddess has in store for you." Then she pulled his mouth to hers and kissed him, giving him a promise of what was to come.

Back on the road, they continued heading west toward the Atlantic. As they drove along, Kate noticed the landscape changing, the rolling green hills dotted with cows and sheep giving way to rockier terrain as they reached the ocean. The clouds had cleared somewhat, throwing sunlight in scattered blocks across the sea, which was churning with waves from the winds buffeting the shoreline. Kate opened the window and breathed in the ocean's scent. She could taste the salt air on her lips and gave a contented sigh. "My god, this place is like heaven," she said, settling back in her seat to enjoy the view and the feel of the wind on her face.

After a short drive north along the coast, Pete turned off the road onto what looked like a walking path toward the ocean. "Almost there."

"Where are we?"

"We're at *Land's End*—a friend let me borrow his cottage for a few days." Pete navigated around a curve in the narrow road where a pretty stone cottage sat on a slight rise, facing the ocean. Wild roses climbed up the side of the house, and she could smell their fragrance through the open window. "This is one of my favorite places on earth." He turned off the engine and came around to open Kate's door. "*Fáilte abhaile*—welcome home," he said, taking her hand. "This is ours for the next two nights."

Kate looked from the cottage to the ocean, then to Pete. "This is one of the most beautiful places I've ever seen. I know I keep saying that everywhere we go, but wow!" She shook her head in amazement.

"Wait until you see inside." He grabbed the bags from the trunk as she headed up the stone path to the front door. She turned and looked out at the ocean, the view sending a jolt of emotions through her, bringing tears to her eyes. Pete joined her at the front door and followed her gaze out to sea. "I know. It makes me feel the same way."

"Thank you. Thank you for bringing me here," she said, trying to keep the tremor out of her voice. "I don't know why it makes me so emotional. Something about this place... it just fills my heart... you know?"

Pete put his arm around her shoulder. "Let's go inside."

Pete knew the cottage wouldn't disappoint. Beautiful, dark hardwood floors with colorful area rugs, overstuffed furniture, and a stone fireplace to take off the chill on those cold winter nights when the winds howled off the sea. They moved through the living room to the kitchen, which was small but well designed and contained every modern convenience. On the counter sat a basket with wine and assorted nibbles. Next to the basket was a large vase filled with wildflowers and a note. *Hi, Pete and Kate. Enjoy Land's End. I've left you some foodstuffs and wine for your arrival. The town is only a ten-minute walk north, either down the road or beach where there's a pub and a market if you need it. Best, Marcus.* Pete smiled, shaking his head. "Marcus is something else—always so thoughtful. He and his husband Aidan are the nicest guys around. Come on. Let me show you upstairs."

They headed up the narrow staircase to a master bedroom encompassing the entire second floor. The view from the windows framed the entire beachfront, as well as gardens and a path leading down to the sea. Their host had decorated the room with rustic furnishings that included a huge four-poster bed. Off the bedroom was an en suite bathroom with a large claw-footed bathtub. From the furniture to the gardens, the entire cottage looked like something out of a quintessential Irish dream. "How do you know Marcus and Aidan?" Kate asked, looking out at the gardens below.

"Marcus is an administrator at Trinity, and Aidan owns a well-known restaurant in Dublin. We can go there on our last night in the city, if you like," Pete offered.

"That sounds great. Hey, how about we go for a walk? The garden looks beautiful and a walk to town would be fun."

They headed out hand in hand, stopping at the car to get jackets against the chill coming off the sea. Down the rocky slope to the water they passed banks of flowers, giving off a wonderful fragrance as Kate stopped to take it all in. "This is incredible."

Pete felt a flood of contentment, knowing she was pleased with the cottage and the view. "Ah wait, there's more to come." He guided her down the path to where it flattened out to a sandy beach. "It's low tide. So, we'll have a clear, dry walk into town this way."

They had just reached the harbor as the sun was setting. Pete stopped and pulled her close, whispering in her ear. "You have to see this." They stood at the railing, watching as the sky turned orange and red through the dark clouds until the sun disappeared beneath the horizon, leaving a vivid purple cast to the sky.

Kate was in awe of the colorful display. "Okay, that was magnificent. Did you plan that too?"

"Nope. I had nothing to do with that. Just dumb luck. Although the sunsets here are spectacular most of the time." He looked at the woman who had stolen his heart. Her hair was windblown and wild, her cheeks rosy and her eyes bright, and he couldn't contain his happiness. "I love you, Kate," he said, pulling her into an embrace, intoxicated by the feel of her against him. "I can't believe how lucky I am." He kissed her, gently at first, but with increasing passion. He broke the kiss on a sigh. "My God, what you do to me. Oh lass, what I'm going to do to you when we get home." He tugged on her lower lip with his teeth until Kate moaned. "Come on. I'd better feed you to keep up your strength. Let's go to *The Harp*. They have wonderful food and traditional music most evenings."

They walked into town and found the pub a block in from the waterfront. The place glowed with hospitality, and like most pubs in Ireland was fitted out with a bar along one wall, and snugs around the perimeter, with a few tables scattered in the center. In the corner was a small area for music, and already there was a crowd gathering.

They were lucky enough to find one of the few remaining tables, and as they settled in, Kate rubbed her hand over the heavy wooden surface. "My dad would love this place."

"Yeah? Why is that?"

"He's a woodworker. I'm sure he could spend hours just marveling at the craftsmanship that went into building this bar."

"I didn't know he's a woodworker. In fact, I don't know that much about your family." Pete noticed her body tense at his comment.

"Oh, not much to tell, really. A mom. A dad. A divorce." She made a half-hearted attempt to laugh it off.

He took her hand, sensing her discomfort. "Katie, c'mon. Talk to me." He watched her take a deep breath, trying to relax.

"Well, it wasn't exactly a Norman Rockwell kind of childhood," she said as the server arrived with their beers. After making their dinner selections, Pete turned his attention back to Kate.

"A Norman Rockwell childhood? Who has that? Nobody I know. I'm serious, Kate. Talk to me." He watched her brows crease as if in an internal struggle and waited, hoping she would trust him enough to open up.

"I hate talking about this," she said, looking at the tabletop. Pete smiled, lifting her chin to meet his gaze. She gave him an appraising look, as if weighing her options. Running her finger around the rim of her glass, she continued. "Kevin Murphy and Gale Chase. You couldn't pick two more distinct personalities." Pete listened as she gave him a thorough rundown on the dysfunctional relationship between her parents.

"Look, I don't want you to think badly of them. They did their best—I guess. I mean, I grew up with a lot of kids who had it way worse than me. After their divorce, my dad moved to Door County, Wisconsin and opened a woodworking shop— he's still there—doing what he loves. He's happy. My mom...." She trailed off for a moment. "I spent the rest of my formative years living with a woman who was looking for... geez, I don't know. Money... status? And as far as seeing my dad? Well, once he left for Door County, that was it. I'd get cards at Christmas and my birthday, an occasional phone call. Oh, I'd spend two weeks up there every summer. Doesn't do much for maintaining a father/daughter relationship."

"Kate, I'm sorry," he said, wanting to do everything in his power to take away the pain she must have felt.

"It is what it is. My dad remarried a lovely woman a couple of years after he and my mom split. I'm glad he's happy. He deserves it. Could he have done more to have a relationship with me? Yeah. But in hindsight, I know my mom couldn't have made it easy for him." She sighed, absentmindedly running her hand along the smooth wood of the tabletop. "Still, sometimes it bothers me he wasn't around for some of those milestones growing up." She shrugged self-consciously. "Dumb stuff like teaching me how to drive, taking pictures at prom, being at my high school graduation.... Ah well, it made me self-reliant." She made a half-hearted attempt at a smile, which made Pete want to take her in his arms.

"What about your mom?"

"Gale? Well, she's on her third marriage, so that speaks volumes, right? I still can't figure out what she's looking for. It's like she has this need that can't be filled. Status and money haven't made her happy. The guy she's married to now is a big corporate lawyer in Chicago. They have a gorgeous condo on the lake and a summer home in Michigan." A grimace flitted across her face. "It's exhausting being around her—I hate to say it since she's my mom. But it seems like I can never measure up."

Dinner arrived, halting the conversation. As they ate, Pete thought about what Kate had shared with him, and it all made sense. How she was so guarded when they met, why she sometimes seemed so wary regarding relationships, her practical, pragmatic nature. Pete winced, thinking about the first time they met when he called her Practical Kate. *No wonder she didn't want to have anything to do with me. Talk about hitting a nerve.* Halfway through dinner, Pete broke the silence. "Thank you for sharing your story with me. I know it's not always easy to share personal histories."

"You've shared yours with me. It was time to share mine. Thanks for listening."

He leaned in close. "You know, I owe Eve a debt of gratitude. She brought you to Salem. I don't even want to contemplate my life without you in it."

"I'm the lucky one," she said, snuggling into his side.

As they were finishing their dinner, several musicians arrived to begin the night's entertainment. A violinist, a piper, an accordion player, and a guy playing a drum called a bodhrán were all sitting in the corner, tuning up. Joining them was a young woman sitting in to sing. They started off with a haunting ballad sung in Irish. The woman's voice was clear and beautiful, quieting the pub and holding everyone enthralled by her talent. When the song was through, Pete watched a flood of emotions cross Kate's face as the pub erupted in applause. "Wow.... She's incredible. They're all amazing," she said.

"I know, right? Most of these folks live in the area. They just come together in the evenings to play. It's such a big part of the social fabric here—everything happens at the pub. It's where the community comes together."

The group played on as the evening continued, and after a few more pints of Guinness and a shot of Jameson, Pete could see Kate had recovered from sharing her family story. The band announced they were going to take a break after the next song and then broke into a raucous rendition of *Whiskey in the Jar*. It wasn't long before Kate was clapping along as people got up to dance and join in. It was a scene of unbridled joy. Pete was singing along, grinning at Kate, feeling like he didn't have a care in the world. He pulled her close and continued singing and laughing as she joined him on the chorus. Before long, he pulled her out of her chair and had her dancing with the locals, laughing and twirling in his arms. The song ended with a cheer that shook the pub.

Her cheeks flushed with excitement, Kate let out a whoop of joy. "Now that was fantastic!" She hugged Pete tight, laughing and breathing in his scent.

Pete looked down at her and felt something shift within himself, a sense of finality, in the best possible sense. It didn't hit him like a thunderclap, but more like a rolling wave, pulling him to shore. "You ready to go?" She responded with a giggle and nipped his ear. "Now, lass. Ye better behave," he growled, nuzzling her neck.

They made their way to the pub door, saying goodnight to the proprietor and promising to return. Once outside, sharp winds and a night sky that was cloudy and dark greeted them. In the distance, thunder rumbled out at sea. Pete looked at the clouds, gauging how much time they had before the skies opened up. He took her hand and started down the road toward *Land's End.*

Chapter 25

P ete unlocked the door as a bolt of lightning slashed the sky. "Perfect timing," he said, pulling Kate into the cottage and locking the door behind them.

"Brrrr, it's chilly out there," Kate said, running a hand through her windblown hair.

"Ah, lass. I know just how to warm ye up," He whispered in her ear using his best Irish brogue.

Kate batted her eyelashes at him. "Why, sir, I don't know what you mean." Pete picked her up, slinging her over his shoulder as she squealed with laughter, getting into the game as he carried her up the stairs. "Sir, stop! Please, I hardly know you! What are you doing?" Kate did her best to act the part of a damsel in distress, but her laughter was getting in the way.

Pete had a thought. Kate was always in control, following the rules. Well, tonight he wanted to give her the chance to let go of all control. He stood her next to the bed and removed her jacket. "I'm doing what I've wanted to do all night." He was getting into the role-playing as well as he grasped her chin, pulling her inches from his mouth. "Watching a beautiful lass like you. All alone in the pub. Don't play coy with me. I will have ye." He growled low in his throat, stroking the side of her breast in a hypnotic rhythm. "No one is around to stop me, is there?"

Kate was no longer laughing—her eyes wide and dark, her lips parted. "No... no, sir," she breathed. Pete took her mouth, consuming her, mindless with want.

"Take off your clothes," he commanded, stepping away from her. Kate did as she was told. Toeing off her shoes, she took off her jeans and socks. She stood in her shirt and panties, waiting for his next move. "Kate..." His voice was hoarse with lust. She gave him a sly smile and slowly unbuttoned her shirt, leaving it hanging open to reveal her black lace bra. Growling, he crossed to her, stopping inches from her body as he grabbed her shirt, pulling it off her shoulders. He ran his hands down her breasts to her waist, then on to her hips. Before she could process what was happening, Pete grabbed her lace panties and ripped them from her. She moaned. "You want this," he said, no longer playing.

"Yes," she whimpered.

Pete pulled her close and stripped her of her bra, leaving her naked to his gaze. "Get. In. Bed," he said, self-control slipping away. She did as he commanded, as Pete moved to the headboard. "Put your arms over your head." Once again, Kate did as she was instructed. "Good. Now, hold on to the headboard."

"Wait. What... what are you doing?" she asked, eyes wide.

"Shhh. We're going to play. Do you trust me?" Kate nodded, her eyes never leaving his. Pete hurried to his suitcase and took out two neckties. Turning, he held them up for Kate to see.

"Oh," she sighed, squirming on the bed.

Gently taking her right arm, he ran his fingers down her skin, making her shiver. He took one tie and with a quick motion, tied her wrist to the bedpost. "Does that hurt?" he asked, inches from her face. She shook her head. He took her other wrist and tied it to the opposite bedpost in the same fashion. Once secured, he moved to the side of the bed and undressed with sensual grace. Kate watched, licking her lips, her breath coming quick and shallow. When he finally removed his pants and briefs, she groaned. He touched himself, stroking his cock and looking down at Kate, his eyes hooded and dark. "So beautiful. I'm going to pleasure you until you scream. Are you ready for that, lass? I'm going to make you come over and over again." He crawled onto the bed to lie next to her and whispered in her ear, "And when you think you can't take anymore? I'm going to bury my cock in you."

Kate pulled on her restraints. "I want to touch you, please...."

"Soon, baby. But now, it's all about pleasure—your pleasure." Pete licked her ear. He looked at her, panting with need, her nipples hard and tempting. He heard her moan, and he chuckled. "You are so fucking ready for me, aren't you?" Kate shook her head and pulled on her restraints, trying to get to him. "You know, I have an idea. I'll be right back." Pete got up from the bed and headed to the stairs.

"Get back here," Kate panted. "Pete!" Chuckling, he made his way to the kitchen. Within minutes he walked back up the stairs with a tray in his hands, holding a bottle of champagne, glasses, and a bowl of fresh fruits. Kate glared and pulled on her restraints. "You picked a fine time to get hungry," she fumed.

He grinned, setting the tray on the nightstand. "My, my... so impatient. I thought you were a poor, innocent damsel in distress." Kate sighed as he took the bottle of champagne and uncorked it with a pop. He filled a glass and sat down on the edge of the bed. "Thirsty?" he asked, smirking. Kate gave him a look, and he laughed deep in his throat, raising the glass to his lips. He stopped. "Where are my manners? Ladies first, of course," he said, lifting her head with his hand and putting the glass to her lips. She took a sip, wrinkling her nose at the bubbles. "Good." Taking a drink, he put the glass on the tray, then picked up a peach from the bowl. He lifted it to his nose and inhaled, never breaking eye contact with Kate. "This peach... it's like you. Soft, fragrant, juicy...." He bit into the fruit, juices running down his arm. Kate moaned as Pete smiled, licking his lips. Once again, he lifted her head, this time offering her the peach. She bit into the fruit, juices running down her neck. Pete licked and sucked her sensitive skin with a languid sensuality, capturing the rivulets of juice.

Kate pulled on her restraints. "Oh, God.... Pete...." He hovered over her and once again bit into the peach, trailing juice down her body to her breasts and down to her thighs. "Sticky..." she breathed.

"Don't worry. I'm going to lick every inch of you clean," he said, beginning his mission to do just that. He started at her collarbone and licked her skin with a featherlight touch, moving down to her breasts, pushing them together. Kate's nipples were hard, and she whimpered when he took his time—first just looking at her, marveling at the sight.

"Pete... please," she begged.

"Please what, Kate?"

"Touch me. Oh God." She pulled on the restraints, desperate to touch him.

"Oh, no. Tonight I'm calling the shots. And I promise you, I'm going to have my hands on every part of your body." He lowered his mouth inches away from her breasts as his tongue darted out, lightly flicking her nipple. She whimpered and squirmed. "The peach is sweet, but you are so much sweeter," he said before taking her in his mouth, first sucking, running his tongue over her nipple, then gently biting, making her buck her hips. He threw his leg over her, whispering in her ear, "You want my cock, don't you." Kate groaned in response. "All in good time, lass. All in good time. First, I think I'll make you come like this." He continued his attention to her breasts, massaging, teasing, pulling one nipple in his mouth while pinching and rolling the other with his fingers. He could feel her getting close, her hips moving of their own accord. "Mmm, such beautiful tits. You love when I do this, don't you? That's it. Let go. Come for me, baby." He pinched hard and covered Kate's mouth with his own, muffling her shouts.

When her breathing calmed, he moved further down her body, stopping to lick the juices until he reached her thighs. He reached over to the nightstand for the champagne, took a drink, then put the glass down in one quick motion. Pete's tongue was still cold when he buried it in her pussy, making Kate shout with pleasure and surprise. He focused on her clit, sucking on the nub, then licking and blowing, bringing her closer to orgasm. Pete listened to the cues her body was sending, and just as she was ready to come, he stopped and looked up from between her thighs. "The champagne is delicious, but it's even better blended with you." He then returned to pleasuring her, sending her into another spiraling orgasm.

"Pete.... Oh.... I... want...." Kate's skin was a sheen of sweat. She tugged on her restraints and tossed her head on the pillow, her hair wild.

He grinned, kneeling between her legs. "This is mine." His fingers slid up her thighs to her sex.

"Yes," she groaned. "Now untie me."

"Not yet, I'm not finished." He rubbed her clit with his thumb and inserted two fingers, widening her entrance. Picking up an intense rhythm, he pushed his fingers deeper while his thumb massaged her as she pushed back against him, desperate for him. Pete was aching for release as he spread her legs wider, positioning his cock at her entrance. Leaning down, he whispered, "Now I'm going to fuck you. I want you to feel me explode in you, baby." Then he rammed into her, feeling Kate tighten around his cock, massaging him, milking him. "Jesus. You are perfect. So tight. So hot," he growled, stilling himself to feel her around him. In one swift motion, he untied her restraints. Kate snaked her arms around him, pulling him tight against her as he began pumping furiously.

"Now," Kate shouted, coming again, crying out her release as Pete followed her over the precipice.

The storm was raging outside as the two of them came back to earth. Kissing and touching, unable and unwilling to stop their intimate contact. Pete rubbed Kate's shoulders and arms. "Okay?"

"Mmm," Kate said, pushing Pete onto his back with her astride him. Her hair wild around her shoulders, her face and lips flushed. She moved her hips in a languorous motion, watching as Pete moaned with pleasure. She sat up, running her hands down to her breasts, teasing her nipples as she rocked her hips. He twitched inside of her as she grinned down at him. "You like that, don't you? Such a dirty boy," she growled, leaning over to kiss him as their tongues danced. "I'm going to make you come again," she whispered, rocking her hips faster.

Pete watched her ride him, her hair flying, tits bouncing, her pussy hot and tight around him. "Ahh, Katie. Jesus, lass," he yelled, digging his fingers into her hips as he came again. With a look of satisfaction, Kate slowed her movements, then settled next to Pete, pulling the comforter up around them like a cocoon while they listened to the remnants of the storm rumbling in the distance.

⸻

The sun was working hard to find its way through the clouds the next morning, giving the bedroom a dusky glow. They woke to the sound of Pete's phone ringing. He rolled out of bed and found his jeans on the floor, pulling his phone out of the pocket. Kate rolled over, rubbing her eyes, and watched Pete standing there naked. She let out a low wolf whistle and gave him a thumbs up as he looked over at her. He posed for her like a Greek god, laughing as he connected the call. "Hello. Hey Rob, what's up?" The conversation continued for several minutes, and from what Kate could tell, they were discussing a meeting before they left Ireland. Pete paced the room, telling Rob they would be back in Dublin on Monday. After a few more minutes, the call ended, with Pete seeming somewhat distracted.

"Everything okay?" Kate asked, as he sat on the edge of the bed.

"Yeah. Declan wants to talk to me." Kate waited, but he didn't elaborate any further. "Oh, okay. Do we need to head back early?" She sat up against the pillows.

"No. But if you don't mind, we'll leave early tomorrow morning. I asked Rob to let Declan know I'd get to his office sometime Monday afternoon." Then as an afterthought, "Oh yeah, Rob and Sarah want to have dinner with us on Monday night. Sound okay with you?"

Kate assured him it sounded like a good plan, but she couldn't shake the feeling something distracted him, and that it had to do with the phone call. She decided not to press the point as she got up and headed to the bathroom. "I'm going to shower. If you aren't doing anything and you'd like to join me, I'd love the company." She shot him a come-hither glance over her shoulder.

Pete jumped off the bed and chased after her. "That's an offer I won't pass up," he said, pulling her into his arms for a good morning kiss.

After a long, steamy shower, Kate and Pete dressed and headed downstairs. Outside, clouds scuttled across the sky and the ocean was still rough after last night's storm. Kate was a little sore from their role-playing the night before and looked longingly at the overstuffed sofa and the bookcase in the corner of the living room. Pete followed her gaze. "I have an idea. How about you make a pot of coffee and I'll make a quick run into town and pick up breakfast? There is a small bakery that does great breads and quiches to go. We could spend the day reading and relaxing. I know we've been on the move since we got here."

Kate walked over and wrapped her arms around Pete's waist, "That sounds perfect." She gave him a kiss, then watched as he grabbed his jacket and headed out the door. She made her way to the kitchen and put a pot of coffee on to brew, then headed out to the little garden by the path leading down to the ocean where she could wait for Pete's return from town. Putting on her jacket, she walked down to the arbor covered in ivy, with a stone bench surrounded by flowers. She looked out to sea and thought about Pete and the week they'd spent in Ireland—a week that was quickly coming to an end. "Thank you," she said to the wind, sending up her gratitude to the universe. Kate smiled, watching the sea birds with their acrobatic moves, at times hovering on the wind, then diving toward the waves. She had never been one to take up meditation, but something about this place settled her mind and she felt a connection and security that warmed her, even in the brisk winds. She once again felt the history of the island and the people, just like she had at the Rock of Cashel, and as she stared out to sea, she heard a now familiar female voice say, *Here, Kate... home.* Kate looked up. "I heard you. Who are you?" She wasn't afraid, but her pulse kicked up a notch with excitement, relishing the experience. "Please, talk to me. I know your voice; I've heard you before." She waited, concentrating on the surrounding sounds, the wind in the trees, the waves in the distance. This had to be more than her imagination. "Abigale?" Kate felt a lavender scented breeze brush her face that felt like a human touch. She sat waiting, but there was nothing more. After a few minutes, she rose from the bench and headed back to the house as Pete pulled up.

"Everything okay?" he asked, meeting her at the front door.

She smiled at him, loving the way the wind tousled his hair, his cheeks rosy, his eyes sparkling down at her. "I'm good. It's so beautiful here. I don't think I've ever felt such peace." Kate took his arm as they walked to the kitchen where Pete dropped a few bags on the counter, loaded with all sorts of goodies. "Did you buy out the entire shop?"

"Bakeries are my weakness," he said sheepishly. "I thought since we're staying in today that I'd buy plenty of stuff. Plus, with the food that Marcus left for us, we won't need to go out again. The staff at the bakery were telling me it's supposed to be a stormy day. So, what better way to spend a day like that then to cuddle up on the couch."

"I agree. I'll get the coffee if you'll get a couple of plates for our feast, then I'll meet you in the living room." Kate put a tray together with the coffeepot, heavy pottery mugs, and a pitcher of cream, while Pete set up a plate with muffins, sliced brown bread, and scones with clotted cream, butter, and jam.

They moved everything to the living room, settling on the couch, facing a large picture window looking out to the sea. Kate looked at the plate of baked goods sitting on the table. "Good God, I'm going to have to go on a diet as soon as I get home."

"No, you're perfect," Pete said, grinning at her as he put a scone on her plate.

"And there's just one more reason I love you." The wind howled around the cottage and down the chimney, as storm clouds formed out over the ocean. They tucked into their breakfast, and Kate thought about the earlier incident outside. "So, here's a question for you," she said, diving right into the subject. "Is it possible ghosts can travel? Or are they tied to one location?" she asked, sipping her coffee.

Pete looked surprised by the question. "Why do you ask?"

"Well, I've had something happen since we've been in Ireland—twice, actually."

"Really? What's going on?"

"Maybe it's nothing, but when we were at the Rock of Cashel, I was standing there, taking in how beautiful it was and feeling so connected to everything around me when I heard a female voice say, 'Here, Kate... home.' I sort of brushed it off as my ears playing tricks on me. But then today, I went outside to sit in the garden to wait for you, and the same thing happened. It was then I realized the voice was familiar—it sounded like Abigale. So, I asked if it was her. She didn't answer, but it felt as if a hand brushed my face."

"Whoa! Really? That is incredible." Pete's eyes widened.

"What does that mean, though? And can ghosts *follow* you?" Kate had to admit that the idea of a ghost following her 3,000 miles to repeat a cryptic phrase kind of gave her the creeps.

"I don't know about the meaning, but I will say that I believe ghosts can travel, for lack of a better word. When Mom visited me in the past, those incidents happened in different locations. If it *is* Abigale, she has a genuine connection with you. Have you ever thought that you might have some psychic ability?"

Kate looked at Pete like he had grown a third eye in the middle of his forehead. "No! Geez, one day I'm a true skeptic and the next I'm a psychic? I don't think so." Still, she couldn't figure out why Abigale felt such a connection to her, or why she would keep telling Kate that she was home. She looked at the plate of baked goods and sighed. "One thing I can predict," she said, holding her fingertips to her temples as if she were getting a message from the ether. "I *can* see another scone in my future."

Chapter 26

The traffic heading into Dublin was heavy, and Kate was grateful that Pete knew what he was doing and where he was going. He had been quiet on the drive back, and Kate couldn't put her finger on what was going on in his head. Maybe he was as bummed out about heading home as she was. But his change in behavior seemed to stem from the phone call the day before. She decided not to dwell on it and instead watched the traffic zooming around them.

Returning to the same hotel they had stayed in when they first arrived in Dublin, the desk staff welcomed them back and handed over the keys, which were to the same room they had on the first visit. They stepped into the elevator, as Pete turned and winked at Kate. "Remember the first time we were in this elevator?" he asked.

"How could I forget? I remember you certainly weren't being a gentleman that morning," Kate said, giving him a sly smile.

"Well, I didn't hear you complaining, Ms. Murphy."

She was happy to see him less distracted, and after dropping their bags in the room, Pete headed off to his meeting at Trinity while Kate went down to the lobby to read a novel she had loaded on her e-reader. She ordered a pot of tea, settled in a wing-backed chair with a sigh, and relived the wonderful memories of the past week. But no matter how happy those memories were, she couldn't help feeling down, knowing tomorrow they would head back to Salem. "I'll be back some day," she said, willing it to be true. Kate thought of the voice she'd heard, Abigale's voice, telling her that this was home. *Was it some sort of sign?* She sighed, thinking of all the responsibilities she had back in Salem with the new business. Dreams were all well and good, but she had to be an adult, at least that's what she'd always told herself. But ever since being with Pete, she had allowed herself to embrace the magical, the unknown, and it felt so much better than constantly policing and editing her own dreams. *Practical Kate.* She shook her head and tried to read the novel in front of her.

After a few hours, Kate yawned, looking up from her book at the clock on the mantle. It surprised her how late it was, and even more surprising that Pete wasn't back yet. Setting the e-reader down on the side table, she asked the attendant if Pete had returned, wondering if maybe he didn't see her sitting in the lobby. The attendant informed her that no; he hadn't gotten back yet, so Kate went back to her chair and sat down, looking out the window.

People were just getting out of work as she watched them move down the street, heading home, or to the pub, or wherever they might go on a Monday night. Kate checked her phone, wondering if she had missed a text from Pete. There was nothing. Now she was getting worried. She was pondering what to do when her phone vibrated in her hand, making her jump. It was a text from Pete.

Sorry I'm late. Meeting went long. On my way. She smiled in relief and texted back, asking if he wanted to join her in the hotel pub. A thumbs up emoji popped on her screen.

Kate found a table, ordered drinks, and looked out the window. Within minutes she saw him walking up the narrow street, the sun licking dark copper highlights on his hair. He had a look of deep concentration on his face, and Kate worried that something might really be wrong. As he reached the corner, he looked up and saw her in the window. She gave a slight wave as his face broke into a grin. Kate exhaled, her entire body relaxing with his look.

"I'm sorry it took so long," he said, kissing her.

"Here, you look like you could use this," Kate said, sliding a Guinness across the table.

"Woman, you're the best," he said, taking a long pull off his beer.

Kate smiled and took his hand. "Okay, Pete. Spill it. Is everything okay? You've seemed so distracted since yesterday."

Pete looked down at their hands, fingers entwined, then looked up to meet her gaze. "Declan made me an offer for a tenured position at Trinity."

Shocked and confused, Kate attempted to hide the pain, pasting a smile on her face. "Wow... congratulations.... When would you start?"

"I haven't decided if I'm even going to take it yet."

"Oh...." Kate trailed off. "But there's no guarantee of tenure at Harvard, right? And you love it here. Seems like a straightforward decision." She stared at the tabletop while desperately trying to keep her tone light.

"I told Declan that I needed a few weeks to think it over. The position won't open until the spring term in January, anyway. This is a big step and I won't jump into it lightly," he said, stroking his thumb over Kate's knuckles. "There's a lot to consider."

Fuck. It's happening. Kate couldn't believe it was going to be Michael Francisco all over again. Only this time it wasn't an eight-hundred-mile distance, it was over three times that. And the depth of her feelings for Pete was far stronger than anything she had ever felt before. Kate could sense Pete looking at her, but she couldn't return his gaze. She was afraid he would see just how much pain she was in. And she wouldn't let that happen. She wouldn't fall apart, not again. *I got through this once before, I'll get through it again.* Once she composed herself, Kate looked up, willing herself to smile. "What's there to consider, Pete?" The words came out a little more flippant than she intended, and she saw the flash of hurt cross Pete's face.

"Well, I just thought that..." he trailed off. "Maybe now isn't the best time to talk about it." He looked at his watch. "Do you still want to have dinner with Rob and Sarah?"

"Of course," Kate said, trying to find her equilibrium. But in her mind, her thoughts were already fast forwarding to the day when they would say their goodbyes. "I'm looking forward to seeing them again."

"Okay, well, I guess we better get ready." He sounded unsure of himself, but he drained his drink, stood, and held his hand out to her.

They rode the elevator in silence until Pete turned, taking her chin in his hand. "We'll figure this out... together. Okay?"

Kate peeped up at him through her lashes, willing herself not to break down. "Okay," she whispered. He kissed her gently as the elevator door opened. They walked down the quiet corridor, hand in hand. "So, when do you have to give them an answer?"

"I'll need to let Declan know by the end of October."

"Oh."

Pete opened the door and stepped out of the way to let Kate enter first. As she passed him, he pulled her into his arms. "It's going to be okay, Kate. I promise you."

She wrapped her arms around his waist and laid her head on his chest, "I hope so." But in her heart, Kate wasn't so sure.

Dish was crowded even for a Monday night, and as they walked in, the hostess, a short, round brunette, gave Pete a hug. "I haven't seen you in ages!"

"Hi Mary," Pete said, wrapping her in a bear hug. "Mary, this is my girlfriend, Kate. Kate, Mary is Aidan's sister. She's lucky to have one of Dublin's finest chefs as her brother."

"Nah, he's lucky to have Dublin's finest hostess." Her face broken into a welcoming grin, shaking Kate's hand. "It's about time you brought a girlfriend over to visit. I was startin' to think you were playing for the other team." She shot a theatrical wink to Kate. "Come on, I'll show you to your table. Rob and Sarah got here about five minutes ago."

They walked toward the back of the restaurant, which was light and airy. It was obvious to Kate that this was where the movers and shakers of Dublin came for dinner. But even though it was decidedly upscale, it didn't feel pretentious. "Here you go, dears," motioning to the table where Rob and Sarah were sitting. "I'll let Aidan know you're here."

"Kate!" Sarah jumped up from the table. "I'm so glad we could get together again."

Kate gave her a hug. "Me too. A perfect ending to an amazing week." And she meant it. Regardless of what might happen in the next few weeks, it had been a once in a lifetime trip that would stay with her for a long time. "Great to see you," Kate said, giving Rob a quick hug before Sarah pulled her down next to her.

"I want to hear all about your travels. Rob told me you spent a few days at *Land's End*. Isn't it gorgeous? Marcus and Aidan have such good taste," Sarah said. "I swear, I need Marcus to come out to the house and give me some tips on decorating."

"Hey, let's not forget we're saving up for a nice vacation next summer," Rob reminded her. "I'm not sure I can afford Marcus's tastes."

Sarah reached across the table to squeeze her husband's hand. "I know, love. I know." Without missing a beat, she launched into questions about Kate's impressions of Ireland. "So, what were the favorite parts of your travel?"

"Being with me," Pete said.

"Well, that's true," Kate grinned. "But really, I love it all. The countryside, the history, and my god, the coastline! Absolutely stunning." She was about to share her impressions of the Rock of Cashel when a short, stocky, dark-haired man dressed in chef gear approached the table.

"Mary told me there was a table full of troublemakers out here. I see she was right. I'm certainly not talking about you, love," Aidan said, winking at Kate.

"Come on, Aidan. You know we bring a certain level of class to the place," Rob said.

Aidan rolled his eyes and turned to Kate, extending his hand. "How did you get involved with this motley crew?"

"Just lucky, I guess? Hi, I'm Kate." Kate shook his hand, liking him immediately.

"Aidan," he grinned. "Chef and owner of this place. So, you're the lass who captured Pete's heart, eh? Well, he has good taste."

She turned to Pete, her heart filling with emotion, thinking about what might happen in a few weeks. Pete must have sensed it, because he took her hand and smiled. "Not only do I have good taste, but I'm one of the luckiest guys in the world." He leaned in for a kiss—the move met with a good-natured round of *awws* and taunts to *break it up*, making Kate blush.

Aidan ran down the evening's menu before he headed back to the kitchen, promising to see them at the end of the dinner service. After the server took their drink orders, the two couples settled in for a relaxing evening. Of course, Pete's teaching offer was a key point of interest, which Rob dove right into. "So, how did it go with Declan?" he asked, eager for details.

"Good." Pete looked somewhat uncomfortable with the discussion. "I'm flattered by the offer, but I haven't decided if

I'm going to take it yet."

"What? But this is what you've been working toward," Rob said while Sarah shot him a look. Kate glanced at Sarah, who smiled in apology.

Thinking she'd better do something to save Rob from his wife's pointed looks and ease Pete's mind, Kate said, "Well, I think it's an incredible opportunity. I'm so proud of what Pete's accomplished—he deserves this." She touched Pete's hand, wanting him to know just how much she meant those words.

"Thanks, Kate. But I'm not ready to decide just yet. There's a lot to consider. Besides, I don't have to give Declan an answer until the end of October."

Rob started to say something, but Sarah cut him off, giving him another one of her dramatically pointed looks. "So," she turned her full attention toward Kate, "you were going to tell us about your impressions of Ireland. Weren't you mentioning something about the Rock of Cashel? I haven't been down there in ages... so beautiful."

Well done, Kate thought. Sarah's concern touched her, so she did her best not to dwell on Pete's upcoming decision. The last thing she wanted to do was mar their last night in Dublin. *What happens will happen,* she thought, determined to let it go.

Course after delicious course arrived, each one more magnificent than the last. Fresh seafood, produce, and every good thing farm-raised on the island seemed to land on their table. They all agreed that Aidan was indeed the premier chef in Dublin. When he came out at the end of the night, the four friends gave him a standing ovation.

"Ah, sit down, you reprobates!" He laughed, pulling up a chair to the table with a sigh. "But I'm glad you enjoyed it." The friends heaped praise on Aidan's culinary skills and shared their belief that he deserved a Michelin star for the restaurant. "You guys really know how to boost my ego. Hey, I've only been open eighteen months, so let's see what next year brings."

After finishing the meal with a round of whiskey, the four friends walked out to the street for their goodbyes. Sarah and Kate promised to email and Facetime to keep in touch, while Rob and Pete talked about a few things that had to be tightened up in their manuscript. Then Rob brought up Pete's next trip to Ireland. "So, uh, at the risk of Sarah pinning me to the ground with one of her stares, when do you think you'll give Declan your decision?"

Pete put his hand on Rob's shoulder and sighed in mock exasperation. "You'll be the first to know. But it won't be until October—so don't keep asking me." Rob raised his hands in surrender and dropped the subject.

As they made their way back to the hotel, Pete was deep in thought. "Thanks for being so supportive, Kate," he said.

Kate squeezed his hand. "You don't have to thank me, Pete. You deserve every success because you've worked so hard." She took a deep breath to ground her emotions. "Whatever you decide, I support you one hundred percent."

"Thanks," he said, sounding unsure.

"You know, I want to thank you, too. This week has been one of the best in my life. You've brought me to a magical place, a country that has always intrigued me, but I never thought I'd see.

And I've made new friends too. Thank you," she said, stopping to reach up and kiss him.

He brushed his thumb against her cheek. "You've helped me see Ireland in a whole new way. It's been great seeing everything fresh through someone else's eyes. A different experience, and better than I can remember," he said as they walked up the stairs and into the hotel. "We'll do this again."

"I would like that," she whispered, hoping there would be a next time.

Chapter 27

K ate arrived at *Potion* early in the morning, the day after her return from Ireland. Jetlag had her on a weird sleep schedule with her body still calibrated to Dublin time. She awoke at four in the morning, disoriented and groggy, looking around her bedroom for a few seconds until it registered she was back home. After a long, hot shower, she dressed and headed into the shop. She enjoyed a leisurely walk in the late summer morning quiet until she found herself in front of the building that had quickly become a home base for her. At the front door, she stopped and took stock of everything that had happened since the chilly January afternoon when she first visited Salem. *Potion* was a comforting reminder of all the good things that had happened in her life since then. She opened the door, smiling as the bells over the lintel gave a gentle, melodic jingle. Jenny stood behind the counter, setting up for the day. "Welcome home, Kate. How was the trip?"

"Great, Jenny. Hard to come back to reality." Kate walked behind the counter and set up the espresso machine, pressing coffee and steaming milk. The coffee was soon sputtering into the cup, filling her nostrils with the rich, dark aroma of espresso. "Oh yeah," she said to herself, inhaling deeply as she poured the steamed milk into the mug. "Boy, did I miss this."

"No coffee in Ireland?" Jenny asked.

"Not like this. But they have the market cornered on tea and whiskey." She added a few lumps of sugar and took a sip. "Is Eve here or is she at Jon's?"

"She's here. Late night last night. We had an open mic, and the place was packed. Eve's probably catching up on some much-needed sleep."

Kate headed back to the office, not exactly eager to get back to work, but knowing that the sooner she did, the sooner she could get caught up. Besides, the work would hold back the thoughts she just didn't want to dwell on. Neither she nor Pete had talked about the job offer anymore, but it was only a matter of time—ten weeks—not that she was counting, before he would have to decide. Kate knew he would take it—it was a straightforward decision. All that hard work and years of research. If it were her, she knew she would do the same.

Sitting down, she sipped her coffee and turned on the computer. She opened her email and found a note from Pete with the subject line, *Welcome home.* Kate grinned and clicked on the message.

Dear Ms. Murphy. I know you are probably in the office at some ungodly hour because you couldn't sleep. Neither could I, which is why I am sending this at 5am. I missed waking up with you next to me this morning. Dinner tonight? Love you, Pete.

Kate grinned and typed her response, telling him that yes, dinner would be great and to stop by whenever he finished up with work. She sat there daydreaming at the monitor when she heard footsteps running down the back stairs. Kate braced herself for Hurricane Eve.

"You're back! I want to hear every detail," Eve said, launching herself at Kate.

"Okay! Okay! Go get some coffee and I'll fill you in."

Within minutes they settled in the office, with Kate giving Eve a minute-by-minute rundown of their trip, taking great pleasure in telling her about their first night in Dublin. "So, I got drunk and told him I loved him." She shook her head at the memory as Eve gave her a wide-eyed look. "I didn't plan on being drunk, or telling him, but it just happened." She paused, "He loves me, Eve." Eve clapped her hands and squealed with delight.

"I knew it! Oh, Katie, I'm so happy for you both. That had to make the rest of the week absolutely wonderful."

"It was." Kate filled her in with the account of the rest of their vacation, including the paranormal incidents, which had Eve almost, but not quite, speechless.

"Are you kidding? This is unbelievable!"

"Freaked me out. One thing I'm certain of, the voice belonged to Abigale. Apparently, she thinks Ireland is my home," Kate said, shaking her head in disbelief. "I know I've been a skeptic, but I think we'll do another investigation in a couple of weeks."

"Whenever it works for you guys, I'm ready to go!"

"Pete needs to get back in the swing of things with his classes, and then we can do it. Probably two weeks, I guess?" Kate looked down at her coffee cup, thinking of Pete's job offer. "There's something else, Eve."

"What?"

"Trinity offered Pete a tenured professor position. They want him to start in January for the spring term. He has to let them know by the end of October," she said, her voice sounding hollow.

There was a long pause. "Oh, Katie." Eve reached over and took her friend's hand. "Is he going to take it?"

Kate shrugged. "He hasn't decided, but come on, he should take it. It's what he's always wanted—plus it would guarantee him tenure."

"How are *you* doing?"

"I don't know. I know this is important to him, his career.... God, it's like Michael all over again." Her voice cracked with emotion as she put her head in her hands. After a moment, she pulled herself together with a brittle laugh. "Isn't this just like me? Profess my love for someone only to have them get an offer to move 3,000 miles away a few days later."

The two sat in silence, sipping their coffee. "Well, try not to project too far. I know that's easier said than done! But I believe this will all work out." She got up and walked over to Kate. "It still sucks, though," she said, hugging her friend. "But you two will figure it out."

Kate shook her head and turned back to the computer, pushing thoughts of Pete living so far away out of her mind, at least for a few hours.

Chapter 28

T he summer ended with a flurry of tourists, all looking to grab those last few days of sun, sea, and fortunately for Kate and Eve, coffee. Even though the days at *Potion* were packed with activity, they reserved one night for communication with Abigale. Eager for an explanation of the cryptic messages she received in Ireland, Kate arranged an investigation right after the Labor Day holiday weekend. But much to everyone's disappointment, Abigale was strangely silent. No matter how they tried to communicate, the building remained quiet, as if breathing a sigh of relief as the evening shadows lengthened and the breezes off the ocean grew chilly. It was only when Kate found herself alone in the office, thinking of Pete and his upcoming decision, when she would feel a breath of air and the faint scent of lavender, which comforted her. Abigale may have grown quiet, but she made it clear she hadn't disappeared.

By October, the leaves on the trees were turning bright shades of red, purple, and gold, and in the air was the smell of wood smoke as neighbors lit fires on cool fall nights. It charmed Kate as she walked along the streets—everything had a magical feeling as jack-o'-lanterns graced the doorsteps of almost every house and business in Salem. The energy changed with the seasons, shifting from a bright summer vibe to an otherworldly, mystical feel as storefronts put out their best Halloween displays, ramping up for the biggest celebration of the year.

And *Potion* was right in the center of it all, hosting events several times a week. Spooky story hour for kids in the afternoons, complete with hot cider and cocoa, with tarot readers, psychics, writers, and music acts filling out the rest of the slots during the weeknights for the adults. The summer may have ended, but *Potion* continued to draw in crowds, especially on the weekends. Eve was in her element, enjoying every minute of the event planning while Kate managed the back of the house. But she was always ready to fill in behind the coffee bar, too. For her, there was nothing more satisfying than watching delighted customers make their way through the door, never being quite sure what would greet them when they arrived.

Eve and Kate kept a casual tally of where their patrons were coming from and were surprised to find their customer base had grown beyond the areas surrounding Boston. Lately, they were seeing an increase in visitors from New York and Pennsylvania. Obviously, word had spread so the two women thought about branching out their advertising and social media marketing. Eve even mused about opening a second location.

However, at the top of everyone's to do list was the planning of the annual Halloween masquerade ball. Both Eve and Kate had been hard at work planning for the event, which drew thousands of people to Salem. The two of them were brainstorming in the office one afternoon when Pete stuck his head in the door.

"Knock, knock."

"Hey," Kate grinned, getting up to give him a kiss. "What brings you over this afternoon?"

"I was wondering if I could steal you away for a late lunch."

"Eve? Can you hold down the fort for a while?" Eve waved them off, and the two headed out to the street. "This is a pleasant surprise," Kate said, taking Pete's hand.

"Yeah, I wanted to talk to you," he said.

"That sounds cryptic." She attempted to make light of his comment, but her heart sank. She knew what the conversation was going to be about. Pete's response was to take her hand, but he said nothing. They walked in silence until they reached the diner. Settling in a booth toward the back, Kate asked, "So, what's up?" She held her breath.

Pete ran his hand through his hair, and Kate's heart ached. "I wanted to talk to you about the Trinity job." She sat silently, not daring to say anything. "So, I've been giving it a lot of thought." Kate shook her head and fiddled with a sugar packet in the dispenser, willing herself to keep it together. "I'm taking the job," Pete said, the words coming out in a rush. "That doesn't change anything with us. I love you. We'll make this work. You can come visit me in Ireland, and I'll come back on semester breaks and during the summer." Kate blinked, trying to hold back the tears as she watched her world slowly falling apart. He grabbed her hand. "I mean it, Katie. We *will* make this work. Please don't doubt it."

Kate looked up, giving him a wistful smile. "I'm glad you decided to take the job. This is an incredible opportunity." She couldn't say anymore because her throat was tightening with tears.

"Damn it! I know what you're thinking, Kate. But you're wrong. This is not like what happened with Michael."

"Uh, huh."

"Come on, Katie." He joined her on her side of the booth, wrapping his arms around her. "Please don't think that. This is so difficult... I...." His voice broke, and he pulled her in tighter, kissing her hair. "This won't break us."

Kate looked up and wiped a tear from his cheek. "I love you, Pete. I always will. Look, I knew this was coming... it's just hard to..." she paused. "Yes, we will make it work." She couldn't bear to see him looking so torn up and, in that moment, vowed she'd be strong, no matter what. "So, when do you start?"

"The term starts right after the New Year, so I've got to move as soon as the semester ends at Harvard. I'll leave in mid-December."

"Before Christmas?" He nodded, a pained expression crossing his face as they sat in silence. Kate's heart broke a little more, and she realized she had to get it together—for both of them. "Well, we have two months before you leave," she said. "And right now, we need to focus on more pressing matters."

"Huh?"

"Come on, Pete! What are you wearing to the masquerade ball? We need to get you a costume!"

"I love you, Kate Murphy."

"Back at ya, baby," she said, while inside her heart was breaking.

Chapter 29

The Halloween season was more than Kate expected, with thousands of people packing the streets for the parade and all the other special events around town. The masquerade ball was held at the Peabody Essex Museum and brought in over $250,000 for local charities. For one night, the museum turned into a mystical forest wonderland. Trees cast spooky shadows in the atrium, with a low fog covering the floor. Of course, Eve and Kate went in big with their costumes. Eve dressed as a fairy sprite, trailing a gauzy swath of sheer fabric of pale blue and lavender behind her, with Jon as her woodland wizard escort. Kate was a forest nymph, her hair braided with ivy and wearing a dark green floor length velvet gown. Pete escorted her, dressed as the Green Man. The two couples made quite a splash, especially since Eve acted as one of the MCs for the charity auction. She was in her element, cajoling the crowd of well-heeled patrons into digging deep in their pockets for their favorite charities. Kate couldn't help smiling at her friend, happy to see her doing what she did best. In fact, the two entrepreneurs had charmed the mayor of Salem so completely he had already tapped them to be on the planning committee for next year's Halloween events.

But after the festivities ended, it was a downhill slide to mid-December and Pete's departure. All of Kate's mental pep-talks, telling herself to stay positive, were beginning to wear on her soul. They didn't talk about the upcoming move very much, just an occasional comment about logistics and the temporary apartment Trinity had secured for Pete until he could pick out his own place. That suited Kate just fine. It was as if the two of them tried to ignore the days quickly moving toward December 15th, the date Pete was flying out.

Pete spent Thanksgiving in Virginia with his father and Mae. He asked Kate to go with him, but she declined, making an excuse that she needed to be at the shop to cover for the staff who were taking time off. The truth was, she couldn't bring herself to get more involved in Pete's family life. She was already disengaging—she could feel it—even though she tried to tell herself this time was different. She knew her refusal to go with him to Virginia hurt Pete, but Kate was in self-protection mode, thinking that maybe the pain wouldn't be so devastating if she could wall off her emotions. And her disengagement went beyond her refusal to travel to Virginia. In the evenings after they made love, she would lie in bed, willing herself not to breakdown, instead turning towards the wall as she listened to Pete's steady breathing.

Kate woke up feeling the aching sadness that had started several weeks prior. Lately she operated almost on autopilot, going through her morning routine without thinking. Because thinking invariably led to more pain. She left the house early, greeted by a chilly wind off the ocean. Inhaling deeply, she smelled the sharp bite of the sea as she looked up at clouds heavy with snow and involuntarily shivered. She turned up the collar of her heavy wool coat, pulling her knit hat farther down around her ears as she walked to *Potion*. The streets were much quieter now than they had been a month ago, and Kate smiled wistfully, passing the storefronts now decorated for the Christmas holidays. Salem had more of a hometown feel to it once most tourists left, and Kate welcomed it. *Potion* was now running on winter hours, opening at their usual time but closing earlier in the day unless they were hosting a special event. This gave both her and Eve a chance to breathe a little easier, especially since they could finally relax from a financial perspective. The relaunch of *Potion* had been more successful than either woman could have dreamed.

The bells jingled as Kate opened the door. Eve was setting up for the day, humming to herself as she readied the espresso machine. "I thought Jenny was going to open today," Kate said.

"She was, but I gave her the morning off so she could get some Christmas shopping done. She'll be in at noon. Besides, I thought we might have a little time to talk. Let me make you a coffee," Eve offered, smiling at her friend.

Kate thanked her, going to the office to deposit her coat and hat. When she returned, a large latte was waiting for her. She sighed and sat down at one of the heavy wooden tables. Eve grabbed her tea and joined her. "How are you doing, Katie?"

"Okay."

"Geez, you don't even make a half-hearted attempt to make that sound believable! Come on, talk to me," Eve said, concern written in the lines on her forehead.

Kate gave her a look. "Count down is on, and Pete will be gone in fourteen days. How should I be doing?" She looked out the window at the quiet street, wishing she could snap her fingers and change everything that was happening. "Just putting one foot in front of the other. Nothing else I can do, right?"

Eve followed her gaze out to the street. "Don't shut me out, Katie. And if I can make a suggestion, don't shut Pete out either."

Kate let out an exasperated sigh. "I'm not shutting anyone out, Eve. I'm dealing with this the best way I know how."

"Well, from here it looks like the door has been locked and boarded shut." She tapped on the table to get Kate's attention. "Look, I know this is hard on you. Do you think this isn't hard on Pete too? He loves you, Katie. December fifteenth is not the end, okay?"

She glared at Eve, who looked exasperated. She rarely saw her like that, which made Kate pause and take stock of things. "Eve.... Look, I'll work on checking my behavior. I'm sorry. I just keep thinking that Pete and I haven't been together that long. *Shit*, not even a year! And now he's leaving. What kind of foundation did we build in that short amount of time to weather something like this?"

"I don't know if your relationship will survive this. I can't tell the future." Eve's face softened. "But you are giving up before even taking the chance. I remember the night when Pete first kissed you. You told me then that you wanted a chance at love regardless of the risks. Well, this is one of those risks."

Kate shook her head, looking down at the table. "I know."

"You need to have a little faith here. Turn off that voice that keeps telling you to expect the worst." The bell over the door jingled, and both women looked up as the first customer of the day walked in. Eve stood, but before she walked away, she said, "Believe. That's all you need to do right now. Believe and trust. Okay?"

Kate shook her head as Eve went behind the bar. She grabbed her phone and texted Pete. *Are you free for dinner?* Within minutes her phone buzzed in response, with Pete saying he would be at her place at five o'clock. She smiled and put her phone back in her pocket. *Believe and trust, that's all I need to do,* she thought, and got on with her day.

Chapter 30

December fourteenth arrived, and Pete would leave the next evening. Kate planned a quiet dinner in for the two of them, and the little house was fragrant with the smell of seafood chowder simmering on the stove and fresh bread warming in the oven. A fire glowed in the fireplace. She poured herself a glass of white wine and turned on some instrumental Christmas music when Pete knocked on the door.

"Brrrr! I can't believe how cold it is out there," he said, rubbing his hands together. Closing the door, he wrapped Kate in his arms, kissing her until her legs felt like jelly. "Now, that's the way to warm up," he said, taking off his coat. "Wow, something smells great."

"Thanks. Would you like a glass of wine?" Pete moved into the living room, smiling at the little Christmas tree she had set up in the corner. "Wine would be great, thanks. I love the tree. When did you get it?"

"Yesterday. That little empty lot near *Potion* is selling Christmas trees. I couldn't resist." Kate handed him a glass of wine. Sitting on the couch, she snuggled next to Pete. "Sláinte," she said, clinking her glass against his. "Dinner should be ready soon." She sipped her wine and looked at him. "I'm glad you could make it for dinner. I know that you have a million things to tie up before tomorrow."

"I submitted my grades this morning and then had an exit interview with the dean this afternoon. Just need to make sure Finn is ready to travel with me tomorrow. The vet gave me a sedative for him, so he doesn't meow his head off during the flight and drive all the other passengers crazy," he trailed off, looking at Kate. "Are you coming to the airport tomorrow?"

She looked down into her glass, hoping that advice on how to handle her heartbreak would miraculously appear in the wine. "I wasn't sure. What do you want?"

"I want you to be okay with this. I want us to be okay. That's what I want. I want to start planning your first visit over and my next trip back. I want this to not hurt so much." He placed their glasses on the coffee table and gathered her into his arms.

Kate touched his face, smiling gently. "I'm okay. We'll be okay too. *Better* than okay. I promise I'll come visit once you settle into the term and sort out your apartment. You are going to be so incredibly busy. It's exciting. Don't let this transition take away from the fun of what's to come. I'll want to hear all the details. Please don't feel you can't share with me because you think it will make me sad or hurt my feelings."

Pete held her tight as they sat, watching the twinkling lights on the little Christmas tree. "Come with me," he said after a long pause.

"What?" Her body went rigid.

"Come with me."

"No." The word came out with more force than Kate expected. Pete's arms went slack around her.

"That was a pretty definitive declaration," he said, hurt filling his voice.

"Pete, look," Kate said, trying to gain hold of her emotions. "We've only been dating for what? Five months? I have a business to tend to. What would I do in Ireland? Sit and wait for you to come home at night?"

"There are worse things in life." he said, a chill coming into his voice. "You could still run the financial end of *Potion* long distance."

The room closed in on her. Every message she'd ever heard from her mother echoed in her ears. *Be successful. Look out for number one. Love isn't always the reason to get married. And make sure when you do marry, you marry up.* No matter how she tried to shut out the ugly voice in her head, she couldn't stop thinking about what would happen if she dropped everything and followed Pete 3,000 miles, only to have him dump her six months later. Then she'd be all alone in Ireland. At least when she was in New York City, she wasn't far from Eve. Or her family, for what that was worth. "Pete, please. Now is not the time for me to pick up and just leave. I'm not ready. It has nothing to do with you." She took his hand, trying to soften her comment. "Please, don't be angry."

"I'm not angry, Kate. It was a selfish request. I'm sorry I brought it up."

Suddenly, the room didn't seem as cozy as it had minutes earlier. She got up and headed to the kitchen. Pete followed behind her. She stood at the stove stirring the chowder, then pulled the bread out of the oven. "Dinner is just about ready," she said, attempting to relieve the tension.

Their meal ended up being a quiet affair, with neither of them saying much. Just small talk and comments about the food. She began clearing the table, and once again Pete joined her in the small kitchen. Taking her hand, he said, "Come on," and led her to the bedroom.

They undressed in silence, and Kate felt her heart was going to break. Something about the night seemed so final. They lay in bed, facing each other in the darkened room. Pete gently smoothed the hair from her brow and kissed her. "Oh Katie, how I love you, lass." Then he smiled, a sad smile that made her feel as if someone were squeezing her heart.

"I love you, Pete," she said, her voice catching on his name. She pulled herself closer to him, needing to feel his skin against hers, to feel the heat from his body, needing all those things so she wouldn't forget when he finally left.

Pete moved his hands down her side, his leg nestled between her thighs, as she willingly opened them, wanting his intimate contact. Kate took his cock in her hand, listening to his breath quicken, loving the sounds he made when he was with her like this. Her skin was beginning to catch fire, flames licking at her, spreading from between her legs and through her body. He slowly entered her, and a tear formed at the corner of her eye. He looked down at her. "Sweetheart, don't cry. Please. Kate." He picked up a rhythm as desperate need burned in them both, trying to obliterate the sadness they felt with the sensations of their intimate union.

After their lovemaking, they lay tangled in the blankets, holding on to each other, hearts breaking in the silence. Kate had her head on Pete's chest, listening to the rhythm of his deep breathing. The emotions of the evening, the finality of their time together in Salem, were almost more than she could bear. Before drifting to sleep, she whispered, "Never forget how much I love you. No matter what, I love you, Pete." He pulled her in tighter and kissed her softly as he watched her fall asleep.

Kate didn't go with Pete to the airport the next day. Instead, she walked to his house in the early afternoon, gave Finn a lingering goodbye hug, then gave Pete a knitted woolen scarf she had made. "I know it gets chilly and damp in Dublin, and I don't want you to catch cold," she said, handing him the scarf, suddenly feeling silly about the gift.

Pete's eyes were glassy with unshed tears as he wrapped it around his neck. "I love it. It's perfect."

Kate had made a promise to herself that she wouldn't cry today. She had done so much of that lately, so she was determined to be strong. She looked up at him and smiled. "Safe travels. I can't wait to hear all about your adventures. Be safe and don't drink too much Guinness."

"I promise I'll practice moderation in all beverage consumption." He smiled, but it didn't reach his eyes.

"Okay, well. I'm going to go now. You don't want to miss your flight." Kate looked around the empty house, and she felt as hollow as the room they were standing in. She took Pete's hand. "I love you, Pete." Her voice cracked, but she held back the tears.

Pete pulled her to him and held her close. "I love you, Kate. I'll call you as soon as I get to Dublin." He kissed her; a long, passionate kiss filled with longing and heartbreak.

Once Kate gathered her scattered senses, she walked to the front door. Turning with tears in her eyes, she smiled. "See you later," she whispered, closing the door softly behind her.

She was a block away from Pete's house before the floodgates opened and she cried in earnest. Walking home, her route led her by the Old Burying Point, where she stopped at the iron gate and looked in at the stand of bare trees close to Abigale's grave. Breathing deeply to check her tears, memories washed over her: the first time she saw Pete standing by the far entrance, their first kiss at the ghost investigation, that night in Ireland when he told her he loved her. A sob escaped her lips as she gripped the fence, her fingers numb with the cold. *I can't do this again.*

In the trees, a mist formed as Abigale watched Kate weeping. Her hands moved to her heart, as if in pain. She remembered her Andrew and the anguish she felt when he left all those years ago. Nothing can erase the painful memory of saying goodbye to the one you love. Poor dear, she sighed, watching as Kate turned and headed for home. Abigale dissolved into the mist, hoping there was something she could do to help ease Kate's broken heart.

Chapter 31

Christmas and New Year's passed in a blur of activity. *Potion* had done a healthy mail order business during the holidays, and Eve and Kate had been so busy they didn't really have time to celebrate the season. Which was okay with Kate, because staying busy meant she had little time to dwell on Pete's absence. He called her every morning, but she knew with the semester ramping up, the phone calls would taper off. She wondered with a heavy heart if that would be the beginning of the end.

"Good morning," Kate said, tamping the snow off her boots and pulling the dark green wool beret off her head. "We got a lot of snow last night."

Eve watched as Kate hung her coat on the hook behind the door. "Hey, I was looking over our financials this morning. I thought with all the hard work we've put in we might want to close shop for a bit, since things really die down around here between January and March."

"Oh?"

"It just so happens that I got an email from an organization in the UK that is hosting a conference and marketplace in London at the end of January. Lots of metaphysical and occult items and books."

"Yes," Kate said, looking at Eve with a glimmer of understanding.

"Yeah, and I was thinking.... I *really* need to see what's new on the market and maybe meet with this artisan jeweler who does really cool stuff that would sell great in the shop. Plus, there are a couple of tea distributors I want to meet." She paused, as if trying to gauge Kate's reaction. "So, I thought wouldn't it be cool if you and I went over to London, made some buys for the shop, and then you could head over to Ireland and surprise Pete before coming home."

Kate grinned, which turned into a laugh. "When do we leave?"

Eve clapped her hands with excitement. "First week in February." She went over to the file cabinet and pulled out an envelope, giving Kate a sheepish look. "I'm glad you said yes, because I already bought the tickets and made the hotel reservations."

Kate shot Eve a look, shaking her head in amusement. "Why am I not surprised by this?"

The two grabbed some coffee and settled back into the office to plan their trip. Kate decided she would surprise Pete by telling him she would be at her mother's place for a week, so he wouldn't call while she was in London. For the first time in three weeks, a bubble of happiness welled up in her. Maybe they could handle a long-distance relationship. *He is going to be so surprised to see me*, she thought, sipping her coffee.

London had been a great idea, not only for the business but also for the two friends to reconnect and share in some much-needed girl time. But after five days packed with activity, they said their goodbyes at the airport, with Eve heading back to Boston and Kate on to Dublin.

Kate had been on pins and needles all week, and now, after checking into her hotel, found herself standing outside of Pete's office building. She entered and raced up the stairs to the second floor, only pausing once at the top. *Deep breaths, slow down,* she repeated like a mantra, as she walked down the long hallway peppered with old portraits of past administrators. Heavy beams spanned the ceiling, dark and solid, giving the impression of permanence. Kate couldn't remember a building like this when she was in college and couldn't help being envious of Pete for having such a beautiful workplace. With her footsteps echoing off the floor, Kate headed down the long hallway toward the open door that was Pete's office. When she was about ten feet away, she heard whispering, and her steps faltered. *What if he's with a student?* she thought. *Well, I'll just quietly put my head in the door.*

Kate was greeted not by the sight of a student deep in conversation with Pete, but instead found Morganne Callaghan in Pete's arms, and it looked as if they were about to kiss. Kate gasped, pulling back as if jolted by an electric current. Pete's head whipped around as he pushed Morganne away. "Kate!" Without a moment's hesitation, Kate turned on her heel and ran down the hallway but not before seeing a look of smug satisfaction on Morganne's face.

"Kate! Wait, stop," Pete said, running after her as she ran toward the staircase. He caught up to her before she could reach them and grabbed her arm. "Kate, don't! It's not what you think."

"Let me go, Pete!" Tears blurred her vision. "Please, just let me go." She pulled her arm from his and headed down the stairs and out of the building, with Pete right behind her.

"Kate, I swear to you, nothing happened! There is nothing going on with Morganne. It's completely one-sided on her part. I thought she understood I wasn't interested, but she cornered me in the office. I was getting a book off the shelf and when I turned around, she pulled herself into my arms. Kate, I swear I have never encouraged her!"

"I knew this wouldn't work. It hasn't even been two months! God, it was stupid of me to think otherwise. This is how it always ends." She pulled away.

"Damn it, Kate! Stop!" He grabbed her arm as students walked by, looking on with interest. "Listen to me. Nothing is going on with that woman, I swear to you. How can you not believe me? Do you trust me so little that you would think I would ever cheat on you? I love you, damn it!"

A series of emotions flooded through Kate—anger, sadness, and a glimmer of hope that he was telling her the truth. "Pete, I...."

"Katie, please. Honey, don't do this." He pulled her into his arms, stroking her back until her body relax. "Come back in and get out of the damp. Come to my office," he said. He guided her back into the building and up the stairs.

Once back in the privacy of Pete's now empty office, Kate heard him breathe a sigh of relief. "Sit down," he said, pointing to the small sofa in the corner.

Kate did as he asked and when he sat down, turned to him. "I don't trust that woman," she said, biting off the words. "Ever since the day I met her, she made it clear how she felt about you. And she doesn't care who knows it! I told you that!"

"I know, Kate. But I don't feel that way about her. You have nothing to worry about! She means absolutely nothing to me. Morganne is a co-worker, an academic collaborator. That's all!"

"Then stop working with her. I'm sure there are plenty of other people you can 'collaborate' with," she said calmly, pinning him with a look.

"What?"

"You heard me. You must have all the research material you need from her. Your book is almost done. Have Rob talk with her if you need anything else."

Pete gave her a look of disbelief. "You can't be serious. I'm not some hormonal teenager who can't control himself, for God's sake. She's a colleague. I work with her, but I have no intention of sleeping with her. My word should be enough for you."

"I'm completely serious. You say you love me? Well, if you love me then you won't work with her anymore."

"Is that an ultimatum?"

"Call it whatever you want. But if you love me, then you'll do what I ask."

"No. I can't believe you are even asking this of me!" Pete's anger enveloped the room. "You are acting like a spoiled child.

This is my job! This is my research!" He took a deep breath, then looked at her coolly. "I'm not Michael Francisco, Kate. And we aren't your mother and father either. You need to let go of that shit once and for all. If you think I'm going to throw away my career because you refuse to trust me, then I guess there is nothing left to say." Standing, Pete walked to his desk, as if needing to distance himself from her.

Kate's face went white. Inside, she was screaming, but she stood and silently walked to the door. She ran her hands over the cool, smooth wood of the doorframe, and the sensation had a strangely comforting effect on her. It felt like an anchor, and if she held onto the frame, her world wouldn't fall apart. She took a shallow breath, then turned and in a barely audible voice said, "That's it then. You've made yourself abundantly clear. Your research is more important than anything else. Sorry to have taken you away from it." Kate let go of the door frame, feeling as if she was being tossed out to sea. Doing her best to keep her composure, she turned and slowly retreated down the stairs and out onto the square, knowing Pete wouldn't follow her, not after what they had said to each other.

———————

Pete sank into his desk chair, putting his head in his hands. "Fuck it," he muttered. "No one is going to give me a god-damned ultimatum." The room was quiet, dark, and smelled like old books. A thought skittered through Pete's brain that his office was a good representation of his life at that moment. As his anger dissipated, regret quickly followed as he replayed the argument in his head and Kate's comment. *Your research is more important than anything else.* A sense of déjà vu grabbed him by the throat and he groaned in misery. He was face to face with a memory he would rather have forgotten.

Pete was living in Cambridge with his wife Jeanine in his last push to finish his dissertation for his PhD, and the stakes couldn't have been higher. It was all about finishing at the top of his class and then getting the plum teaching gig his professors had alluded to if his dissertation was up to their standards. Everything was riding on his research, which was why he spent little time at home with Jeanine. His drive to succeed was like a set of blinders blocking out anyone or anything else happening in his world.

Pete shuddered at the memory of the night he and Jeanine got into that horrible fight. She had just wanted him to take a break and see a movie, hoping it would relieve some of the stress at home. Instead of taking a few hours away from the library and his research, Pete dug in his heels, telling Jeanine she was being selfish, that she wasn't taking their future seriously. After a heated back and forth, Jeanine grabbed her coat and before walking out the door left him with a last parting shot—the accusation that his research was more important than anything else. She filed for divorce a month later, citing irreconcilable differences.

Jesus Christ. What the fuck am I doing? He picked up the phone, determined to make things right with Kate.

Kate stood under the stream of hot water and let the tears flow, sobbing uncontrollably. Pete's angry words kept running through her brain, and she knew there was truth in some of what he'd said. She stepped out of the shower and wrapped herself in a robe, then curled up in the bed and burrowed under the covers while her phone vibrated on the nightstand. Without looking, she knew it was Pete leaving messages. She didn't bother listening, and instead deleted each one, knowing there was nothing left to say. He'd made it clear that he considered her damaged goods, unable to separate her past from her present and possible future. *Maybe he's right,* she thought as the tears started again.

An hour must have passed, as she drifted in and out of sleep, when the hotel phone rang. Warily she picked up, knowing Pete had no idea where she was staying in Dublin. It was Eve, and she sounded frantic.

"Katie," Eve said, the sound of jet engines in the background.

"Yeah...." Her voice raw from her tears. She cleared her throat and sat up in bed.

"Pete called me."

Kate let out a brittle laugh. "Where are you?"

"I'm still in London. My flight was delayed. Katie, are you alright?"

"I'm fine. As soon as I can get a flight out of here, I'll be on my way home."

"Kate, talk to Pete. He's frantic."

"Right. Well, he can be as frantic as he likes. I'm done." Kate started to cry again. She looked at the ceiling, willing herself to get a grip.

"He told me what happened. Don't you believe him?"

"This was a mistake. All of it. I never should have gotten involved. I let you fill my head with possibilities. Well, I'm done. Practical Kate has returned, hurting like hell, but much wiser now." Anger and sorrow welled up, and Kate felt as if she would suffocate from the emotions.

"Oh, Katie.... Please don't do this to yourself."

"Look, I'm going to get off the phone. I need to call the airline and try to change my reservation for a flight tomorrow morning. I'll text you as soon as I have it sorted." Kate sounded like she was working on a business deal until she heard Eve sniffing back tears. "Oh shit, don't. I'm okay... or I'll be okay." She tried to laugh, but it came out as a shaky sob. "When are you leaving London?"

"We're getting ready to board in a few minutes. Are you sure you'll be okay?"

"Yes. I'm going to order some room service and maybe watch a little TV. Don't worry, please. I'll see you at home."

"Okay. I love you, Katie."

"I love you, Eve. Safe travels."

"You too.... Are you sure you're okay?" Eve asked again, worry floating over the phone line.

"I will be." Hanging up the phone, Kate sat in the quiet room with only the muted sounds of Dublin traffic in the background. After a few minutes of trance-like silence, she sighed, grabbed her phone, and set the wheels in motion to get back to Salem, to get back home.

Chapter 32

U sually, Kate found that if she could keep herself occupied by working or walking, she could keep thoughts of Pete from overwhelming her. But even as she walked along the quiet street, Kate kept wishing she could turn back the clock on the last few weeks. Though she hated to admit it, her own personal demons had gotten her into the mess she was in. But instead of admitting she had a part to play in the breakup with Pete, she doubled down and walked away from what she now realized was the love of her life. *Yeah, but he....* She couldn't finish the thought, knowing in her heart that the victim card wouldn't work anymore. But without those feelings of anger, what did she have left? *Pain. Plenty of pain.* She blinked against the cold and continued to walk, burying her hands deeper into her coat pockets.

Essex Street was quiet, and she soon found herself in front of the local antique shop. There was a sign in the window that said *Estate Jewelry—New Acquisitions*, and on a whim she went in to look around. *Maybe a little retail therapy will help.* Her mother's birthday was coming up at the end of March, and maybe she could find her a suitable gift. *Suitable gift.* She grimaced, thinking back to past gift giving incidents. Kate figured she was averaging about a 60 percent positive rating from her mother when it came to birthday gifts. *Well, it's not easy winning the gifting game when your mother shops at Tiffany's on the regular.*

Kate opened the shop door and waved to the owner, Sally McBride, a diminutive, white-haired woman of indeterminate age who was always immaculately turned out in a certain *Town and Country* style. "Hello, Sally," she said, her voice sounding raspy in her ears, as if she hadn't used it in days.

"Good afternoon, Kate. I'm surprised to see you. I thought you and Eve were in London or someplace."

Hoping she hadn't visibly winced at the reminder of *London or some place,* she plastered on a smile, hoping it would cover up her shredded emotions. "We were in London picking up new items for the shop. But that was three weeks ago. I'm just enjoying a few weeks of peace before we gear up for the season."

"Are you looking for anything in particular?"

"Birthday gift for my mother—and anything else that might catch my eye. I saw the estate jewelry sign and thought I might find something interesting and a little different."

Sally ushered Kate to the jewelry case and brought out many beautiful pieces of Victorian jewelry. After looking at several brooches and necklaces, Kate settled on a pair of delicate drop earrings for her mother. The gemstone was a deep garnet, and Kate knew they would look beautiful against her mother's pale blonde hair and ivory skin. As she was getting ready to make her purchase, she noticed a small gold mourning locket engraved with an intricate seascape on the front. "Could I see that?"

"Certainly. This is quite an interesting piece. It was discovered in the old Hastings building." Sally looked at Kate with astonishment. "That's where your shop is, isn't it?"

Kate could feel her skin prickling as she cleared her throat. "Yes, yes, it is. Do you have any history on the piece?" She wondered if the recently silent Abigale was sending her some sort of message.

"Yes. Actually, it tells its own history," Sally said, pushing on the small clasp on the locket.

Kate's breath caught. On one side was a lock of sandy blonde hair behind a thin piece of glass. Engraved on the other side were the words *In Loving Memory of Andrew Michaelson, 1847–1869*. Kate clutched the counter, trying to process what was in front of her. "He was Abigale Hastings' fiancé at one time," she said, as much to herself as to Sally. "How... how much?"

Sally quoted her a price and Kate agreed, taking both the earrings and the locket, then hurried out of the shop. She walked to *Potion*, and unlocking the door, headed back to the office. The shop was quiet, since Eve and Jon had taken a few days off to go on a ski trip in Vermont. Alone, Kate sat down at the desk and opened the bag containing the jewelry. She unwrapped the locket with a shaking hand and held it up to the light. For such a small piece, it felt heavy. Slowly, she latched the chain around her neck as the locket fell to the hollow of her throat. She closed her eyes and wondered if it had belonged to Abigale. She touched the locket, now warm from the heat of her skin, and felt a slight breeze, along with the faint scent of lavender. For the first time in many months, Kate felt comforted and smiled.

In the weeks following their breakup, Pete found himself thinking about Kate in the most inopportune moments. In the middle of a lecture, shopping in the market, or in a department meeting, invariably something would happen, triggering a memory of her. He was having trouble sleeping at night, and during a meeting with Rob about their manuscript, Pete snapped at him when he asked about a specific historical date.

"Hey. Dial it back, alright." Rob gave him a look that said, *I love ya, bro, but you're treading on thin ice.*

Pete was more than a little embarrassed by his inability to control his temper. "Sorry.... I've not been sleeping very well."

"I can see that." Rob paused, as if weighing whether or not to comment. "Look, why don't you just call her?"

"Do you think I haven't tried?" Pete shoved his hands through his hair. "She won't talk to me. Besides, it's over. We've said everything there is to say to one another—more than enough."

"Well, you're going to have to sort yourself out, okay? The manuscript goes to the printer at the end of the week, so I really need you to focus right now." Pete sat, shoulders slumped, looking exhausted and miserable. "Look, why don't you plan on coming over for dinner on Friday. Sarah's been asking how you've been getting on—it will do you good. Get you out of the house," he said, patting Pete on the shoulder.

"Thanks, Rob. I could use a night out, and some of Sarah's cooking as well," he said, more than grateful to have a friend who not only called him on his unacceptable behavior but also supported him. "I'm going to head back to my office for a bit. I have some grading I have to see to before my class next week."

As he walked back to his office, Pete tried to keep his mind off anything that would remind him of Kate. *It's been almost two months. I have to focus.* Settling in at his desk, he sorted through the mid-term exams he needed to grade and focused his attention on the task at hand. An hour later, he was interrupted by a knock on his door. It was Morganne.

"Hello, Pete. I thought I'd stop in and see if you were free for lunch."

"Thanks for the offer, but I'm trying to catch up on some grading." The last thing Pete wanted was to spend any time alone with Morganne. It made him feel guilty, even though he had done nothing to feel that way. And that irritated him.

"Oh, come on. A fellow has to eat. I've been looking at the last proof of your manuscript—Declan sent it over to me—it looks fantastic. I thought we could start the conversation on your next book." She gave him a warm smile.

If I refuse, I'll look like an ass, he thought. *Besides, I do have to eat.* The fact he was feeling guilty for no reason piqued his irritation. *Screw feeling guilty. I'm single, she's attractive, why not?* He gave her a smile. "You're right. I'd love to have lunch."

The pub was crowded with a mix of students, businesspeople, and faculty. "So, how does it feel to have your manuscript completed?" Morganne asked, as they grabbed a table.

"It's not completed yet. I won't be able to relax until I see it in print. But it feels great to see the results of all of that research on the page. To see years of work in print. It's a dream realized for both Rob and me. Of course, we couldn't have done it without you. Your knowledge of ancient Celtic mythology was integral to our research. Thank you."

"You're welcome. But no reason to thank me. If I'm being honest, I did it for selfish reasons," she said, lowering her voice and looking at him through her lashes.

He felt uncomfortable and slightly out of his depth. "Selfish reasons? Not sure I understand."

"Don't you? I think you do. You must know how I feel about you."

"Morganne, look..." he said, trying to cut her off before the conversation went any further. His idea of throwing caution to the wind now didn't seem like such a good idea. There was no way he could use someone just to get over his feelings for Kate. "I'm flattered. Really. But I don't share your feelings. If I've led you on in any way..."

She held up her hand. "No, don't be ridiculous. You've been nothing but professional, more's the pity." She gave him an admiring glance. "I just thought we could spend some time together, get to know each other better and see where it goes."

Looking at the woman across the table, he realized her direct manner impressed him. She was lovely and successful. But she was a poor substitute for Kate. He could feel a wave of sadness crashing down on him. "I'm sorry, I can't. There's someone else."

"Kate? But I thought you two broke up."

"We did. But I..." He couldn't hold it back any longer. "I love her." Just saying the words out loud tore him apart but also made him want to take action, any action that might bring her back. "I... I have to go." Without waiting for a response, he got up and rushed from the pub, taking in deep breaths as he tried to calm down. Heading for home, Pete was desperate for solitude and some sort of plan to get back to Kate.

Chapter 33

The month of March came in like a lion, roaring and gnashing its teeth, and it seemed as if it would go out the same way. Thunderstorms one day, then snow the next. Things at *Potion* were ramping up, with new deliveries arriving every day and local customers stopping in for their morning cup of coffee. Between serving their loyal regulars, Eve and Kate, with Jon's help, had rearranged the shop by expanding the seating area and building a small stage along one wall. The special events were becoming the ticket for entertainment, both for tourists and locals alike, and they needed a space to accommodate them.

Kate was back in the office, balancing the books and paying invoices when Eve came downstairs from her apartment. "Hey Katie." Kate looked up, seeing the concern in her friend's eyes. She knew she looked like crap—tired, pale, and far too thin. As much as Eve had tried, Kate refused to talk to Pete, or talk about Pete, telling Eve it was better that she not think about him at all. In a constant state of mourning, her heart had all but shut down.

Eve squeezed Kate's shoulder. "Hey, I'm heading into Boston with Jon this evening. Are you going home soon?"

"Yeah. I just want to finish this up for the accountant. He's trying to wrap up our taxes," she said, giving Eve a faint smile.

"Well, you need to take a break. Forecast is calling for another thunderstorm, so make sure you go home before it starts, okay?"

Eve waited for a response.

"Don't worry. I won't stay late."

"Good. I'll lock the door behind me. I'll see you tomorrow."

Kate returned to the computer, continuing her work until she heard a rumble of thunder in the distance. She stood and stretched, then walked to the front of the shop and looked out the window. Storm clouds were gathering, and it reminded her of that first night on the ghost investigation when Pete had kissed her. "Stop it," she told herself. "You have to stop doing this to yourself—it's like torture." It felt as if there was nowhere Kate could go to escape her memories. Not work, not home. Wherever she went, memories of Pete followed her.

Thinking she might as well get going before the rain started, Kate turned to go clean off her desk when she felt a draft of cold air raising the hairs on the back of her neck. She tried to shake it off as she walked toward the office until she heard someone whisper in her ear, *Kate*.

She stopped abruptly. "What do you want?" she asked, her voice shaking.

Home, the voice said.

"Isn't this your home, Abigale?"

Your home. Go.

"You say this, but I don't know what you mean. I wish I could help you," Kate said. "But don't worry, I'm going to go home now." She grabbed her coat then stopped, remembering the incidents at the Rock of Cashel and Land's End. "Abigale, was it you who spoke to me in Ireland?" Silence. "What do you want from me?" Her voice rose in frustration.

Be happy.

Kate's face crumpled as she began to cry. As she picked up her purse, she caught the fragrance of lavender. She stopped and stood in the middle of the office, her fingers touching the locket she'd worn every day since she found it. Warm and smooth under her fingertips, it calmed her. A hand touched her shoulder, a cool but comforting touch. "Thank you. I'm not sure what you want, but thank you."

She turned around, hoping to see Abigale, but no one was there, just the faint scent of lavender. Turning off the lights, she headed to the front door, locking it behind her and making it to her car moments before the rain began.

Kate tossed her keys on the side table, breaking the silence, then moved into the living room. She watched the storm and replayed what had transpired in the shop—trying to sort it out in her mind. Restless, she walked into the kitchen to make toast, the only thing she had been eating for days. As she prepared her dinner—such as it was—she decided to worry about what Abigale was trying to tell her tomorrow. Now, all she wanted to do was eat her toast, go to bed, and try to forget about how her heart was breaking.

However, sleep didn't come easily for Kate. Tossing and turning, she would wake up after a recurring dream. In the dream Pete was getting married—or at least it looked like a wedding. She couldn't see who the bride was, but the location was unmistakable. It was at *Land's End,* on the west coast of Ireland. Kate could see Pete standing outside by the arbor overlooking the ocean, looking down the aisle expectantly. Every time the dream progressed to where she might see the bride; she would hear someone whisper her name. And each time she would sit bolt upright in bed, shaking. What was unmistakable was that the voice sounded like Abigale's. After the third time, she gave up and crawled out of bed, exhausted. She thought about calling Eve, but then stopped herself. She would see her in a couple of hours. Instead, she went to the kitchen and made herself a pot of strong Earl Grey tea, figuring if she was going to get up, she might as well fortify herself with caffeine.

Turning on the cable news channel, she curled up on the sofa, pulling her robe around her like a cocoon and inhaling the mug of fragrant tea. After a mindless hour of staring at the chirpy newscaster, Kate took a shower and checked her email before heading into the office. Startled, she saw Pete had sent something several hours earlier. She hesitated to read it. He hadn't tried to contact her in over a month, and Kate was just getting to a point where she didn't feel like a snake was going to bite her whenever she opened her browser. After sitting and staring at the screen for a few minutes, she finally opened it, her heart racing.

Dear Kate,

I hope you read this and that you are doing well. I'd be lying if I said I didn't think about you every day. I wish you would just talk to me—if we could just talk this through, then maybe we could... I don't know, find a way back to where we were. I miss you, Kate.

I wanted to let you know my book is going to launch the first week in May. There's going to be a reception here at the university. I've attached an invitation with the date and time. I would love for you to be there. Rob and I are happy with the results and the advance response has been good. Sarah and Rob ask about you all the time. Sarah says she hasn't heard from you in weeks.

I'll send you a copy of the book as soon as I get it from the publisher... or you could come to Dublin for the launch party. I wish you would come, Kate. I miss you so much.

Love,

Pete

Kate sat, staring at the monitor. Her eyes filled with tears as she put her head on the desk. "What am I doing?" she choked back sobs. "I can't bear this anymore. My heart can't take it." She was crying in earnest now, letting the pain wash over her, until she heard her name being called as the smell of lavender surrounded her. Kate sat up quickly, feeling the room turn cold.

In the corner of the room stood a woman in Victorian dress. She smiled sadly at Kate. "Abigale?" Kate asked, wiping the tears from her eyes. The woman slowly nodded. "What? Why are you here?"

"Go home, Kate."

"I don't know what you mean by that."

"Ireland." Abigale moved a step closer to Kate, her transparent image shimmering like glitter and smoke.

"But Ireland isn't my home."

"Go to Pete."

"What?"

Abigale looked at her with kindness. "Kate, do you love him?"

She began to cry again, thinking of Pete and what she had lost. "Yes. More than anything in this world."

"Then go. He loves you. Don't waste the time you have on this earth being afraid. He is true to you, Kate." Stepping closer, she reached out and touched her cheek. Kate felt the cold, but wasn't afraid.

"Why me? Why did you do this for me?"

"Because you deserve a love that lasts a lifetime—more than a lifetime." Abigale turned, stepped away, and faded from Kate's vision.

"Abigale, wait!" Kate touched the locket around her neck. She unclasped the chain and held the locket in her palm. "This is yours. I've kept it safe, but you should have it. I will never forget what you've done for me." She hesitated, not sure how she could give it to the ghostly figure. Holding out the locket, she watched as Abigale held out her hand and grasped the chain. The locket swung in the air as Kate released it.

"I always felt close to Andrew when I wore this locket. Thank you for finding it." Abigale put the locket around her neck with a sad smile. "Kate, don't make the same mistakes I did. Don't push away the love that is waiting for you. There is so much more to life than you can imagine." She gave Kate a look of affection and slowly dissipated into the air along with the locket.

Kate sat in silence for a long time, no longer sad, but feeling determined. She picked up her phone and dialed Eve's number. "Eve. Are you back from your ski trip?"

"Yeah," she said, groggy from sleep. "Everything okay?"

"Couldn't be better. Meet me in the shop in fifteen minutes."

She grabbed her purse and headed out the door as the sun rose, giving the sky a shimmery pink glow, erasing the storms from the night before. Inhaling deeply, Kate smiled at the scent of damp earth and lavender as she listened to the birds singing to welcome the morning. All her senses seemed heightened. She played the morning's visit with Abigale over and over in her mind as she walked along the slowly awakening street. With each step, her heart became lighter. She knew what she had to do, and she was ready.

Chapter 34

K ate's flight to Dublin had been delayed for hours. As she sat at the gate, freaking out and constantly checking her watch, she had plenty of time to second guess her decisions leading up to this moment. *Why didn't I leave yesterday? I'm not going to make it in time.* For weeks she had been making plans to surprise Pete at the reception for his book. In her mind, Kate had imagined a scene that would put the best romantic movie to shame. She had even splurged on a brand-new dress—a burgundy wrap number with a deep vee neckline—perfect for telegraphing just how serious she was about seducing Pete. Although she hoped it wouldn't take that much effort. In her planning, Kate had printed out the invitation Pete sent to her, then scoured the Trinity College website to find a map with the exact location. In her mind, the plan was going to go off without a hitch. The only thing she hadn't planned for was the huge storm system currently hovering over Ireland. She thought, foolishly she now realized, she could get into Dublin the day of the event, check into her hotel, and then spend a relaxing afternoon getting ready to surprise Pete. It looked like Mother Nature had other ideas.

She paced the concourse in front of the gate, trying to talk herself down from the ledge she was on while the chaos of the airport swirled around her. All she could think about was Pete and the fact she wouldn't make it to the reception. Kate was just getting ready to text Eve and tell her she was going to come home when an announcement came over the PA system saying her flight would board within the hour. She checked her watch and did a mental calculation, hoping against hope she could see her plan through.

———◦———

Pete checked his watch, then reviewed the notes for his speech. He had given hundreds of public presentations, so he wasn't nervous about that. He knew the work he and Rob had completed would stand on its own merit, regardless of how tough the audience of academics could be. Still, he was nervous. Pete kept thinking of his invitation to Kate the month before. But the reality was he didn't know if she had even read his email because he never received a response from her. *Maybe it is time to let her go. She's obviously trying to move on, and you should too.* He heard footsteps and laughter coming down the hall, followed moments later with Rob and Sarah peeking their heads around the corner to his office.

"Ready to go?" Rob asked.

Pete gathered up his notes and plastered a smile on his face. "Let's do this."

As they headed out the door, Sarah touched Pete's arm. "Have you heard from Kate?" Pete's smile faltered for a moment, then he shook his head and kept walking.

———◦———

The plane tossed around in the sky, and if Kate had not been focused on getting to Pete, she might have been clutching her seat and praying to every deity in the universe. Instead, she checked her watch again as they made their approach into Dublin. 6:02pm. The reception had just started. *How long will it take to get through the airport?* She tried to calculate her journey through immigration and baggage claim. The plane made a sudden dip, flipping Kate's stomach. *Damn it, I didn't get this far to go down over the Irish Sea,* she thought with resolve, looking out at the rolling waves below.

Within twenty minutes, the pilot navigated them safely to the ground while a round of applause erupted from the cabin. As soon as the plane reached the gate and the seat belt sign was turned off, Kate jumped out of her seat. *Why did I check my bag? Come on people, let's go! How long will it take to get a taxi into the city? Can't you all move any faster? Okay, calm down. Breathe.* Kate did her best to tamp down her frustration.

Kate maneuvered through immigration and baggage claim with minor delays, and after standing in the pouring rain for ten minutes at the taxi stand, found herself heading into the city. She checked her watch as the taxi pulled up to the front gate of Trinity. 8:27 pm. She paid her fare, grabbed her wheeled bag, and sprinted across the campus. By the time she reached the right building, she was a mess. Her hair, clothing, and spirits were drenched. *No time to stop.* She raced down the hall, looking for the right room, dragging her luggage behind her.

She found the room where the reception was scheduled and gave a tentative pull on the door. The reception hall was almost empty, just the custodial crew cleaning up the remnants of the event. Heart sinking, she closed the door quietly. "I missed him...." She leaned against the cool stone wall, trying to hold back tears. For a few seconds she stood there, not sure what to do next, as the plans she had so carefully made disintegrated before her eyes. Everything was supposed to be perfect, but now.... Kate wandered back toward the lobby, thinking she would go to her hotel, dry off, and figure out what to do next. Looking out the window, the rain continued, so Kate waited it out for a while, sitting on a stone bench in the empty lobby. It was the first time she hadn't been in constant motion for hours. As she sat in the quiet, her exhaustion and emotions got the better of her. Nothing had gone the way she had planned. *Isn't this a life lesson?*, she thought, as the tears flowed. "Oh, damn it, stop crying," she said, digging through her travel bag for a tissue. As Kate emptied the contents on the bench beside her, looking for the elusive package of tissues, she didn't hear the footsteps coming down the hallway.

———◦———

Pete sat in the quiet of his office, thinking of all that had transpired. *Manuscript done after two years of hard slogging. Career set in the place I've always wanted to be. Hell, it's time to think about my next book. This is everything I wanted....* But the hard reality was that it didn't feel like success. Instead of feeling energized, he felt brittle, as if one little push would see his world break into a million pieces. *She didn't come. I was so sure she would be here. Well, there's your sign. Accept it and move on.* He looked at his watch. *Better go if I'm going to meet them at Dish,* he thought, knowing Rob had made a reservation for a celebratory dinner. As if on auto-pilot, Pete put on his trench coat, locked the door, and headed down the hall, his footsteps echoing off the stone walls.

As he walked towards the exit, doing his best to push away the disappointment, he stopped dead in his tracks. Sitting in the lobby, looking through her bag, was Kate. It was all Pete could do to not run to her. Instead, he took a deep breath and slowly approached her, afraid she might be an illusion that would disappear into the ether. But the closer he got, he knew it was real—she was real. He stopped in front of her, eyes filled with love. "You look like you could use some help."

—————◦•◦—————

She continued sorting through her bag, embarrassed to be caught crying by a complete stranger. "I'm fine thank you; I can't find my...." She looked up at Pete and jumped off the bench, launching herself into his arms.

"Kate. You're here. My god, you're actually here," Voice rough, he held her close.

"I was in the neighborhood," Kate said. She pulled away just enough to look up at him, smiling through her tears.

"Oh, Katie, lass. How I've missed you."

"I've missed you. I missed your book launch... my flight was delayed... I'm sorry."

"I don't care about that. God... I love you, Kate." He kissed her deeply, holding her tightly as if he were afraid she might disappear into thin air.

Kate broke the kiss and looked up at him. "I love you, Pete. I'm sorry I ever doubted you. I was a stubborn fool."

"Shhh, don't say that. What's important is you're here," he said, kissing her again. He pressed against her, and she felt his hardness, thinking she might faint from wanting him. She had dreamed of this moment for the past month. Pete's hand moved to cup her breast.

Kate moaned softly, then remembered where they were. "Wait. Maybe this isn't the best place to get reacquainted."

He took a shaky breath. "Right. Yes. Let's get out of here," he said, with more than a hint of lust in his voice.

Pete started collecting her luggage as Rob and Sarah, who were leaving the building, greeted them. Sarah grabbed Kate in a bear hug. "Oh, Kate! We're so happy to see you!"

Rob leaned in to give Kate a hug and whispered, "He was lost without you."

"I was lost without him," she said, eyes shining with happy tears.

"We're going to leave now," Pete said. "I think I'll take a pass on dinner, okay?"

"I'm hurt you don't want to spend a night out with your best friend and co-author." Rob slapped Pete on the shoulder. "Get out of here. We'll talk to you later."

Thanking their friends, Pete and Kate headed out of the building into the spring evening. The hard rain had stopped, leaving a soft mist coating the buildings and greenery. Pete grabbed Kate's hand and strode across campus and onto the street. "Where are we going?" she asked, keeping pace with him.

"My place. It's not far from here."

Within minutes, they were on a quiet street lined with Georgian townhouses. At the end of the block, Pete guided Kate to a blue door. "Reminds me of your place in Salem," she said. He smiled as he unlocked the door, where Finn greeted them immediately. "Finn, buddy! I missed you," Kate said, rubbing the cat behind the ears as he purred with satisfaction.

Pete took her hand and led her up the stairs, pulling her into the bedroom. "You can get reacquainted with him later." Pete took Kate into his arms. "You really are here," he said, looking at her as if it was a dream.

"Yes. I *really* am here." Kate touched his face, reveling in the feel of his skin.

He kept his gaze fixed on her. "I kept telling myself not to hope...."

Kate started loosening his tie and unbuttoning his shirt as she spoke. "Never give up on hope," she said between kisses, her pulse kicking up as she pulled his shirt off. She kissed his neck, moved to his chest and licked his nipple, hearing his quick intake of breath. "I have been waiting a month for this moment. To touch you, taste you, to tell you how much I love you." She trailed off and turned her focus to his belt—unable to stop herself.

"Jesus, Kate," he groaned, helping her with the buckle and quickly lowering the zipper on his fly. As soon as they dealt with his zipper, she yanked down his pants and briefs in one movement. "Honey, wait," he panted, toeing off his shoes and stepping out of his pants. As soon as he was free, Kate stripped off her wet jeans and shirt. "Fuck me, you are beautiful," he breathed, as she stood in a plain white bra and panties.

"Oh, I plan on fucking you," she said with a full-throated laugh of joy, and freedom, and certainty. She unfastened her bra and threw it over her shoulder, never losing eye contact with him, a smile on her face the entire time. "You know, I had this sexy dress I was going to wear for the reception. I thought it would be a great way to let you know I wanted to jump your bones. But I guess this will have to do. Come here," she ordered.

Pete scooped her up, tossing her onto the bed and falling next to her with a laugh. "Kate... Kate," he said, pushing the hair away from her brow. "This is so much better than a stodgy reception for my book." Then he kissed her and neither one of them was laughing anymore.

An hour later, tangled in the sheets and listening to the muted sounds of evening traffic on the Dublin streets, Pete turned to Kate, who had a look of absolute bliss. "How long are you staying?"

"Well, I booked a return for a week from tomorrow. I hope that's okay."

"No, it's not okay. I wish you weren't leaving at all," Pete said, pulling her close.

"I know. But at least I'm here for a week, right?"

"I'll take what I can get. I've got two classes tomorrow and then I'm free. We'll plan something fun for the weekend, okay?"

"I already thought we were doing something fun," Kate said, as she ran her hands down his back.

"Oh, there will be plenty more of that, lass." He kissed her neck. Suddenly Kate's stomach grumbled. "Are you hungry?"

"I am. I haven't eaten since yesterday before I left for the airport. And I couldn't eat on the plane—for some reason I was too nervous to eat."

"Come on. Let's go down to the kitchen and I'll make us something," Pete said, taking Kate's hand and pulling her from the bed.

"I need to get some dry clothes out of my suitcase."

"Why," he asked with a grin. "I think you look fine just like that."

Kate rolled her eyes. "I don't much feel like parading around in what God gave me."

Pete headed over to his dresser and pulled out a Trinity rugby shirt. "Will this do for now?" he asked, handing her the shirt. Kate pulled it over her head. The shirt came almost to her knees, and she had to roll up the sleeves. "Here are some socks, too. The floors are chilly." He gave her the socks and kissed the tip of her nose.

"Perfect. Thanks," she said.

Pulling on a pair of sweatpants and tee-shirt, he held out his hand. "Let's get you fed, woman," he said, pulling her close, not wanting to be apart from her for more than a moment.

The kitchen was bright and modern, with blond wood cabinets and stainless-steel appliances. Pete opened the refrigerator and pulled out two bottles of Guinness, as well as a large container. "I hope you don't mind; it will be leftovers tonight. I made a pot of Irish stew earlier in the week. Okay?"

"Great. I'm starving! Can I help with anything?"

"There's a loaf of soda bread in the breadbox on the counter if you could grab that and the cutting board. Let me see what I've got for a salad." Pete went to the fridge and pulled salad greens out of the crisper. Suddenly he stopped and looked at Kate. "You really are here. I keep thinking I should pinch myself to make sure I'm not dreaming all of this." He paused a moment. "What made you decide to come?"

Kate smiled at the memory of what led her there. "Let's just say there was a ghostly intervention on my behalf."

"What?" Pete poured her a beer as she settled at the kitchen table.

"Yeah. You know the day you sent me the email about the book reception?" Pete nodded. "Well, I had a visit from Abigale. Twice within several hours. Once at *Potion* and then at home early in the morning." Kate sipped her beer and shared her story about Abigale's fateful visit.

Pete looked stunned and pale. "I can't believe it."

"Yeah, well, the next thing I knew Abigale was talking to me, telling me to come to Ireland, and that I shouldn't give up on love—that you were true to me." Kate teared up. "Oh, Pete. She made me realize I had to stop being afraid. That I needed to trust in love... your love. So, here I am." She walked across the kitchen and put her arms around him, resting her head against his chest.

"This is incredible. I have to tell you something," he said, holding her tight. "The night I wrote that email? Well, I had been so depressed. I missed you so much and I didn't know what to do. I felt paralyzed, you know? I... I was in bed, trying to sleep." He took a shaky breath. "I had a visit that night. From my mom."

Now it was Kate's turn to look shocked. "What? Helen?"

Pete nodded. "Mom came to me and told me not to give up—that you loved me. I decided to write to you after her visit. I thought if I didn't hear from you then I would do my best to move on." Pete grabbed Kate's hands. "Oh Kate! When I saw you tonight...." He touched her face. "When you didn't respond to my email, I didn't think there was a ghost of a chance I would see you again." Pete laughed in amazement, "Can you believe it?"

Confused, she tried to put it all together. "Do you think Helen and Abigale were tag teaming us? I mean, could it be they were working in tandem to bring us together?"

Pete shrugged. "Well, however they did it, it worked. This has certainly been an interesting couple of months, eh?" He turned to put the stew on the burner as Kate sat at the kitchen table, still puzzled by everything that had happened.

"Seriously, this has to be the weirdest... I mean... how can this be?" she mused.

"I think this is one of those things we just have to roll with, you know? There are a lot of things about the paranormal that we just don't know. Maybe it will all be made clear at some point... or maybe it won't. All I know is I'm not complaining."

"I'm not either. Hey, I'd like to propose a toast. Here's to Helen and Abigale. Two unstoppable women who know how to get our attention."

Pete raised his glass to Kate. "Here, here. Cheers to them both."

Chapter 35

P ete left early the next morning for his classes, leaving Kate to sleep in and recover from her jetlag. She woke around ten o'clock, and it took a minute to remember where she was. But then the memories of the previous day came flooding back. She grabbed her pillow and hugged it, smiling to herself at how things had transpired. After a few minutes of basking in happiness, Kate got up and headed to the bathroom, where she found a note on the mirror.

Hey sleepy head. I love you. Check your text messages. - Pete

Grinning, she went about her business, then went back to get her phone from her bag and headed downstairs to make some coffee. She scrolled through her texts and found one from Eve— filled with heart emojis. Kate sent her a quick text peppered with her own litany of heart and kiss emojis, with an eggplant thrown in for good measure. Then Kate saw Pete's text:

I should be home around noon. I made plans for us for the weekend. xoxoxoxoxo

She grabbed a cup of coffee and headed back upstairs, humming to herself as she went. *Life is good, girl.* Putting the coffee mug on the bathroom sink, she turned on the shower taps. For a moment she let herself wonder. *What happens when the week is over? How are we going to make this work?* Her thoughts briefly skittered to her past with Michael. "No," she said, scolding her reflection in the mirror, shaking the worrisome thoughts from her mind. "I'm happy, Pete loves me. We'll figure this out!"

An hour later, Kate was sitting in the living room snuggling with Finn when Pete walked through the door. "Hello, love," he said, joining her on the sofa and kissing her soundly. Finn gave a loud, plaintive meow at being rudely ignored. "Finn, she's mine. Go get your own," he laughed, rubbing the top of Finn's head until he purred in appreciation.

"How were your classes?"

"Great. I've got a graduate research group and they pretty much run with whatever I throw their way. The undergraduates take a bit more prodding, but they are all fantastic students. I love teaching here." Pete stood and pulled Kate to her feet. "Let me change clothes and pack a few things and then we'll head out, okay?"

"Sure. Where are we going?"

A smile broke across Pete's face. "One of your favorite places I seem to recall."

"*Land's End*?!" Pete nodded as Kate clapped excitedly. "Hurry up and let's go," she said, pushing him playfully toward the stairs.

It was a glorious spring afternoon, and the sun was shining warm and bright. Along the road were banks of wildflowers flashing brilliant colors as they drove along. Kate thought of just how familiar this country had become to her—how much it now felt like home. She thought of Abigale's message and wondered where this path would lead. Kate looked over at Pete, relaxed as he drove along the motorway, absent-mindedly humming along to a tune on the jazz station. Her heart swelled with love. As if sensing her attention, he turned to give her a quick grin. "A penny for those thoughts, woman."

"I was thinking about how much I love this country... and you," she said, touching his arm. "Heading back next week is going to be tough."

Pete took in the glow surrounding Kate as the sun shone behind her, setting her auburn hair shimmering in the spring sunshine. "I love you," he said simply, taking her hand and kissing it. "All is right with the world since you arrived." He turned his attention back to the road, and they drove on, watching the changing landscape as they got closer to *Land's End*.

Along the coast road, only a mile or two from the cottage, the sea was like glass, with only a slight breeze ruffling the tall grass. "I saw Marcus on campus this morning. He told me the housekeeper left us a picnic hamper. So, if you like, we can take it down to the beach for a sunset picnic," Pete said, breaking the silence as he turned off the main road toward the house.

"That sounds great," Kate said, as they pulled up to the house. She got out of the car and stretched her legs, inhaling the salt air. "Now this is just what I need," she said, turning toward the ocean view.

Pete came around the car and took Kate in his arms. "This is just what I need." He kissed her, slowly, almost reverently. Kate pulled herself closer to him as the kiss deepened and their tongues met. He pressed against her, and she sighed. Breaking the kiss, he chuckled as he took Kate's face in his hands. "All in good time, lass. Come on, we've got a picnic waiting for us." Pete grabbed the bags from the back of the car and they headed to the front door.

Once they deposited their things in the bedroom, they checked out the kitchen. Sitting on the counter was a beautiful wicker hamper and a note from the housekeeper, letting them know of all the provisions in the refrigerator. She also informed them where to find beach blankets and hurricane lanterns. Kate quickly got to work putting dinner in the hamper while Pete went to scout out the blankets and lanterns. Soon they were headed down to the beach and the glassy sea.

"Does this look like a suitable spot?" Pete pointed to a little protected area backed by sea grass and a low dune.

"Perfect! Magnificent view of the ocean, and it looks like we'll have a gorgeous sunset—the sky is so clear," Kate said, looking out to the horizon. She put down the hamper while he arranged the large blanket with hurricane lamps on each corner to keep the breeze from moving it.

He sat down, holding out his hand to Kate. After placing the hamper within easy reach, she settled down next to him, sighing. They sat, looking out at the seabirds as they soared and dipped toward the water. She rested her head on Pete's shoulder, quietly enjoying the view, the warmth, and especially the love.

As the sun set, Pete lit the hurricane lamps as Kate opened the hamper and set out their meal. "Marcus' housekeeper has excellent taste—paté, salad, a cheese board, and water crackers. And this wine," she said, holding up the bottle, "A lovely rosé—

and bless her, she didn't forget to include a corkscrew!" After setting everything out, Kate looked quite pleased with the presentation. "I think that's everything. Now just cue that gorgeous sunset," she said, pulling her jacket a little closer as the breeze reminded them it was still early May.

"It's not quite everything," Pete said quietly, looking a little nervous. Kate gave him a questioning look. He busied himself uncorking and pouring the wine, then turned to face Kate, taking her hands. "Remember that first night at *Sabatino's* when we met?"

Kate giggled, "Oh my god! I was expecting some dude in a Ghostbuster's tee shirt who lived in his mom's basement. You destroyed my theory of what a paranormal investigator would be like. Although technically, the first time I met you was at the Old Burying Point when I thought you were a stalker!"

"You took me by surprise too," he said. "I wasn't expecting a green-eyed, redheaded reincarnation of the goddess Áine." Kate blushed. "Who drives me to distraction when she blushes," Pete said, kissing her.

When the kiss broke, Pete sat back a little and pulled something out of his jacket pocket. "Kate, I think I started falling in love with you that night when you called me ghostbuster. When I got on the plane to move here, I didn't know if I could live without you. Then, when you came to visit and there was that dust-up about Morganne...."

Kate cut him off, grabbing his arm. "Oh Pete, don't go there! God, I was so insecure."

"The thing is, I realized when I saw you sitting on that bench last night, I don't want to live without you." He fiddled with a small velvet box as Kate felt her heart race in anticipation. "So... my beautiful Kate Murphy, I'm asking you, here, on this beach with nature as a witness, will you marry me?"

Kate looked down at the ring nestled on a bed of black velvet. A diamond surrounded by small emeralds winked in the light of the setting sun. She looked at Pete and cried. "Yes! Yes! Absolutely, yes!" With shaking hands Pete put the ring on her finger. "Pete, Pete... I love you so much," she said, kissing him and laughing with abandon.

Under a clear evening sky twinkling with stars, Kate and Pete made plans for their wedding. Almost in unison, they agreed the wedding would take place right there at *Land's End*. Kate thought back to the dream she had and knew it truly had been a message from beyond, as she sent a silent prayer of thanks to Abigale and Helen for not giving up on them.

Chapter 36

I t was a perfect July morning as Kate stood on the empty beach; the sun warming the sand beneath her feet. She breathed deeply and looked up at the cloudless sky. "How did I get so lucky?" Turning, she looked up the hill to the cottage where a large tent had been set up on the lawn the day before. In the garden, underneath the arbor where Kate had sat almost a year before, a small altar had been set up for the wedding ceremony that would take place in a few hours. She looked back toward the sea and sat down on the warm sand, thinking about the past few days. So much had happened. From making sure there were enough rooms for guests at the local hotel, to worrying about her parents seeing each other after so many years. Fortunately, her worries were needless since her mother was on her best behavior and was gracious toward Pete and his family. Pete's dad really hit it off with Kate's father, and the two were already making plans to get together once they returned to the states.

And then there was Eve. Thinking of her friend, Kate got a lump in her throat. Eve had arrived with Jon earlier in the week and took care of the wedding logistics with the vendors and caterers, leaving Kate to relax (as much as she could) and enjoy visiting with family and friends. Of course, her friend dropped everything at *Potion* to be there to help—didn't matter that it was their busy season—Eve wouldn't hear of not being there to support Kate. She had even arranged yesterday's rehearsal and dinner, which was lovely, with everyone gathering on the beach for a casual feast laid out on tables underneath the stars. Eve really had worked magic for the event—a New England meets Ireland seafood boil. It had been beautiful, sitting next to her husband-to-be in the moonlight, while all the people Kate cared most about in the world were there on that lovely beach. She smiled at the memory and closed her eyes, feeling the sun warm her face.

"Hey, you," Eve called, settling down next to her friend. "Don't get sunburned right before the wedding!"

Kate grinned and put her arm around Eve's shoulder. "I won't. Just wanted to savor a few minutes of quiet before all the craziness begins." She hugged Eve. "Thank you. That doesn't seem like enough, though. You've helped me through so much. Not only the wedding plans, but... life."

Eve waved off her thanks. "No need to thank me. This is what we do for the people we care about. By the way, before everyone arrives, and we get swept up in all the professions of love and fidelity," she grinned, pulling out a small jewelry box, "I wanted to give you this." Eve handed her the box.

"Eve. You've done so much for me already," Kate protested, opening the box. It held a meticulously handcrafted silver and lapis lazuli pendant, shaped like the pagan triquetra, hanging from a thin silver chain. "Oh, Eve! It's beautiful." Kate's eyes filled with tears as she put the necklace on.

"Lapis signifies friendship and truth. The triquetra is a Celtic pagan symbol. The interlocking triangles represent the connection between mind, body, and soul. Or earth, sea, and sky. May it always connect you within yourself and your world, my dearest friend." Eve blinked away tears as the two hugged. "Now, in a few brief hours, this place is going to be filled with people expecting a wedding. Let's go get you ready, okay?" They headed back to the house arm in arm, ready to face the day, but not before they had their morning coffee.

Pete had never felt so happy or anxious in his life as he waited under the arbor with his Rob as his best man. The sun was shining through the ivy and flowers, scattering sunlight across the cobbled walk where they stood. "You ready?" Rob asked.

"More than ready." Pete smiled, looking out at the guests sitting in the garden. In front of him sat his father, Jacob, with Mae by his side, beaming at Pete with pride, while behind them sat family, friends, and co-workers. Jacob was truly in his element, being back in Ireland and visiting with family. Pete focused his gaze to the other section of seats on the bride's side and saw Kate's mother Gale, looking cool and chic in a pale buttery yellow Chanel suit with matching shoes and bag. Kevin Murphy waited by the back row of chairs, looking dapper but somewhat uncomfortable in his formal tuxedo, his red hair touched with gray glowing in the sunshine, as he waited for his daughter to enter.

"Try to remember as much of it as you can. The day will pass in a flash," Rob said to Pete, looking toward his wife with a soft smile. Sarah gave him a wave and Rob mouthed, *Hello love* to her. She returned his smile and sat back in her chair.

Soon the minister approached the altar, and Pete's heart kicked into high gear. "Reverend," he acknowledged.

The minister, a kind-looking woman with long gray hair tied back in a loose braid, and wearing a cream-colored robe with accents of kelly green and royal purple, turned to Rob. "Do you have the rings?" After checking his pockets, Rob nodded. The minister smiled at Pete. "Then I think we are ready to begin." Minister, groom, and best man turned to face the congregants to wait for the bride.

Kate and her father stood in the doorway of *Land's End*, watching the minister approach the altar. "Well, Katie, I think they are ready for us," he said, turning to his daughter. Tears shone in his eyes. "You look beautiful, sweetheart," his voice gruff with emotion.

"Thanks, Dad." Kate squeezed his hand. "I'm so glad you're here." In that moment, all the missed opportunities between them seemed to fade away; the proms, the driving lessons, and other things that happened when she was a teenager. She realized they could start from today and make memories to last a lifetime.

On cue, a small string quartet played old Celtic folk songs and Eve, acting as Kate's maid of honor, started down the aisle, holding a small bouquet of wildflowers. Her long dress of pale lavender moved gently on the breeze, and she looked almost like a garden fairy with her short, jet black hair topped with a wreath of wildflowers. She winked at Jon, who sat on the aisle, grinning from ear to ear as she passed him.

Once Eve made her way to the altar, the music changed to a hauntingly beautiful solo violin. Kate stepped forward wearing a gown of ivory Irish lace that draped off her shoulders, nipped in at the waist, then cascaded to the ground with a small train. She held a bouquet filled with ivory-colored roses, lavender, and sprigs of rosemary. Her hair was crowned with lavender and ivy. The lavender and rosemary held special significance for Kate. The lavender was to honor Abigale, and the rosemary signified a remembrance of those who had passed—especially Pete's mother, Helen. Pete stood by the altar with a look of pure love. Kate knew that look—she remembered it from her dream. Squeezing her father's arm, she let him know she was ready.

Kate could see Pete barely holding back tears as she walked down the aisle toward him. In her soul she knew—he was her beginning, her ending, her everything. When they reached the altar, Kate's father kissed her cheek, and with tears in his eyes, turned to Pete. "Take care of my Katie," his voice breaking as he said her name.

"I will, sir," Pete said, taking Kevin's hand and pulling him in for a hug and pat on the back. As Kevin moved away to take his seat, Pete turned and took Kate's hands in his. "I love you, lass," he whispered.

"And I love you," she said.

The ceremony was heartfelt and memorable, with an abundance of laughter and tears. Afterwards, the guests moved to the tent, where everyone was treated to a delicious feast created with the best that Ireland offered. After dinner, the reception turned raucous, with music, dancing, and imbibing in

Ireland's finest whiskies and beers. Several hours into the festivities, Pete found Kate talking with a group of friends. She smiled as he approached. "Sorry to interrupt this party, but I'd like to steal my wife for a bit." Taking Kate's hand, he led her back to the garden where the ceremony had taken place, giving them a few moments of solitude in the middle of the celebration. A full moon hung over the sea, giving everything a peaceful, mystical glow. "Mrs. O'Brien," Pete said, taking Kate in his arms.

"Yes, Mr. O'Brien," Kate said, her heart fluttering at his touch.

"Isn't it about time we send these people packing?" he asked in mock exasperation.

"Aren't you having a good time?"

"I'm having a wonderful time, but I want you all to myself. There is nothing I want more than to make this marriage *official*." Pete kissed her, giving her no doubt about what he meant.

"Soon, love. Soon." Her head resting on his chest. They looked down to the beach, awash in moonlight. There was a slight movement down by the water. "Pete, look there."

Appearing out of the ether were two women, one in Victorian dress and another in more modern apparel. "Mom," Pete said. "Oh, Mom...."

"And Abigale..." Kate said. "Helen, thank you for being with us on our wedding day. I will love your son all the days of my life." Kate's eyes filled with tears. "Abigale, thank you for helping me to not give up on love."

"Isn't she beautiful, Mom?" Pete asked, as Helen nodded in agreement.

They watched as another apparition took form. It was a man, and he turned toward Abigale and took her hand. Kate let out a gasp. "Andrew?" Abigale flashed a knowing smile in response as the three spirits faded from view.

"Who is Andrew?" Pete asked.

"That is a love story for another day," Kate said, reaching up to kiss her husband.

Pete and Kate stood, arm in arm, looking out at the moon over the water, when they heard people approaching. Turning, they watched Rob and Sarah walk down the path toward them.

"We wondered where you two headed off to," Rob said.

"Just trying to get a few minutes alone with my wife." Pete grinned, hugging Kate close.

Sarah smiled at the two of them. "We won't keep you love birds. Just wanted to let you know that we're heading out. Looks like the party is winding down."

"We were just on our way back up to the house," Kate said. "We want to thank everyone and see them off." The four friends headed back toward the sound of laughter and conversation in the tent. Eve was dancing dreamily with Jon, as if they were the only two people on earth. Kate smiled and was turning to say something to a departing guest when she saw her mother standing off to the side, watching the newlyweds. Gale motioned to her daughter. Taking a deep breath and wondering what her mother had to say, Kate headed over to where she was standing.

"Kate, I'm going to be going now. My flight out of Shannon leaves early tomorrow morning." Gale motioned vaguely toward the car waiting at the end of the drive.

"Thank you so much for being here, Mom," Kate said, wishing she could let down her guard with her mother, but not trusting that it would be well received. "Have a safe flight back to Chicago."

"Kate, before I leave there is something I want to say to you."

Kate braced herself for the onslaught of negativity that seemed to follow her mother around like a cloud of expensive perfume. "Oh... okay...."

"I'm not very good at this," Gale said, looking down at her hands, twisting the expensive rings on her fingers.

"What is it, Mom?"

Gale looked directly at her daughter. "Well, I will tell you I had my reservations about all of this." Kate felt herself stiffen in response. "Leaving your job, moving to Salem... then a marriage and moving to Ireland...." Gale trailed off for a moment and looked around her, her eyes resting on Pete, who was talking with his father—his arm around Jacob's shoulder. A faint smile crossed her face. "But, after seeing you here with Pete... seeing how happy you are and the friends you have around you... I was wrong to have any reservations. I've always just wanted the best for you, Kate." She raised her hand to touch Kate's cheek and smiled. "Pete seems like a wonderful young man, and he obviously loves you very much.... I haven't been the best parent," she said. Kate tried to cut her off, but Gale held up her hand. "We both know I never would have made mother of the year." She looked at her daughter wistfully. "You have worked so hard your entire life, you deserve happiness. I love you, Kate." She leaned into her daughter and kissed her cheek.

Kate grabbed Gale and hugged her tight. "I love you too, Mom."

Across the room, Pete watched the interaction between the two women and smiled. He excused himself and headed over to where Kate and Gale were standing. He took Kate's hand in his, pulling her close for a quick kiss. "Gale, you aren't leaving, are you?" he asked.

"Yes. I was just telling Kate that I've got an early flight tomorrow morning."

"Well, come back and spend more time. We'd love to have you," he said.

"Thank you. Maybe I'll do that. I've always wanted to learn more about Ireland, and from what Kate tells me, you are the man who knows the history better than anyone," she said.

"Well, I don't know about that, but we would love to have you come back for an extended visit," Pete offered.

With that, Gale said goodbye, leaving her daughter standing dumbstruck.

"You okay?" Pete whispered in Kate's ear.

Kate shook her head. "I never thought I'd hear those words...." As the car pulled away, she turned to Pete. "This day has been magical. But now, I think it's time we created a little magic of our own. What do you say, husband?"

Pete grabbed Kate and lifted her into his arms as the last of the guests hooted and cheered. He waited until everyone quieted and said, "Thank you all for joining us. It has been a memorable day, and it is because of all of you being here to celebrate with us." Pete looked at Kate, who grinned up at him. "But now, if you will excuse us, my wife and I will take our leave." Pete carried her over the threshold as Kate waved goodbye over his shoulder. He did not put her down until they were alone in the rustic bedroom they had shared on their first visit to *Land's End*.

Kate walked to the window and looked out at the moon casting a glow on the garden below and the sea beyond. She could hear the last of the guests saying their goodnights and smiled at the memory of the day. Walking down the aisle as the sea breeze gently brushed her face, seeing Pete so handsome in his tuxedo, waiting for her at the altar, feeling as if her heart would burst with happiness. Kate sighed as Pete turned off the light on the nightstand and moved behind her, wrapping his arms around her and kissing her neck. "I love you, Mrs. O'Brien. Standing in the moonlight like that, you are even more bewitching—if that is possible."

Kate turned to face him—her husband, the love she never thought she would find, her soulmate. "Pete," she said, running her hand along his jaw, reveling in the warmth of his skin, "You are my life, my love... my world is forever changed for the better because of you." Pete kissed her gently and Kate melted into him, finally understanding what it meant to be home.

Epilogue

Kate walked down Grafton Street to the empty storefront on the corner. It was early and Dublin was still on the sleepy side of morning. She unlocked the door and stepped in out of the late autumn chill, scanning the large empty space. "It's perfect," she said. Eve's early flight should have landed around five, so she expected her to arrive soon. As Kate walked around the main floor, she imagined where the coffee bar and tables would go, as well as the merchandise area. She had given it a lot of thought and had run the numbers—the business had come so far in two years. Maybe it was time to expand *Potion*. And Grafton Street was prime real estate—lots of locals and tourists. Kate said a silent prayer that Eve would agree on the location, since she had already drawn up a preliminary contract with the solicitor. All the contract needed was their signatures.

A knock on the door interrupted her musings. She turned to see Eve waving and hurried to let her in. "You made it," Kate said, hugging Eve and pulling her in out of the early morning chill.

"Katie! I've missed you! Wow, this place is fantastic," she said, putting down her bag and surveying the main room. "How's Pete?"

"He's great. In the thick of the semester now and working on a new book with Rob. He's looking forward to seeing you. How's Jon," Kate asked.

Eve's eyes lit up, and she held out her hand. On her finger was a beautiful diamond engagement ring. "Oh, he's okay," she said, casually draping her hand on Kate's arm.

"Oh, my god! Eve! Congratulations." Kate hugged her tight. "I am so happy for you. Have you set a date yet?"

"Nothing solid yet, but we were thinking about next August."

"In Salem?"

"Well, we were thinking about having it here in Ireland. If you wouldn't mind helping me with the planning? Oh, and being my matron of honor?"

Kate's eyes welled with tears. "Oh Eve, of course!" Then she did a few mental calculations and laughed.

Eve gave her a quizzical look. "What's so funny?"

"Well, you and I never do anything by half measures, do we? Let's expand the business, get you married, and.... Well, the O'Brien's will add a plus one to the wedding guest list."

"What? Praise the Goddess! You're pregnant?"

Kate nodded, glowing with happiness, then put her hand on her belly. "Pete and I had it confirmed last week. I'm due in mid-May."

After spending the morning talking about wedding plans, baby names, and ideas for the international version of *Potion*, the two women headed out on to the street, which was now alive with Dubliners and tourists alike, starting their day. Eve surveyed the people walking by. "Soon, they'll be able to get their morning cuppa from us," she mused.

"Does that mean we are a go for the space?"

"Oh, absolutely! It checks off all the boxes as far as location, size, charm," Eve said. "But there is one thing we need to make sure that it does have."

"What? I thought I had covered everything," Kate said, somewhat puzzled.

"A ghost!" Eve laughed.

Kate grinned and rolled her eyes. "Well, I guess we'll have to investigate. But lucky for us, I'm sleeping with the hottest ghostbuster around!"

Acknowledgements

They say it takes a village to raise a child—well the same can be said for writing a novel. Thanks to Lynne Pearson at *All That Editing* for editing my manuscript in the middle of a pandemic —let's hear it for technology! Maybe someday we'll meet in person. Special thanks to the three professorial divas in the PNW Department of English, Dr. Bethany Lee, Dr. Heather Fielding, and Sarah White who got me through my master's thesis about the romance novel—my romance novel. You women rock the literary world! I'd also like to thank my cover illustrator, Karin Star, for capturing the spirit of *Ghost of a Chance*, and my photographer, Albert George, for capturing my spirit. A special shout out to my beta readers, Darlene Beaman and Linda Jeffreys. Finally, thanks to Craig Long. Your support, patience, and phenomenal kitchen skills have kept me going. None of this would have been possible without you. I love you to the moon and back—now let's go to Ireland!

What's Next?

Lily's Luck (working title) will be the next novel released by Nikki Long. If you enjoyed Kate and Pete's adventures in romance, then you'll love Lily and Evan. What's not to love about a picturesque lighthouse on the coast of Ireland, a whiskey distillery, and an ever-so-sexy movie star? Mix in a nosey but well-meaning real estate agent, a psychic witch, and a group of otherworldly visitors who didn't get the memo that it's the 21st century, and you'll be transported to a place of beauty, magic, and of course, love!

Here's a sneak peak of *Lily's Luck*.

Prologue

The neon lottery sign in the convenience store window flashed the updated total for the weekly mega-millions drawing: $365 million. "Wouldn't that solve a lot of problems?" Lily Keegan whispered as the light from the neon cast her face in a pink glow. Shrugging, she continued down the street. Thirty-five, recently divorced, and soon to lose the house she'd lived in for the last ten years, it was difficult for Lily to see her luck turning anytime soon. Having spent the last two weeks trying to find an apartment in the college town of Ann Arbor, Michigan, she quickly realized that everything was either too expensive or too depressing to consider.

Adjusting the wildly colored knit scarf that set off her long, red hair, Lily worried about her 'to-do' list: finish packing up the house, find an apartment, get a job—well, a better-paying job. And all of this two weeks before Christmas. But Lily knew what would happen if she didn't check all those things off her list. She'd end up on her mother's doorstep. In Florida. That alone made her shudder. Who the hell wanted to live in a place that had alligators? Alligators! The modern world's answer to dinosaurs! On top of that—and as much as she loved her free-spirited mother—Lily knew she couldn't possibly survive sharing an apartment with her mom in a gated retirement community. *Yeah, that would just about put the nail in the coffin of my life.* Stopping abruptly, she turned around and headed back to the convenience store. *Oh, what the hell. What's one lottery ticket going to hurt? It's not like I'm going to win, but still....*

Be sure to check out Nikki's website at nikkilongwrites.com for the release date of *Lily's Luck*.

About the Author

Nikki Long started writing romance novels because she loves reading them. After completing her master's degree in English, she decided it was time to publish her own stories about contemporary women who aren't necessarily looking for romance, but it finds them. Her novels are filled with humor, friendship, sometimes a dash of the paranormal, and romance with heat.

Nikki shares a home in the woods near Lake Michigan with her husband and a menagerie of dogs and cats. When she's not writing, she enjoys throwing dinner parties for friends or enjoying a fine whiskey—preferably in Ireland with her husband.

Visit her online at www.nikkilongwrites.com, on Twitter and Instagram @nikkilongwrites, and on Facebook at www.facebook.com/nikki.long.96558/

Made in the USA
Las Vegas, NV
04 February 2022

43152042R00176